# PRAISE FOR RACHEL VAN DYKEN

"*The Consequence of Loving Colton* is a must-read friends-to-lovers story that's as passionate and sexy as it is hilarious!"
—Melissa Foster, *New York Times* bestselling author

"Just when you think Van Dyken can't possibly get any better, she goes and delivers *The Consequence of Loving Colton*. Full of longing and breathless moments, this is what romance is about."
—Lauren Layne, *USA Today* bestselling author

"The tension between Milo and Colton made this story impossible to put down. Quick, sexy, witty—easily one of my favorite books from Rachel Van Dyken."
—R. S. Grey, *USA Today* bestselling author

"Hot, funny . . . will leave you wishing you could get marked by one of the immortals!"
—Molly McAdams, *New York Times* bestselling author, on
*The Dark Ones*

"Laugh-out-loud fun! Rachel Van Dyken is on my auto-buy list."
—Jill Shalvis, *New York Times* bestselling author, on *The Wager*

"*The Dare* is a laugh-out-loud read that I could not put down. Brilliant. Just brilliant."
—Cathryn Fox, *New York Times* bestselling author

## The Seaside Series

*Tear*
*Pull*
*Shatter*
*Forever*
*Fall*
*Eternal*
*Strung*
*Capture*

## The Renwick House Series

*The Ugly Duckling Debutante*
*The Seduction of Sebastian St. James*
*An Unlikely Alliance*
*The Redemption of Lord Rawlings*
*The Devil Duke Takes a Bride*

## The London Fairy Tales Series

*Upon a Midnight Dream*
*Whispered Music*
*The Wolf's Pursuit*
*When Ash Falls*

## The Seasons of Paleo Series

*Savage Winter*
*Feral Spring*

## The Wallflower Series (with Leah Sanders)

*Waltzing with the Wallflower*
*Beguiling Bridget*
*Taming Wilde*

## The Dark Ones Saga

*The Dark Ones*
*Untouchable Darkness*
*Dark Surrender*
*Darkest Temptation*

## Stand-Alones

*Hurt: A Collection* (with Kristin Vayden and Elyse Faber)
*Rip*
*Compromising Kessen*
*Every Girl Does It*
*The Parting Gift* (with Leah Sanders)
*Divine Uprising*

# DANGEROUS EXES

Liars, Inc., Book Two

# RACHEL VAN DYKEN

SKYSCAPE

Text copyright © 2018 by Rachel Van Dyken
All rights reserved.

Published by Skyscape, New York

www.apub.com

Amazon, the Amazon logo, and Skyscape are trademarks of Amazon.com, Inc., or its affiliates.

ISBN-13: 9781503904514
ISBN-10: 1503904512

Cover design by Letitia Hasser

Printed in the United States of America

*To Grandma Nadine, for once again inspiring another fun character that left me smiling long after I typed The End.*

# Prologue

**Los Angeles**
**2015 Emmys**

My heart was in my throat as I weaved past hotel guests and down the hall. My entire world felt like it had just fallen sideways.

It was going to be fine.

I just needed proof.

I needed to know whether I was right—or crazy.

I prayed for crazy as I pulled my key card from my purse with shaking hands. Drunk couples walked by me. It was supposed to be a party, I was supposed to be having fun, enjoying myself.

Three a.m. and people were still drinking and networking, and I was . . . panicking, overanalyzing, controlling, as per usual . . . everyone but my fiancé.

Up-and-coming Hollywood director Wayne Alvillar, even his name sounded like something you'd see in bold script flashing across the big screen in giant black letters.

I calmed my breathing, pushed my shoulders back, and shoved open the door.

The lights were on. That should have been my first clue. If he was sleeping, they'd be off, right?

I quietly stepped into the Presidential Suite and surveyed the pristine marble floor, the way the lights bounced off the white rock. The fireplace was on and the sleek flat-screen TV was blaring a *Friends* rerun. I made my way down the hall, past the fully stocked wet bar and into the main bedroom. The shades were pulled, creating a dark glow across the king-size bed. Wayne was sitting there watching TV as if he really had decided to escape the madness of the party like I'd been told.

Then again, I'd also been told he left on the arm of a Hollywood actress.

I was clearly going crazy.

"Hey, baby." He flashed me that million-dollar capped smile and patted the side of the bed. "You wanna watch a movie? I thought I was tired then saw the news. My speech was so good." He shook his head in disbelief. "I was so damn nervous."

"It was . . . perfect," I said, kicking off my heels and joining him on the bed.

He turned and nuzzled my neck with a kiss.

Yup, I really was losing my mind.

He wasn't cheating on me with an actress.

He loved me.

His hand moved to my breast as he pressed an open-mouthed kiss to my neck.

I sighed into him and fell asleep.

Two hours.

I was in his arms for two hours.

Two peaceful hours of knowing that we really did belong together, that my perfect life really was as amazing as it looked on TV.

I had it all.

With a sleepy grin, I got up from the bed and walked to the bathroom, and nearly tripped over the rug. I straightened it then saw Wayne's crisp white shirt bundled in the corner under a towel.

I rolled my eyes, the guy was sentimental, so he'd want the shirt he'd won an Emmy in. I grabbed it and froze.

Perfume.

Lipstick smudges.

More perfume.

Blonde hair wrapped around a few buttons. Blonde hair I recognized because it was so glaringly different from my own dark hair. My hands shook.

I dropped the shirt like it was diseased as rage and pain filled my body so quickly that I had to hang on to the door to keep from passing out. I sucked in a harsh breath, and then another.

We were engaged.

I had a plan.

I was looking at houses.

I'd ordered invitations for the wedding.

I tried to get my breathing under control but it was no use, the rage won out over all the hurt, over the sound of my heart breaking. I charged into the room and slammed a pillow over his head until he jolted awake, then punched him in the face.

And when he recovered.

I did it again.

I wish I could say that I walked out after that, but I took him back.

Again.

And again.

And again.

Until I found them together and almost smashed a bottle of wine over his head after he tried to stupidly explain what went wrong and where I could do better.

Yes.

Better.

And that's where my story starts.

In a wine shop yelling at the man I thought was going to be my husband, falling apart in public only to lock eyes across the room with someone who looked like she'd had an even worse day than me.

I thought my life was over that day in that wine shop.

And then I met my soon-to-be-best-friend Blaire and realized . . .

It had only just begun.

# Chapter One

There was a very fine line between love and hate.

Or in my case, a very thin fence where hate decides to set up across the street and stare at you through binoculars even though you've repeatedly threatened to get a restraining order.

I glared. Jessie freaking Beckett.

Ex-target of Dirty Exes, the PI company my best friend and I built from the ground up.

Ex-quarterback.

Ex-pain in my ass.

I heaved out a breath, that's a lot of exes. A hell of a lot of exes. He gave me a small wave.

I flipped him off.

"He still there?" Blaire Hunter, my best friend and business partner, asked, turning the page of *Cosmo* while reaching for another piece of licorice.

"Yup." The *p* popped on the word, my chest ached with misplaced anger—it wasn't him I was angry at, it was the situation, the entire situation. I slammed the binoculars down, causing our receptionist, Abby, to jump in her seat.

Blaire held out the bucket of licorice. "Maybe it will help?"

"He's trying to ruin my company, how is sugar going to help?" I paced in front of my desk and tried to think of all the ways it went wrong.

Maybe it was the fact that for the first time since building the PI company, we were wrong about a target.

His wife was our client and had hired us to catch him in the act, but she had been the real cheater in the marriage, the user, the manipulator—but all the signs at the time had pointed to him. Every damn time.

I stretched my arms above my head and then pulled my tuxedo jacket tight over my plunging white blouse. I didn't do well with chaos.

I was a planner.

I had one Erin Condren planner for work, and another for home and recreational activities like my biweekly running and yoga sessions.

I even mapped out my meals on the front of my fridge in different-colored chalk for each day of the week. I'd never faltered in my routine, I never forgot to highlight, to color code. It was my life.

Until Jessie.

He was the wrench you throw in the perfectly good engine, causing it to sputter to its death.

I picked up the binoculars again, despite Blaire's heavy sigh. "He's just . . . staring right back at us. Leaning against his stupid Tesla like he owns the world. Why is he even driving a Tesla?"

"Why are we mad about his car again?" Blaire asked in a bored voice.

I glanced over my shoulder. "Don't you have a date with your perfect man-bun-wearing millionaire hotel-empire-owner slash bartender?"

"I love that you actually included the slash." Blaire laughed. "And yes, yes I do." She walked over to me and jerked the binoculars from my death grip. "Give it a rest, he's just trying to get into your head. He's still pissed about everything that was leaked to the press."

"That wasn't our fault and you know it." I put my hands on my hips. "That was his blood-sucking wife trying to make us and him look bad."

I'm a professional.

I'm in control.

Breathe in and out.

Everything is fine.

I'm co-partner of one of the premier PI companies in Hollywood.

I'm the Beyoncé of catching cheaters with their pants down.

Everything.

Is.

Fine.

"Right." Blaire nodded slowly. "But in the end it just made him look stupid in front of the entire world—in front of a world that he's trying to make a better place through all of his charity endeavors, which means, even though he's not a terrible person, everyone now thinks he is."

A headache pulsed behind my temples, I rubbed my head and tried to think of a solution. It's what I did. I fixed things. I fixed broken marriages, relationships, and if a client was too far gone and in a free fall, I handed them a safety net and made it better.

Yet every time I thought of Jessie Beckett I either wanted to inflict violence on his person, or just . . . huh, I guess all I really wanted was to fight him.

I was tall.

He was muscular.

I would lose.

He would laugh.

Plus it would mean touching him.

I shivered.

"Cold?" Blaire grinned.

"You're still here?" I said, confused.

She shoved me toward the door. "Go talk to him, throw up the white flag, and move on. Thanks to the news, we didn't get the short end of the stick, and have a client load that's going to force us to take on another employee."

I sagged a bit. "Right, you're right. Okay, I'll just tell him it's over. How hard can it be? He has to be bored out of his mind anyway. He's been there all day."

Blaire smiled and then gave me an encouraging nod before walking to her car. I gulped at Jessie and stared him down, all six foot four of him.

There were so many things wrong with him as a human that I was offended just thinking about them.

For one, his eyes were too knowing, like he'd already done a search on every single part of your body that responded to male touch and memorized it just in case he got the chance to corner you.

His light eyes against tan skin, dark hair that was a bit longer in the back, curling at the ends and making a girl think about giving them a tug.

And don't even get me started on his muscular build.

It said one thing, in bold colors above his head, that he put physical perfection above all else and wanted everyone else to not only know it, but comment about it, appreciate it—he basically had a big giant freaking "You're Welcome" sign hovering over him. And it irritated me.

It irritated me that when I'd tried to get close to him during our investigation, he didn't play into my hands as easily as I was used to with most of our targets.

And to be honest, it stung a bit that when I dumbly threw myself in his face in order to distract him from Blaire—he looked at me like I was a sad excuse for bait. I'd never had a guy react to me in that way, typically it was easy to distract them, tempt them to default to their cheating tendencies, catch them on camera, and be done. But Jessie . . . Jessie hadn't even blinked in interest—if anything, I annoyed him. Which in turn annoyed me, made me try harder to push his buttons, until he relented and we became friends.

He gave me another small wave.

I steeled my gaze and made the slow, painful walk across the street.

From friends.

To enemies.

In one final swipe.

Bastard.

# Chapter Two

## JESSIE

There was something both gorgeous and terrifying about a woman with a tuxedo jacket and red spiky heels. Isla was the type of woman who could become an army general and terrify even the biggest jackass of the group. Her words had a way of slicing right through a man, causing irreparable damage. And the way she held her body? She was always positioned to strike. A lesser man would have been intimidated. Isla was the type of woman who would wear stilettos until her toes bled then lie about the pain just to see your reaction.

Five minutes.

That was all it took—five minutes after being introduced to her I decided that I wanted to strangle her more than I wanted to kiss her. She'd followed me around like a puppy that first night—she even went as far as to stalk me to the bathroom and lock the door behind her while I was mid pullout—all in an effort to throw me off her scent.

The scent of a general in a tuxedo jacket.

A wolf dressed like a stupid-ass sheep.

I crossed my arms again and waited as the sound of her heels clicking against the pavement got closer and closer, and it seemed more purposeful, like she hoped the loud noise would scare me away.

Bullshit, I was going to destroy her the same way she destroyed me, from the inside out.

I rubbed my chest.

Irritated that I still felt upset, heartbroken, betrayed—those words didn't even begin to cover the feelings I had toward Isla and what she'd done to my reputation. Granted, my ex-wife didn't have to go to the press. But she wouldn't have been as pissed as she was if it wasn't for Isla and Blaire.

Blaire.

I shook my head.

My best friend's girlfriend.

Yeah, didn't see that coming. I'd been pursuing her for a month when I finally found out my best friend had already done the conquering and planted his flag where mine should have been all along.

Which brought me back to Isla. Everything always came back to her—she'd conveniently shoved them together while pulling me and Blaire apart.

I could forgive a lot of things.

And it's not like I enjoyed watching her through binoculars like a stalker.

She grimaced and nearly tripped on the sidewalk, as her breasts tried to slide out of her sheer blouse.

Definitely not a hardship watching her.

At least when she wasn't speaking.

"Jessie." She said my name like an expletive. I tried not to be turned on by the way her breasts slid against that silky material but I couldn't pull my eyes away—I was a red-blooded male, sue me, I didn't have to like her to appreciate the gift of her banging body.

But the fact still remained.

The minute she and Blaire poked their heads into my business, I was put on the fast track to disaster. My ex-wife went to the press, told every dirty detail about our falling-out and the reasons behind it—mainly because she was pissed she didn't get any money in the divorce—and here we are.

I was asked to step down from my job as chairman of the charity I helped build. The same charity that helped get clean water into third-world countries and build schools and orphanages. I'd poured my life into that charity. But the board of directors didn't think it was wise for me to be the face of the charity anymore.

And I couldn't blame them.

I was on every fucking gossip rag in America.

Even some in the UK.

And every article speculated on my relationship with my ex-wife, the farce I kept up with, the lies I helped her tell. Isla didn't just give my ex, Vanessa, the means to ruin me, she helped her do it.

Yeah, I could forgive a hell of a lot.

But I'd bled for the reputation I had.

My worst fear had come true.

And I only had one person to blame.

One person who was currently eyeing me like she'd rather run me over with her car than say one word.

But I refused to be the first to speak.

Her right eye twitched. "Did you need something, Jessie?"

I shrugged. "Just bird watching."

"Bird." Her chest heaved as she stutter-stepped. "Watching."

"That's what I said." I grinned. "Been walking in heels long?"

"There was a pothole." She sniffed and looked away, then back at me. "Look, there has to be a way we can discuss this like normal adults, not ones who stalk with binoculars and make petty threats."

"Oh, so now my threats are . . . petty?" I took a step toward her. "I'm not making empty or petty threats—I fully intend on ruining this little business of yours, maybe then you'll know what it feels like to lose everything." I tried not to flinch at the guilt that poked me in the chest, the guilt that I was also bringing down her business partner,

Blaire, who I used to date a long time ago and who was now engaged to my best friend, Colin.

Blaire? She would be just fine.

Blaire? Wasn't as emotionally invested as Isla now that she had Colin, at least that's what I told myself.

And that was the point.

Isla breathed this business.

Blaire merely worked for it because she wanted to stick it to any guy who tried to cheat.

But for Isla? It was personal. It was beyond personal.

It was her life's blood.

Her face was cold as stone.

Damn, she was brutally frigid.

Not one straight black hair out of place.

Bright-red lipstick and just enough makeup to be taken seriously but not so much that you got lost in it.

Every accessory thought out, from the gold bangles on her wrist to the tiny teardrop necklace that plunged down her blouse.

She didn't move a muscle.

Didn't even blink.

And finally said, "I didn't do anything. That was all your ex-wife, so if you want to point fingers, I think she's somewhere in Hollywood trying to sleep her way into the next *Avengers* movie."

"You"—I jabbed a finger toward her—"took her on as a client based on false information."

She scowled. "Everything checked out, we do our homework. Now if you'll excuse me, I have a two o'clock I can't miss."

I pressed my lips together in a smug grin. "Another life to ruin, Isla?"

"Jessie." Her façade cracked, and I felt my resolve weaken. "I'd like to think we used to be friends—"

I flinched at the word.

Yes. We were friends.

We were friends until I realized she'd stuck a knife in my back in order to further her business, her career, until I realized she was on my ex-wife's team all along. She betrayed me.

"Friends," I rasped, "don't screw each other over. Do you even know what people are saying about me? The gossip is through the roof! Didn't you know? I'm a liar. A cheater. I'll do anything to look perfect. I'm a sick fuck, that's what they're saying. My reputation is shit because I chose the wrong woman who in turn chose you to fix something that never could be fixed in the first place. Our marriage was already too far broken, so don't sit there and talk to me about friendship."

I shoved past her and got into my car, then turned on the engine.

She stood in front of the car, arms crossed, then finally hung her head and stepped out of the way as I spun out.

# Chapter Three

ISLA

By the time I made it to my appointment I was fuming! He had no right to blame me for his ex-wife's behavior. Sure, did we take her on as a client in an effort to find out if he was cheating?

Yes. But that's what PIs do! It's our job. Literally.

I grabbed my necklace and gave it a little tug before I cut off the engine to my Lexus GS hybrid.

He was just angry.

And when people were angry they were hardly rational—I should know, I was in the business of angry couples.

After a few weeks he'd cool off, he'd see that we weren't in the wrong, and everything would be fine.

Totally. Fine.

Feeling immeasurably better, I snatched my white leather purse from the passenger seat and opened my door. The warm LA winds tangled my hair around a bit as I maneuvered my way toward The Ivy.

It was my least favorite restaurant to meet people at, mainly because it was a place most people wanted to be seen.

And I hated the limelight.

After years of being in it by way of my stupid director fiancé, the last thing I wanted was to run into him while he was tongue deep in yet another actress, or worse—actor. Because the lovely thing about him? He was a lover, not a fighter. Didn't really pick sides, that one. He just loved attention and would take it any way he could get it.

Female.

Male.

Horse.

Plant.

Okay, slight exaggeration, but I still found great humor in imagining him trying to seduce a horse then getting trampled to death.

I plucked off my sunglasses and approached the small brown table. "Yes, I have lunch reservations under Isla Turner."

She beamed up at me through black spectacles and a toothy smile. "Right this way, Mrs. Turner."

"Oh, it's Miss." I tucked my hair behind my ear. "Actually."

I got Mrs. a lot.

I told myself it was because I looked classy—not old.

Single.

Unattached.

I glared into my water glass. "Could I get some extra lemons, please?"

"Absolutely." She handed me a menu. "Your waiter will be arriving momentarily."

"Thank you." I glanced back to my pristine menu and tapped my fingernails against the table, a bit irritated my new client was late.

A shadowy figure appeared near my right, I glanced up and choked on the sip of water I'd just taken as Jessie Beckett plopped down in the seat opposite me.

"Okay, you're seriously taking your stalking to the next level." I gritted my teeth and pasted a fake smile on my face as people started whispering and staring. Great, just great. The last thing I needed was more attention, especially since my client had requested a semi low profile.

Then again, why The Ivy?

I shook my fuddled head just as the waiter approached. "Would you two like some more time?"

"He's not staying," I hissed.

Jessie just grinned that cocky grin and looked smugly up at the waiter. "I'd love to see the wine list."

"Sweet cheese and crackers," I muttered under my breath. "He doesn't need the wine list, because he's not staying."

The waiter looked between us in confusion.

"Don't mind her, she's just hangry." Jessie nodded. "Wine list, and let's start with two Caesar salads and some calamari."

"I'm allergic to calamari," I lied.

"Extra calamari." Jessie winked at the waiter.

"Alright . . . then." The waiter slid a wine list onto the table and walked off.

"Go away!" I leaned in and jerked the wine list from Jessie's hands. "You've already done enough damage, my client should be here any minute!"

"Oh, he's here." Jessie blinked innocently. "Sitting across from you, gazing into your venomous eyes, and wondering how your brand of manipulation got my ex to burst into tears with your lies. Don't people like you recognize each other?"

I took a soothing breath and reminded myself that murder would land me in prison, even if it was justified, the bastard. "You tricked our secretary into booking an appointment with me? Why?"

"I didn't have to trick her." He shrugged his muscled shoulders. "I just told her I was a potential client and willing to pay out the ass if I could have an appointment with you."

I scowled. "You're paying for lunch."

"A gentleman always does," he said, confusing me further.

His light eyes twinkled a bit before he shut down whatever he was thinking. "You're a menace to society."

I let out a breath and leaned back against my seat as a headache pulsed between my eyes. "And you're like a dog with a bone. We don't do anything illegal and this isn't going to make you feel better. Shutting down my business may seem like the solution, but think of all the other things you could do with your time!"

"Shutting down your business," he said calmly, "shows the press that I was caught in a bad situation, it tells the charity that I was wrongfully fired, and hopefully proves I was wronged. At least the media gets to feel sorry for me—I can find a way to get back on top."

Anger burned through my chest, making it hard to swallow. "It's all the same with you power-hungry celebrities, isn't it? If life isn't perfect. If you aren't on top, if the cereal isn't perfectly alphabetized just in case someone takes a picture of your freaking pantry and sends it to TMZ for the world to see what an OCD freak you are!"

He growled low in his throat, his teeth snapped together. "That has nothing to do with this."

"It has everything to do with this," I said softly. "You want something back, something you think has been wrongfully taken from you, by me, but I think if you look at the facts you'll see that being on top only means one thing—"

"Oh yeah?" he snarled. "What's that, Isla?"

"There's always further to fall when you aren't the golden boy anymore," I said softly, reaching out and touching his hand on instinct, because it's what I did in my sessions with clients, because it's what I did when I put my heart into things I had no business putting my heart into.

He stared at our touching hands as a tether of awareness slithered through my fingers like he'd just caressed me.

A few seconds went by, both of us staring down.

I would have been happy to spend the rest of the lunch trying to figure out why my skin tingled.

Except a whiny voice interrupted. "You sure move on fast."

I pulled my hand away and stared up in horror as Jessie's ex glared at both of us with disdain then looped her arm through her poor date's arm.

My ex-fiancé.

Wayne.

It was suddenly hard to breathe.

Hard to think.

"Hi, Isla." He grinned like he owned me, like he was seeing my naked body respond to his touch, like he had a right to look beyond my clothes.

I felt my entire body pale.

And then Jessie's hand was on mine again, not soft, but firm. He gripped it tight and then glanced up at Wayne and said the unthinkable. "Who exactly are you?"

I wanted to groan.

I wanted to throw myself off a cliff.

Or maybe just crawl under the table and hide from his leering eyes.

Wayne's smile was still in place, but it was fake. I knew that smile, I'd been on the receiving end of it more times than I could count. He was pissed that Jessie didn't recognize him.

"Wayne Alvillar." He held out his hand.

Vanessa beamed. "He just directed the last action series to make over half a million in a weekend! We're out celebrating!"

I just bet they were.

Stomach suddenly queasy, I tried to keep my posture perfect, my smile in place, my eyes from watering down my cheeks.

"Huh." Jessie looked so comfortable, so normal. "Doesn't ring a bell." He shrugged. "Then again, I'm more of a stay-at-home-and-watch-old-movies sort of guy, right, baby?"

He was looking at me.

I was baby.

He had no idea how much he was saving me.

I played right into it, leaning toward his hand and winking. "My favorite thing to do with you." I scrunched up my nose. "Okay, maybe top five, you know what number one is."

He laughed, and then I swear his eyes smoldered. "Don't I ever . . ."

My stomach dropped to my knees, damn it, that smolder, damn it to hell!

"We were just going, lost track of time." Jessie stood, threw a crisp one-hundred-dollar bill onto the table, making my eyes widen briefly before he grabbed my purse, handed it to me, wrapped his arm around me then called over his shoulder, "Have a great lunch."

We walked out of the restaurant with heads held high.

Unfortunately I was parked on the other side, and they were immediately seated in the outside patio where they could see us.

"Still watching," I said under my breath while Jessie turned me around in his arms and dragged his mouth over my surprised lips.

He tasted like lemon water and spice.

It had been so long.

So damn long since I'd been kissed that well.

Maybe ever.

I clung to the front of his shirt, the combination of heat from his skin and bulging pec muscles was enough to give any sane woman a stroke at thirty-three.

He placed his hands on either side of my face, gently guiding the kiss, stroking his tongue along mine like he'd been doing it for years.

When we broke apart, his chest was heaving.

And I was leaning too close, like I didn't want him to stop.

He kissed me again.

Then grabbed my hand and walked me to my car.

Of course he knew where it was parked.

I sighed as he pushed me up against the door, my eyes flickered to Vanessa and Wayne, both glancing our way still.

Jessie's eyes met mine as he cupped my face. "You know him?"

I nodded as tears filled my eyes.

Jessie pressed his body against mine. "He still staring?"

I nodded again, afraid if I spoke I'd blurt out the whole horrible story and then get snot stains on his shirt. I'd never worked past it. I didn't want to. I figured if I did, I'd lose all the anger that kept me going on a daily basis, the anger that helped me have perfect focus on my job.

Jessie's forehead touched mine as he left one last lingering kiss on my lips and whispered in my ear, "This isn't over."

"Stop stalking me," I whispered back, ducking my head against his chest as he wrapped his arms around me.

"You're a good kisser, Isla." He tilted my chin toward him. "But it's not enough—I will shut you down, that I promise."

He walked off leaving me hot, breathless, and pissed.

I opened my car door and tossed my purse in the opposite seat, then pressed my fingertips against my lips and cursed the universe for doing the impossible. Making me feel alive again—by way of my enemy.

# Chapter Four

## JESSIE

I motioned to the bartender, who just happened to be my best friend, and sat on one of the stools.

He jerked his chin in my direction then went and grabbed me a pilsner. He knew me well. I drank whiskey because it appeared more refined, I drank beer because I actually liked it.

And today.

Today I needed it.

I could still taste her.

Two protein shakes. A Snickers bar. A piece of beef jerky, and now beer, and I could still taste Satan on my lips.

It sparked a memory I'd kept shoved into the furthest recesses of my mind. I battled that memory like a soldier every fucking day—because I could still smell her when I thought of it.

I could still feel her.

I could taste her in the air.

*"You make me depressed." Isla plopped down next to me at the bar at the resort we were staying at. My ex-wife just got on a plane, my best friend was currently screwing my ex-girlfriend Blaire, and I was getting drunk.*

*That, at least, was the plan.*

*Isla elbowed me. "Come on, let's do something crazy."*

*"Says the crazy person." I took another shot of Jack.*

*She scrunched up her nose. "If you don't say yes I'm just going to pester you until you do."*

*"Charming." I finally glanced over at her, she was wearing a low-cut black dress that fell loosely around her lithe body. I was having a hell of a time looking away from the teardrop necklace that kept bouncing between her two perfect breasts.*

*"Eyes up here." She grinned and then held out her hand. "Come on, we're doing this."*

*"I never agreed to—"*

*Her heel caught on her dress as she stumbled into my arms, her hands gripped my biceps so hard that I found myself flexing to keep both of us steady, and then her eyes heated, and there was one brief moment of insanity where she locked onto my mouth with a wanting gaze before clearing her throat and looking away, tucking her hair behind her ears.*

*"Deal," I found myself saying. "So what's this crazy thing we're about to do?"*

*She just shrugged. "Dance."*

*My eyebrows shot up. "We're going to dance?"*

*She nodded and then grabbed my hand and drew me to the dance floor. The lights darkened and then her hands were on me, and my hands were on her hips as we moved in sync to the music. The music slowed, forcing us closer together.*

*Our mouths almost touched.*

*She smelled like sweet wine.*

*I could sense her want.*

*It matched mine.*

*And I was vulnerable to the way she looked at me, the opposite of my ex . . . as if she wanted me more than anything else, and when she looked at me, she only saw me.*

*And for once in my life, I wanted to hold on to that feeling just a bit longer, selfishly take it so I could remember what it felt like to be with a woman who saw me as a man.*

I snorted into my first glass of beer and emptied it just as Colin brought me a second. Yeah, that memory was doing me no favors right now.

"Rough day?" He leaned over the bar, his snake tattoo poking out from underneath his tight black shirt.

"Don't patronize me with your bullshit." I rolled my eyes. "You're not my therapist."

"Thank God for that." Colin grinned. "Even I feel sorry for your therapist, didn't the first one actually fire you?"

I glared. "She quit."

"Is that normal? For therapists to just quit their clients?"

"Is this you being helpful? Because it feels like the opposite." I shoved my empty glass toward him and grabbed the full one.

"Seriously, anything I can help with?" He had that look, the look that said he knew what was on my mind but was dating Isla's best friend and had already told me he wasn't going to take sides (at least if he could help it). Besides, he was so happy that I felt guilty for even thinking about pulling him back into my life's drama. He already couldn't avoid my ex-wife since they were blood relations.

I drank deep and placed the glass back on the bar. "No."

"Uh-huh." Colin's eyes narrowed. "This wouldn't have anything to do with you hanging outside Dirty Exes all morning like you were part of a stakeout, would it?"

"Blaire needs to keep her mouth shut," I grumbled. "And I was trying to be intimidating."

Colin choked on a laugh then nodded seriously. "Good call, I always think stalkers are intimidating, especially ones who wear three-piece suits and drive Teslas. What did you think would happen? You'd smolder her to death? Look, I know you're pissed—"

"No." I clenched my fist. "They ruined everything!"

Colin's smile disappeared.

"Everything." I said it again as rage pulsed through my body. "I had the perfect trajectory, things were finally calming down. My wife signed divorce papers, I was free from her brand of crazy and ready to move on with my life, hell, I was gonna get a dog!"

Colin's jaw nearly came unhinged. "You're not even a dog person."

"I was branching out," I grumbled. "The point is, the minute everyone found out that Vanessa had Dirty Exes investigating me, my credibility went to shit. My reputation is completely fucked because of them."

Colin moved the beer to the side and leaned over the bar. "Look, it's going to blow over, this shit always does. Until then, just lie low. You're only going to make it worse by camping outside their place of business and taunting them. Plus, you can't really do anything by watching her through binoculars."

I smirked. "Yes I can . . . I'm in her head, and soon . . . I'm going to be the only thing she sees, everywhere. She thinks it's bad now? The war hasn't even started."

Colin held up his hands. "Just leave me out of it."

I snorted. "I wouldn't expect you to help me anyway."

"Why's that?"

"You're getting laid."

He nodded. "Solid point, you're on your own."

"Some best friend you are."

"A best friend who's getting laid on the regular by a goddess with a fascination for tugging my hair? Um, yeah, hard pass."

I groaned in red-hot envy and downed the rest of my beer, my brain going a million miles a minute.

It was the only solution.

Shutting her down, proving to the world and all those shitty reporters that they weren't even a legit PI agency.

One more wrong move.

And she'd be forced to close her doors forever.

Blaire and Colin would live happily ever after with his millions.

And Isla?

She'd be on the street wondering where the hell she went wrong.

And I'd be there waiting with a smug-as-fuck smile on my face.

I grinned as I paid my tab.

Even though my insides churned.

Tit for tat.

She deserved everything she had coming to her.

# Chapter Five

ISLA

The universe was plotting against me. It started when I spilled coffee on my new white blouse, continued its downward spiral after I nearly got clipped by a motorcyclist and then dodged a bird who was clearly hell-bent on suicide, making it so I had to park across from my great-aunt's retirement home and jog across the busy street in heels.

A warm breeze picked up.

I shivered.

And paused.

The damp stain chilled my skin as my teeth chattered for a few seconds. I scanned the parking lot. Something felt wrong, out of place, off.

Foreboding washed over me. Why were there so many cars? I always visited on Tuesday afternoons and I'd never had trouble finding a spot before.

The wind swirled and moaned around me again.

I was being ridiculous.

Paranoid.

And I'd had maybe three hours of solid sleep last night—ever since Jessie's kiss I'd been consumed by the heat of his mouth until I woke up moaning like he was in my bed ready to pounce.

It was unfortunate that I hated him.

And that he hated me just as much, possibly more.

My heels clicked against the concrete as I quickly made my way into the LA Hills Hollywood Retirement Plaza. It was an upscale retirement community for older movie stars and industry professionals.

It had four pools.

A freaking Starbucks.

And basically anything an old rich person could possibly want except for cabana boys—apparently that's where they drew the line no matter how many times my aunt had her friends sign a petition.

They almost won last year.

She went as far as putting up posters of Efron to Hemsworth around the retirement community and inviting Bieber to do a benefit concert to help their efforts. Shockingly, Justin said no.

I couldn't imagine why it wouldn't be appealing to perform half-naked in front of eighty-year-olds. Where was the kid's sense of adventure?

I grinned and waved at Henry, the sixty-year-old volunteer receptionist who asked me out for coffee and the early-bird special every weekend.

Sometimes I took him up on it.

Best dates I've ever had were with Henry.

And we always split the bill.

He blew me a kiss, his blue eyes twinkled as he nodded his head to the main activity center.

Frowning, I weaved my way down the hall toward all the chatter and laughter. My Aunt Betsy, or Goo-Poh (what I called her in front of others as a term of respect), wasn't in her usual blue chair, which was odd considering that chair wielded more power than the United Nations.

Wars were won in that chair.

Wars about what activities would be participated in, who was allowed to date who, and which dessert would be served on Funday Friday—she was essentially the queen bee of a very old hive, and it fit her, kept her busy. She'd been a director in another life—bossing people around, me included, was her life's calling.

"Isla!" I heard her call my name but didn't see anything except a crowd of people tittering over something in the middle of the room. That sense of dread intensified until it was hard to breathe.

And then the crowd parted.

Betsy grinned up at me with a wide smile then wrapped her arm around a man I could only describe as a perfect representation of Satan.

"Jessie," I said through a clenched-teeth smile. "You're . . . here."

"I wouldn't miss this for the world . . . pumpkin."

I flinched.

He noticed.

I hated him.

So. Much.

My stomach fluttered as he leaned in and kissed my aunt's cheek, and then set her on her feet. "We were just having a nice chat."

"A nice . . . chat," I finished. "About what? World hunger? Why the hell are you following me everywhere?"

Silence ensued.

I crossed my arms as my face flushed.

"Pumpkin, I thought we talked about this." Jessie smirked. "You said every Tuesday you visit your favorite aunt, and you promised this Tuesday I could come with you."

"Right."

Jessie shrugged. "I could have misheard you, you do mumble in your sleep."

About five women clutched their chests while the elderly men elbowed each other.

Fantastic.

Goo-Poh gave me such a happy smile I didn't have the heart to tell her that not only was I not sleeping with Jessie, but I had actually scheduled time to plot his murder later and was planning on doing it drunk off my ass.

"Goo-Poh." I pulled her in for a tight hug. "Let me just . . . talk to my pumpkin really quick and I'll be right back."

"Oh, honey"—Goo-Poh gave him a once-over and visibly trembled—"you take your sweet time." She winked at Jessie and returned to her giant blue chair while her little friends gathered around her like her niece had just snagged the Sexiest Man Alive.

I scowled.

So he'd been on the cover of *People* twice.

But that was at least three years ago.

Maybe two.

I hardly noticed.

I tugged at my blouse while Jessie's eyes raked over me. "You."

"Me." His smile was back.

Hold it the hell together, Isla!

I grabbed his hand and jerked him toward the far side of the room. I had a feeling that it wasn't far enough—I knew the majority of our audience was hard of hearing, but they could read lips. I had proof when Goo-Poh's gaze focused on my mouth as I was getting ready to verbally spar with the best of them.

I learned of her skill the hard way when I lost my virginity to Aiden my senior year of high school and excitedly told my friend at one of the football games, not noticing my aunt's eagle eyes. My Goo-Poh threatened to tell my parents, and I told her I'd take care of her until her death if she kept it to herself.

She thought I was joking.

And yet here I am, upholding my end of the bargain, spending every Tuesday with her like a champ. Though if I was being honest, I did it more for myself than for her silence, and I think she knew it too.

What started as a bribe became a relationship that developed into so much more than I could have possibly imagined. She was all I had left once my parents died—and she was my favorite person in the world, but I had no way of knowing that at eighteen when I made the deal.

As she got older, whatever filters she had kept disappearing, making it impossible for me to discuss certain topics without blushing, and now I could only imagine what was going through her head.

"Look." I shoved Jessie into the hall. "This is going too far. You can't involve my family in whatever crazy plan you have in that thick skull of yours."

"Why not?" He frowned and crossed his arms. "It makes so much sense for me to infiltrate your world, your privacy, the way you did mine—how's it feel? To know someone's always watching, someone's always waiting for you to . . ." He hesitated and then leaned forward and whispered in my ear, "Break."

I gritted my teeth. "It's not the same. This isn't your job, which only makes it creepy."

"You mean a charity visit from an ex-NFL star who loves helping others . . . is creepy? Even when it's to his girlfriend's aunt? How could anyone possibly take that wrong?"

And just like that, Henry approached with tears in his eyes and held out his hand. "Thank you, Mr. Beckett, we're all so excited to have you as the host of our annual Christmas ball this year, and the donations to the local elementary school we sponsor every year, well—" He wiped an actual tear from his eye. "Some of our most treasured people here don't have family, it was absolutely inspired that you would help pair some of the orphaned foster kids with those who want someone to take care of this Christmas, after all, it's never too early."

He walked off.

I smacked Jessie so hard in the chest my palm stung.

Then did it again.

"What the hell!"

"Orphaned. Children!" I hissed. "You're the actual spawn of Satan, aren't you?"

"Because I help children?" He looked genuinely confused.

"NO." I jabbed him in the chest with my finger. "This, this isn't over, it's just begun, if you think I'm going to let you stomp all over the life I've worked my ass off to build, you've got another think coming. Stay away from me. I'm warning you."

"Or what?" Jessie grinned at me like I wasn't even a small threat. "You're gonna tell your aunt on me? Admit it, you're stuck."

And it suddenly hit me.

I was stuck.

And alone.

I couldn't tell Goo-Poh the truth.

And Blaire would ask too many questions.

Which left me with nobody but . . . Jessie.

He didn't say it. Maybe he didn't have to.

It stung more than it should.

Even though I'd readjusted my armor in order to battle harder, the arrow had just enough time to slide through and prick me in the heart.

I stared at his chest as tears filled my eyes.

I begged them not to spill over.

"Isla—" Jessie reached for me.

I jerked away, wiped my cheeks, and then stomped back over to my aunt. Only a true bastard would remind me of the things lost.

And all the things he had to gain by removing everything I'd built, and leaving me with nothing.

# Chapter Six

ISLA

I abandoned Jessie to the elderly.

I felt zero guilt about it, especially when Henry started asking questions about Jessie's football career. Soon he had at least ten elderly gentlemen telling him about the good old days while I snuck my aunt out and escaped to her room.

"Well." She placed a bowl of japchae in front of me and scooted it across the table. "That's the most excitement we've had since Carol got drunk and took off her top during the Lord's Prayer."

I groaned and grabbed a fork, but it was quickly replaced with chopsticks.

Always the chopsticks with my aunt.

I was only half Chinese.

It wouldn't matter if I was one percent Chinese, I still had no choice when I was in her domain.

The last time I tried using a fork she threatened to stab me with it.

I also wasn't allowed to use her given name in private, it was a respect thing, so there I was with my Goo-Poh, great-aunt, wondering if she would try to stab me again just so she could brag to her friends that's how she kept me in line.

Sometimes I wondered if Chinese foreplay was just a lot of yelling and waving of sharp objects.

With a sigh, I dug into the noodles even though I wasn't hungry.

I knew the expectation was to eat every last bite, otherwise I'd suffer an hour-long one-sided conversation where I'd be forced to look at family albums and defend my lack of eating to my dead ancestors.

I was always too thin when I didn't eat.

Too fat when I did.

I never won.

I gritted my teeth.

"So, he's your boyfriend." Goo-Poh took the seat across from me and rubbed her hands together. "He seems . . . muscular."

The noodles revolted in my stomach and then danced around as if saying, *Hell yeah, he's muscular, let's touch him!*

I shrugged and kept eating. Ducking my head closer to the bowl.

"Isla," Goo-Poh tsked. "Why did you not tell me about him?"

Oh you know, because he was my mortal enemy. "It's kind of new."

She gasped. "And you've already given him your treasure chest!"

I groaned. "Not this again. Aunt Betsy, I'm thirty-three years old, the treasure's been discovered—"

"That Aiden boy never did deserve it first." She sniffed.

I leaned back in my chair. "Not this again."

"He had small hands." She said it so factually I was at a loss about whether I was supposed to agree or just wait for her to keep talking. I chose the latter. "And he looked his nose down at our bowls."

"He asked for a plate. Hardly a crime," I grumbled.

"And then laughed when I said we didn't have any!"

I sighed. "Goo-Poh, I came to relax and talk about anything not personal or work related, can we do that?"

She slid the bowl away from me and then handed me a cup of hot spiced tea that made my tongue burn. I choked it down anyway. "What's this have in it? Whiskey?"

Her eyes twinkled.

"Just add day drinking to my list of new things to try." I lifted the cup into the air and sighed.

"You're not happy," she pointed out. "How is that male god not pleasing you? Does he not know how to . . ." She leaned in. Oh hell, her whisper was more of a yell when she said, "Pleasure your treasure?"

"Okay, first off"—I set the cup down—"stop referring to my girly bits as *treasure*, it's weird, second, he's . . . fine."

She gasped. "Fine!"

"No, no, Goo-Poh—"

It was too late.

She was already up.

Halfway to the door.

My stilettos against her brown Hush Puppies.

I was out of breath by the time I made it back into the activity center. Jessie was still in the crowd of men when my aunt approached.

I briefly contemplated punching an old person in the face just to distract everyone from the upcoming disaster.

Instead, I stood rooted to the floor while Goo-Poh poked Jessie in the chest with her finger and started talking so fast I couldn't catch every word.

But the words I did hear . . .

"Tongue, patience, squeeze—"

It was enough for me to have nightmares for life.

Jessie turned redder by the minute.

And oddly enough, rather than get more embarrassed, I felt empowered as I sauntered over to them and winked while Goo-Poh finished with "I've drawn diagrams before, you just let me know, I email you." She elbowed him. "You aren't the first to experience this, you know, not the last either. I've had my fair share of sexual letdowns too."

I nodded in agreement while Jessie's jaw went slack.

She patted him on the back and yawned, then turned to me and kissed both cheeks. "Exhausted. I go to nap now, honey."

She left with a group of her little friends while the men around us coughed uncomfortably before filtering out of the room, leaving the buzz of the TV on around us and the tension of a thousand awkward moments.

"So." I rocked back on my heels. "You learn anything?"

"More than I'd like to, yes." Jessie shuddered. "I'm almost afraid to ask what brought that on, because it sure as hell wasn't my lack of performance, believe me." He tilted my chin toward him. "If you were with me, you wouldn't be able to walk for days."

He dropped my chin.

Stepped back.

And just.

Left.

I stared after him.

Hating him more and more.

Hating my body's betrayal because it should have been completely on board with the mental daggers I sent sailing toward his body.

And when my thighs clenched.

I blamed the muscle spasms on trying to sprint in heels.

It wasn't him.

Or any effect he had on me.

This was war.

And I was going to win.

# Chapter Seven

## Jessie

I sighed in contentment.

My house was quiet.

Everything had its place.

From the alphabetized cereal to the white walls and perfectly designed art pieces I'd chosen myself.

I hunted down a bottle of wine and let it breathe, just as the doorbell rang.

Chinese takeout.

It was the perfect ending to a day of warfare.

Isla wouldn't stand a chance in hell once I was through with her.

My plan went like this: follow her, wreak havoc on her control-freak nature, and make sure she saw me in every area of her life until she woke up in a cold sweat.

I wanted her to go to her local grocery store and look over her shoulder.

To watch her favorite movies and wonder if I was watching too.

I wanted her to be as consumed with paranoia as she made me.

Perfect. Plan. I was going to throw her so far off her game that she'd be begging to go to the press and clear my name, which in turn would destroy hers.

I cracked the door open and pulled out a few twenties, then looked up when I didn't hear the total.

"You," I spat.

Isla grinned and waltzed in right past me, a bag of Chinese food in her hand. She put it carefully on the table and started pulling out all the different tiny boxes.

"So, how was your day?" She helped herself to a glass of wine and sat.

"What the hell do you think you're doing?"

"What?" Isla asked. "Aren't you hungry?"

My stomach growled at the most inopportune moment.

She grinned. "Sit."

"Are you poisoning me?"

"Too easy." She scrunched up her nose. "Besides, what makes you think I didn't already succeed in doing that?"

"Well, if that's not terrifying," I grumbled, moving to the other barstool and grabbing a fork.

She slammed it out of my hand so fast that it clanged against the floor.

She blushed and then gulped. "Sorry, old habits. Here." A pair of chopsticks was placed in my hand. "Eat it right or don't eat at all."

Good thing I actually knew how to use the bastards.

I dug in with fervor, too exhausted to ask her why she was stalking me and eating my food, and too oddly content having someone to share a meal with to shatter the moment with my voice.

"So." She wiped her mouth. "What do you think about red?"

"Red," I said dumbly. "Red what?"

"Walls."

I choked on a piece of rice. "I don't do color."

"Right, but if you have any chance of selling you'll need to make the walls more interesting, maybe add in a few throw pillows."

"Not selling, don't need paint, don't need pillows. Sell your crazy elsewhere, Isla."

"Oh." She looked crestfallen. "I guess I assumed wrong then."

With that, she got up, grabbed her purse, and slowly made her way to the door.

Curiosity had me following her. "Are you drunk?"

A bright smile spread across her face. I sucked in a breath, hating the way it made my body ache for things it had no business even thinking about wanting. "No, why?"

"You're acting crazier than normal."

"First off, never call a woman crazy, at least to her face, and is that all you have to say after I paid for your dinner?"

"Why exactly would you do that again? We aren't friends." At least not anymore.

She leaned up and kissed me on the cheek, the scent of her citrus perfume filled my nostrils. "Just trying to be neighborly."

It didn't click until I watched her walk out of my house and take a hard right. Directly into the guesthouse I'd agreed to rent out on a separate part of the property.

The one I told my real estate agent to handle without me.

The one that my ex used to live in.

She turned on her heel and blew me a kiss, then let herself inside.

"What the actual fuck." I breathed out another curse for good measure and then lifted my head and smiled in her direction. "Well played, Isla, well played."

# Chapter Eight

ISLA

My victory was short-lived when I realized that in all my hastiness I hadn't thought to bring sheets or a pillow. I hadn't even really planned on moving, but when I'd used my powers—my PI powers, that is—for evil . . .

I'd discovered that this little beauty was on the market as a rental.

It was like finding the holy grail.

I'd made an offer the agent couldn't refuse, thanks to the money I'd stockpiled over the years, and picked up the keys that afternoon.

I hadn't even moved out of my own apartment.

Or given notice.

Being this rash wasn't like me—not even a little bit—but if I was going to win, I was going to have to drive him just as crazy as he was driving me.

And that started with infiltrating his inner circle. Thankfully, I had all the dirt on him because of our investigation.

He liked white.

Alphabetized cereals and never ate them.

Didn't even like whiskey.

Secretly co-owned a gym with his best friend.

Liked roses in his garden, but only white ones—shocker!

And volunteered as much as possible, only to come home to a solitary white yet modern house to watch Netflix, then wake up and do it all over again.

He. Was. Predictable.

He said red gave him hives.

And the last time someone asked him what music he liked, he said he was confused by the question.

Either his ex zapped all the interesting things out of his body in order to use him as her boring sex slave, or he really was just . . . average.

In my mind, Jessie was a muted beige in a world full of magenta.

And if that wasn't tragic, what was?

The only thing he had going for him was that he was the most attractive ex-football-player alive.

I almost yawned just going over the data I'd grabbed from my office.

I set up shop in the kitchen, thankful that he'd at least furnished the place with pots, pans, couch, flat-screen, and a coffee table that looked shiny enough to eat off.

By the time midnight came, I had my battle plan ready.

But still no pillow.

The couch would probably be comfortable enough.

But.

I smiled.

And then very hastily dressed in a pair of silk shorts, pulled off my bra, added my silk tank top, then made the trek back to Jessie's house.

I knocked.

The lights were all off.

I knocked again, this time harder.

Jessie jerked the door open wearing nothing but low-slung Nike joggers and a smile made for sin.

I gaped.

His half-lidded gaze raked over me like I was a feast and he hadn't eaten in days.

I licked my lips and took a step forward, his chest rose and fell slowly.

"Pillow," I whispered.

"Pillow," he repeated. "One word. How the hell am I supposed to know what that means? You want to smother me with a pillow? Have pillow talk? Your pillow's too flat? Help me out, Isla, because I have a meeting in six hours."

"Seven," I corrected.

He glared. "Got my schedule too, did you?"

I just smiled. "May I please borrow a pillow, I forgot mine."

He groaned and opened the door wide, then stomped into a room I could only assume was his. I followed close on his heels as he grabbed a pillow from a large bed and chucked it at my face.

I caught it with one hand, then squeezed with both arms as my breasts spilled over it.

His eyes immediately lowered.

It was all part of the plan.

Why not drive him crazy in every way possible?

I was passably attractive, with smooth skin, dark features, and good bone structure, according to Goo-Poh.

I used to model.

And I knew how to use my body to my advantage—any good PI knew how to.

I could have sworn he muttered *fuck* under his breath when I looked down and shrugged. "Everything . . . on the up and up?" I dropped my gaze to his waist and then lowered as I bit my lip.

He gripped me by the shoulders and turned me toward the door, then whispered gruffly against my neck, "This is a dangerous little game you're playing, pumpkin."

For some reason I was okay with the nickname this time.

"I think I can handle myself," I said in a clear voice.

He jerked me back against his rock-hard body, his rock-hard every-thing. Blood pounded between my ears as my body slacked against his. "You just keep telling yourself that."

I walked on wobbly legs all the way to the guesthouse and shut the door.

*Point, Jessie.*

# Chapter Nine

ISLA

"You're more high-strung than normal." Blaire handed me a cup of coffee and waited for me to respond. My mind was reeling. I'd slept like crap again.

Thanks to Jessie.

And his body.

And his . . . other, the other parts of his body. Damn it!

"I've never seen that look on your face before," Blaire said in wonder. "It's like you want to take over the world but don't know how. Who foiled your plans?"

She was teasing.

But there was truth to it. All of it.

"I'm going to kill Jessie Beckett," I announced to Blaire and our receptionist, Abby. I was still pissed that Abby hadn't put two and two together and realized that Jessie wasn't just another paying customer but a client scorned. Then again, he probably sweet-talked her. Abby was easy to please, all you had to say was "thank you" and she was putty in your hands. I glared at Penny, the other traitor by association. Didn't cats hiss? Was that not a thing? Could she give a bit of a warning next time? Geez!

I made a face at her.

Penny meowed in agreement while the other two just stared at me blankly like it was normal to have stare-downs with cats. The phones kept ringing. Abby ignored them while Blaire grabbed another piece of licorice and made herself comfortable.

"What?" I looked around nervously. "He followed me to my aunt's retirement home! He sent them orphans!"

"Whoa, back up, he sent orphans to a retirement home?" Blaire asked in a confused voice. "Is that legal?"

"Keep up!" I thrust my coffee mug into the air. "So naturally my only option was to move into his rental!"

Abby spit her coffee onto the newspaper, and Blaire's licorice dropped out of her mouth.

"That's perfectly normal behavior," I said defensively. "I'm a PI, sometimes we do the crazy things in an effort to get the cheater."

"You do realize Jessie isn't a target anymore, right?" Blaire said softly, like she was seconds away from patting my hand and asking if I needed a good cry. "Besides, he's pissed at us, that doesn't mean you need to move in next to him and make his life a living hell."

I grinned. "He's breaking into my circle of trust, I'm going to blow up his. It's as simple as that."

The phone rang again.

Abby finally answered it. "Yeah, I'll get her." She covered the phone with her hand. "Isla, line two."

I confidently marched over to my desk and shoved away all irritation with Jessie. "This is Isla Turner, how can I help you?"

"I heard you're the best." The woman sounded troubled. "I need the best."

Back in my element, I took down all her information and tried to soothe her when she started crying about the state of her marriage. Apparently her husband had been cheating for at least a year, and she needed proof before she filed for divorce. Blood roared in my ears. This,

this was why we started Dirty Exes! To protect those who needed it. To make sure that no woman was left with nothing postdivorce when she was the innocent party. I thought back to Wayne and shuddered. I was going to bring down her man and shove my success in Jessie's face once and for all. Preferably in front of the world, on live TV, and if that didn't work, at least, you know, in front of Penny.

By the time I hung up I was refreshed beyond reason. "New client!"

"Isla," Blaire groaned, "we have to hire another investigator as it is, we can't just take on a new client."

I sat and fired up my laptop. "Look, I have a feeling about her. This case should be an easy pop-in, pop-out, not full-scale Dirty Exes warfare."

"Okay, fine, but if anyone gets to be bait, it's you."

"Deal." I winked. "Now let's get started!"

See? Everything was looking up.

I was going to drive Jessie absolutely crazy.

He was eventually going to have to back off.

And everything would return to normal.

I ignored the hollow feeling the word *normal* brought to my body, like I didn't want normal anymore, but that was ridiculous.

I liked order in my life.

Not the chaos that Jessie brought.

I'd lived that life before, and I was in a better position now. Right? That was why I felt in control. Calm. Completely calm.

# Chapter Ten

I had her entire schedule.

I visited her office with a box of donuts and charmed her office manager, Abby. When Abby told me about her long, hellish day, I sent her to Colin's bar and told her that she and her husband should order anything they want, on me . . . but not before swiping the keys to the office.

And boom.

Schedule obtained.

Life. Ruined.

I grinned.

I knew it all.

Where she ate. Where she visited on Tuesdays.

Her fucking routine was mine to memorize.

And I only felt slightly guilty about it, mainly because it was an invasion of privacy and I knew I'd clearly lost my mind if I was planning my day around driving her insane and making sure she knew I wasn't going to back down.

For one minute.

I'd second-guessed myself.

And then I'd stupidly turned on the TV to see news of my old charity's annual holiday gala.

And the anger returned tenfold.

Had she never taken my ex on as a client, embarrassed the living hell out of her, and basically used entrapment—I wouldn't be sitting on my couch upset over my life's work getting stripped from me based on rumors and bad publicity.

Blaire was in on it too.

But for some reason I blamed Isla more.

Isla had made me feel like she genuinely liked me. She made me think she was real, that our friendship was real, not just a way to get at me in order to expose something that wasn't even true.

A falsehood.

She'd thrown our friendship, or whatever the hell it was, away for a paycheck.

And I wasn't sure I would ever forgive her for that.

For giving me a taste of what it could be like. What it should be like.

And ripping it the hell away.

I checked my watch and smiled when her Lexus pulled up. "Right on time."

Part of me had to respect the rigorous schedule she kept, another part of me was horrified that there was another human being on the planet as punctual as me.

The woman probably only had sex in one position and preferred the lights off.

I scowled.

Where had that errant thought come from?

She jumped out of her car and grabbed a black duffel bag. Her leggings hugged every inch of skin like she was poured into them, and her bright-pink shirt only made me stare longer than necessary at the expansive cleavage getting pushed up by her pink-and-black-striped sports bra.

Maybe this was a bad idea.

Or the best idea I'd ever had?

I snuck in behind her and winked at the receptionist I'd bribed, then casually strolled right into the hot yoga studio.

The doors closed with finality behind me.

I cringed.

The last time I did yoga I couldn't walk for weeks.

But the receptionist had convinced me this was a beginners class, that I'd be just fine as long as I had no health issues. I almost felt the need to remind her who she was talking to but didn't want to come across like a jackass.

If I can stay in the NFL for eleven years as a star quarterback, pretty sure I can handle an hour of hot yoga.

I eyed Isla, grabbed my mat, and then rolled it out right next to hers. "Hey, neighbor."

"Son of a bitch," she hissed under her breath, knocking her water over in the process of trying to scurry away from me.

I grinned at her horrified expression. "You miss me?"

"Like I miss my braces and feathered bangs."

"You? Feathered bangs?" I reached out to touch her silky black hair, but my hand was slapped away with a burning sting.

"Stop that." She scooted to the edge of her mat and sat with her legs crossed. "You're taking your creepy stalking to a whole other level if you're following me to yoga class, you psycho."

"Psycho." I rolled the word around in my mouth and grinned. "Kind of has a nice ring to it, also maybe next time you should say that while looking in the mirror since you're the one who basically moved in with me."

"I did not move in with you." Her cheeks flashed pink. "I merely saw an opportunity to drive you insane and took it."

"And yet here we are." I spread my arms wide. "In yoga class."

"You gonna go to my gyno appointment with me Monday too?" she snapped, then regained her composure just as fast as she'd let the mask slip.

Gotcha.

I smirked. "It's a dentist appointment, and though I'd love to watch you get your teeth cleaned and mouth tortured, I think I'll take a hard pass, I hate the dentist, don't even like walking into the office."

Her eyes widened in fear as she hissed, "How the hell did you get my schedule?"

I just looked her body slowly up and down, then shrugged casually, as if to say I had to use different means, like my sexuality, to get it.

It was a lie.

I knew it.

She knew it.

And her blush, damn it, her blush was worth every lie I told.

An instructor in nothing but a black sports bra and black yoga pants turned on some weird new-age music and smiled at the class, spreading her arms wide like she was gathering our souls to her bosom before sacrificing them on the sweaty altar of hot yoga. She started rocking back and forth from foot to foot like she was doing a mating dance, her braid swung with her.

"What the hell is she doing?" I said under my breath.

Isla was gaping at me. "Then how do you have such nice teeth?"

"I think I'm lost."

"The dentist. You refuse to walk into the building."

"Does she always do that?" I pointed to the instructor.

"I mean they're really white." She leaned in like she was seconds away from asking me to open up so she could inspect.

The instructor inhaled deeply through her nose. "She seems really into this."

Isla elbowed me. "Are you ignoring me on purpose? And she's getting rid of all the bad energy."

"Bad energy," I repeated. "You're kidding." I panicked as I watched the students start mimicking her movements like there was literally bad air and energy in the room. They moved their arms and legs, and then shut their eyes. What. The. Hell. Finally my lust seemed to cool a bit, so I answered, "I have a friend who's a dentist, he makes house calls."

She rolled her eyes. "Of course you do. And no, not kidding, this is yoga, we don't really lift heavy things and expect someone to clap for us or pay us millions of dollars when we can throw a stupid ball."

"Twenty-eight million, actually," I corrected with a wink. "A year."

She scowled and returned her attention to the instructor. "No wonder your dentist makes house visits, do you even grocery shop on your own?"

"Isn't that what Amazon is for?"

"Unbelievable," Isla said through clenched teeth. "You know what? This isn't even about me anymore, is it? You're just so bored and I'm the easiest target in a sick scheme to find some sort of meaning in your life outside of football!"

"Bored?" I repeated, hating how it actually made me feel like less of a man when she pointed out one of the things I had struggled with until finding the charity. "Nah, just . . . angry. Very. Very. Angry. So. Fucking. Angry. That the one thing I had to hold on to was ripped out of my fingers by a bitter, selfish woman and her ignorance."

"So I'm ignorant?"

"No." I gritted my teeth.

Her eyes flashed with hurt and anger.

"No!" the instructor shouted in my direction. "We leave our anger at the door."

Isla leaned in, her eyes wild with rage. "She means literally."

"Go on," the instructor said in a fake soothing voice. "Walk over to the door and just . . ." She rolled her shoulders back and forth as if my anger was weighing them down. "Leave"—she let her arms go limp—"all the anger."

"Just like that, huh?" I said in disbelief as I stood and walked over to the door, then made a dropping motion with my hands. "All gone."

"Don't you feel better?" She smiled wide.

No, actually, if anything, I just collected everyone else's anger that they'd supposedly left at the door and carried it back with me to my mat, where a grinning Isla was waiting.

"Yup," I said quickly.

"Good." She rubbed her hands together. "Shall we get started, class?"

I sat down on my mat while Isla laughed softly next to me.

I may have scooted as close as physically possible to her.

She stopped laughing.

And I stopped thinking altogether as the room filled with a sickening heat, and as beads of sweat started rolling down her toned arms.

I just . . . watched.

Appreciated.

And then entered into actual hell when the instructor called out movements that I'd seen but never performed.

"And back into cobra." Sweat pooled from my arms to my fingers. "And hero pose!"

I stole a glance at Isla, who was seamlessly moving her body into each pose like she was born in yoga pants chanting *ooohhhm*.

My foot slipped.

My face collided with the mat with a loud thunk.

"You alright, big guy?" Isla smirked at me in her perfect pose, sweat slid down her cheeks and onto the mat. My eyes zeroed in on the moisture collecting on her lips. I licked mine instinctively, only to have her mimic me as her breathing picked up.

I may want to destroy her.

But I was still a guy.

A guy who knew how damn tempting she was, especially when the next pose was called out and her ass went straight into the air.

A sharp intake of breath had me nearly choking on my tongue as I tried to focus on making it through the next—holy shit, it had only been ten minutes.

"And chaturanga." The instructor moved to a plank position.

*That* I could do.

I let out a groan of pleasure as my muscles stretched and flexed, my shirt glued to my body. In frustration I tugged it over my head before going back into the pose.

Isla scowled next to me. "Do you even eat fat? Cookies? Ice cream?"

"What?" I grinned at the way she refused to look at any part of my body except my face. Hell, the woman wasn't even blinking. "Of course I enjoy the finer things in life . . ." I lowered my voice. "Wine, chocolate, anything I can lick . . ."

She gulped, her eyes fluttered to my ass before meeting my gaze again. "I prefer something I can sink my teeth into instead . . ."

My cock hardened.

She bit down on her lower lip.

I swear I could almost feel those lips wrapped around me, sucking, toying.

"Don't put down a good licking, Isla," I whispered. We both moved into different positions, our bodies completely in sync, as I tried to hide the situation under my thin joggers. "I mean biting's good, but a good lingering lick? A deep pulsing lick . . ." Her body flinched as she shut her eyes and gave her head a shake. "Perfection."

"I'll just take your word for it." She looked away, completely shutting me down. I wasn't used to being ignored, and I just realized something very vital.

She may appear controlled.

But the woman's body burned for touch. It was in the way she eyed me, the way her body leaned in when her brain told her not to.

So I touched.

I ran the back of my fingertips across her thigh, and when we changed to yet another position, I grazed her ribs, lingering near her breasts only to pull away.

"Pity," I whispered.

Her neck craned. "What's a pity?"

"That you're taking my word for it." I eyed her mouth one last time before turning my attention back to the instructor.

I painfully ignored her the rest of the class.

And was still in such dire straits that I knew if I stood up when class ended she'd see just how much I wanted to lick her dry.

Isla didn't move.

People walked around us.

She laid back against the mat while the instructor gave us a wink and closed the doors behind her. A clinking sound burst through the air like a bomb, a very loud, angry, sexually tormented bomb.

"Those didn't lock, did they?" I wondered out loud as Isla made a beeline to the doors and gave them a pull.

Nothing.

They didn't budge.

How the fuck was I supposed to stay in here without mauling her? Already my body was prepping, jumping with joy that we were alone.

"When's the next class?" I asked in desperation.

Isla turned to me slowly. "One hour."

"One hour," I repeated, voice hoarse.

"Sixty minutes." She nodded slowly.

"Thirty-six hundred seconds." I hung my head then grabbed a nearby towel and slowly ran it down my chest.

Isla's eyes bulged before she banged on the doors with both fists.

# Chapter Eleven

"Hello!" I slammed my fists against the doors, then rattled them hard in the vain hope they'd magically open. "We're stuck in here!"

I was a woman crazed.

Horny.

Sweaty.

And desperate.

I could feel his testosterone pulsing to the rhythm of my estrogen, our hormones dancing around each other, flirting, lingering, toying.

No!

"Help!" I screamed again.

And then a very hard male body was pressed up against me from behind, sliding his hands over my grip on the handles. He gave a tug, and my body jerked back against his.

I sucked in a breath. Sweet. Crackers.

Did yoga normally do it for guys?

Send all the blood rushing to a giant . . .

Huge.

I gave my head a shake.

No more adjectives.

I needed out.

Otherwise I was going to crumple beneath the temptation of a six-pack, blinding white smile, and triceps.

Hot damn, those triceps.

Enemy. Enemy. Enemy.

Jessie gave the doors another shake. I was too lost in my lust to think to keep holding on to the handles, so I fell back against him.

All of him.

For a second time.

A third would probably cause a spontaneous orgasm.

That's what men like Jessie did to a woman with a pulse. Too bad he had that nasty habit of wanting to destroy my life. I could almost get on board.

"No luck," Jessie said, still not moving.

"Doesn't look like it." Great, and now I was breathless. "I guess we just wait."

"Yup." He still didn't move.

The tension between our bodies was this swirling, thick, pulsing creature, and the more silent we were, the more it fed.

It fed on our inability to flee.

I was the first to move.

And he was the first to grab my wrist and stop me. Slowly, he turned me around so that we were chest to chest. Skin to skin, sweat to sweat. Something very hard and ready pressed against me.

"Isla—" He lowered his head.

I met him halfway.

And the doors magically opened with us in that exact position.

Along with enough camera phones to put the paparazzi to shame.

# Chapter Twelve

ISLA

"What the hell were you thinking?" Blaire paced in front of me. "Never mind, you clearly weren't thinking! We've had paparazzi outside the building since the news broke an hour ago—people are wondering if you guys were dating while we tried to prove his infidelity. You kissed! Isla, this is bad, I need you to know how bad this is!" Blaire dug into the licorice tub and pulled three ropes free, chomping each of them down before facing me again. "It hurts our credibility. He was the ex of a client!"

"I know." I held out my hands like I was trying to protect myself. "Let me just think, I can fix this. I know I can." Everything was spiraling out of control, and my normally calm demeanor was shattered thanks to Jessie. Nothing was helping me regain my composure, not the pacing, not even the yoga breathing.

Jessie chose that moment to stroll right into our office, freshly showered, scowl still in place. "Question, do you ruin people's lives on purpose? Or is it just a happy accident?"

"You!" Blaire pointed at Jessie like he was getting scolded in the principal's office. "Sit."

Colin, her boyfriend, walked in moments later, smirked at both of us, and then kissed Blaire on the mouth. "Haven't been so excited to watch the news in years. Hey, Jessie, maybe next time wear something other than joggers."

"Fuck." Jessie hung his head in his hands while I tried not to laugh from hysteria.

"And you"—Colin pointed at Isla—"with the headlights on, hell, a blind person could take a look at you two and know exactly what you were doing behind closed doors."

"Nothing happened," Jessie said quickly.

It stung a bit, that he'd so casually deny what was about to happen, what would have happened had the doors stayed closed ten seconds longer than they did.

"Like I said"—I sent him a seething glare—"I can fix this, the company's rep, our reps. It's what I do. I fix marriages—"

"Do you, though?" Jessie just had to add.

I shot him a look that would have made a lesser man cower in the corner and suck his thumb. "Every problem has a solution, give me a few minutes to come up with something—anything."

"Fact." Colin crossed his arms. "You girls could easily lose your company if the masses assume you were double dipping—dating the very guy you were supposed to be investigating. It doesn't matter that it's not true, what matters is it looks damning."

Blaire hung her head. "It's what we were afraid would happen last year when all of this started." Jessie's wife at the time (our client) threatened to go to the media with text messages between Jessie and Blaire, even though she was flirting with him as part of the job. Our fear then was, again, the public perception. And we'd never had a client turn on us like that . . . then again, we'd never dealt with Satan before.

"Idea, let's just blame Vanessa?" Jessie joked.

Just kidding, Satan was sitting across from me.

"We need a story," I finally said, my rusty mind working double time, mentally oiling the gears so it would work faster. "A believable story."

Blaire's eyes narrowed. "Isla, the only story you have is the truth, and nobody's going to believe it, not after seeing you and Jessie in a yoga studio looking ready to sex each other up. Not after pictures of you guys kissing at The Ivy and the news of Jessie donating his time at your aunt's retirement home. Not after you decided to rent his guesthouse."

I stood and went back to pacing, then made myself two cups of coffee. Everyone watched me in silence while I chugged the first cup, set it down quietly, and stared into the second, waiting for an answer from the coffee gods.

"Isla?" Blaire's soft voice returned me to the present. "Any thoughts? Ideas? Anything?"

Our phones were ringing off the hook. I could hear Abby fielding questions from the press and clients about my relationship with Jessie.

My mind whirled.

Everything pointed to a relationship.

Everything pointed to me basically doing the unthinkable.

"If we ignore each other, it just causes more speculation." I drummed my fingertips on the table. "It looks like we're hiding something."

"Agreed." Blaire handed me a piece of licorice, while Colin and Jessie shot each other worried glances.

"So we lie." I straightened my shoulders. "And in the end, both of us get something out of it."

"Come again?" Jessie stood and faced me. "How is lying supposed to help anyone?"

"Easy." I spread my hands wide. "It helps because we get married."

The room fell silent.

Jessie laughed, and then stopped. "You're serious? How the hell did you get from lying to marriage?"

"I second that." Colin's expression narrowed in on me. "Is this normal for you? This behavior?"

Blaire smacked him on the chest. He winced.

I rolled my eyes. "Look, it's easy, Jessie's still pissed—"

"Rightfully so." Jessie just had to interrupt.

"If people see that he's in a committed, loving, noncheating relationship, doing all the things that a doting fiancé would do, it puts him in a good light because the very woman willing to put his ring on *her* finger is the very one who was hell-bent on exposing his cheating ways."

Jessie's jaw dropped as Colin did a slow clap.

I almost patted myself on the back when Blaire gave me a wink.

"You." Jessie dragged out the word with more bite than necessary. "What do you get out of all of this? It seems to help me more than you."

"Stop saying *you*." I gritted my teeth. "And it helps because I'm able to tell our love story without people wrongfully assuming I'm the other woman."

Jessie snorted. "So now we're in love? And people are just going to believe that after having the"—he air quoted—"perfect marriage crumble, I'm just going to jump right back into the saddle? Or maybe you like the term *ball and chain*?"

"Technically the ball and chain both attach," I pointed out. "Maybe that's why the first one didn't last, you were doing it wrong."

Jessie took a menacing step toward me.

"Sore subject?" I said the minute we came chest to chest.

"Yeah," Colin said slowly. "People are totally going to buy that love thing . . ."

Blaire separated us and then stood in the middle. "If this is going to work, you guys need to start looking like you love each other and not like you want to rip each other's heads off."

"Easy." I pasted a sweet smile on my face. "Right, pumpkin?"

Jessie eyes narrowed. "How long?"

"Until it blows over. Until another celebrity shaves their head or cheats, or confesses to showering with clothes on because they're afraid of their private parts. Got it?"

The room was silent.

"I don't need to remind you guys what's riding on this." I had to say it, I needed him, I couldn't lose this. He had money and fame to fall back on.

I had nothing but the business Blaire had helped me build.

It was my life.

It was literally all I had.

If I lost it, I'd be losing a part of my soul—and I remembered too well what it felt like to lose your identity and come out the other side questioning everything about yourself and your place in the world.

I controlled my world.

My destiny.

My damn business.

Jessie held out his hand.

I took it.

He pulled me to his chest. "I would say to get our terms in writing, but that's just something else for them to find . . . I will say this, if you make things worse, I will shut you down."

"So you've said." My voice was wobbly as I released his hand and flashed Blaire a smile. "See, like I said, fixed."

Jessie leveled me with a stare that went straight through to my soul. I shivered.

"We'll see."

# Chapter Thirteen

Six hours since I left the office and my chest still burned, making me think I was either coming down with some sort of cold, or maybe feeling the effects of the strenuous workout followed by the almost-make-out session.

I told my cock to calm the hell down, but it was pointless, I'd probably die with images of her ass flashing before my line of vision.

Too bad I didn't trust her.

Maybe it was my distrust of women in general, maybe it was the fact that her smile wasn't as confident as it usually was—I wasn't sure why I was so bothered, but it left me feeling chaotic.

And I did not perform well around chaos.

In any shape or form.

Straight lines.

Black and white.

Control.

And Isla, well, she was like a giant splotch of red paint on a fucking dalmatian. It didn't do well for my anxiety that somehow the press was going to get wind of yet another character flaw on my end or worse—another bad decision with a woman——and fillet me alive.

I walked over to the kitchen and pulled out one of my favorite red-wine glasses from Saks, monogrammed with a *J* on the middle and thicker around the stem, making them more masculine.

It helped they were pure crystal.

The wine had been breathing for the past half hour while I stared out the window at the devil herself flicking on lights in my guesthouse only to turn them off again. Part of me wondered if she wasted electricity on purpose to see if I'd notice, or to see if she'd win this insane little war that she started back when she took on my ex-wife as a client and decided to screw up my perfect life.

I hesitated at the word *perfect*.

Stared at the white granite and winced.

It was the exact word Vanessa had uttered over and over to me, fucking hammered it into my world until I was sick of it, sick of pretending, sick of being what everyone expected all the time.

And yet.

I was caught between being fake and being afraid to be myself—because who wants that guy?

The guy who'd rather stay at home and watch old movies? The beer drinker who was more loner than socialite? The one who honestly didn't give a shit if he wasn't seen at parties and events?

I'd like to think the nonprofit was helping me in more ways than one. I was starting to become myself again, not the self my ex had fabricated for me.

But the one who actually went up to a bar and ordered a beer, even though in our circle it wasn't as refined.

The guy who allowed himself to wear jeans instead of head-to-toe Prada.

The guy who wasn't afraid to show emotion in public for fear someone would get a bad picture.

The guy with the permanent smile.

That was me.

The last time I was *People's* Sexiest Man Alive, they captioned the cover story "The Man Who Has It All."

I scowled harder then poured a full glass, just as my doorbell rang. I took two long gulps then walked to the door and opened it.

Isla's hair was pulled into a knot on the top of her head, she was wearing Under Armour joggers and a black tank top that kept falling off her shoulder each time she crossed her arms.

And, thank God, a matching black sports bra.

And a pair of black Uggs that had my fingers twitching to grab and toss into the fireplace.

"Steal those?" I pointed at the boots.

She rolled her eyes and shoved her way past me.

"Sure, come in, not like I have company since apparently I'm getting engaged and trying to hide it from everyone I know."

"About that." Isla whirled around. "I think a public engagement would be best."

"Of course you do." I sighed, praying for patience. "You wouldn't happen to be one of those girls that has a scrapbook full of wedding ideas just in case the right guy comes along, would you?"

She traced a droplet of wine on the pristine white counter with her fingertip and shrugged.

My eyebrows rose. "A Pinterest board too?"

She jerked her head up. "If I did, it would be a secret board, so don't even try to find it."

I smirked at the sudden blush on her cheeks. "You have your colors picked out then?"

"Black and white," she said with a straight face before bursting into laughter. "You should have seen your eyes light up!"

It was my turn to blush as I swiped my wine from the countertop and took two more healthy sips. "Pretty sure my eyes would never light up over wedding talk—I wasn't planning on ever walking down the aisle again."

"Guys don't walk," she said with a wink. "But if you want me to be at the end of that aisle, all you gotta do is ask, baby."

"I'm not drunk enough for you yet." I drank more.

She grabbed the bottle and lifted it to her damn lips, then tipped it back before I could stop her. "Ohhhhh, that's a nice red blend."

I clenched my teeth. "People use glasses."

"Point one out, and I'll use one," she said with a wide smile.

"You aren't going away, are you?"

"No."

"Care to tell me why?"

"Care to find me a glass?"

Scowling, I went to the cupboard, pulled out another crystal glass, and handed it to her.

Our fingers brushed.

I shouldn't have even noticed.

I hated that I did.

I hated that her eyes flickered to my mouth before she turned away and poured herself a glass as big as mine.

The kitchen felt too small for the both of us.

And I felt awkward just standing there while she took her first sip. It felt wrong to stare at her lips like I hadn't just tasted them. Pieces of hair curled by the back of her neck, had she just showered? Did she have naturally curly hair? Why the hell did I even care?

I lifted my hand.

Then dropped it to my side as she walked away from me and sat in the adjoining living room. I assumed she wanted me to follow, so I grabbed my glass and the bottle, and sat next to her on the white couch, praying the whole time she wasn't a spiller.

"So." I leaned back. "The reason for this late-night visit?"

"Couldn't sleep." Her eyes darted from the wine bottle to me, then back again. "I also thought that maybe . . . we should call a cease-fire."

"Cease-fire?" I leaned forward and clasped my hands together. "What do you mean?"

She blew out a breath like she was annoyed, then turned to me. "Look, we can't constantly be at each other's throats if we're supposed to be showing people that we're a happy couple."

My stomach filled with dread.

My eyes burned like I'd just had acid dumped into them.

"You should go." I stood.

Isla looked around the room then back up at me. "What did I say?"

I didn't realize how much anger I still had inside.

Anger at being controlled.

Allowing myself to be a puppet.

Allowing a woman to tell me how I should live my life, and why.

And I sure as hell wasn't doing it again.

"I'm not your child, Isla." I didn't mean the words to come out so aggressively. "I can't—" I lost my voice.

"Whoa, whoa, whoa—" Isla set her wine down and reached for my hands. It was so unexpected that I collapsed onto the couch as she pulled me closer. "That is not what this is."

"Isn't it?" I countered. "Fake marriage for the cameras? You think the universe is just trying to fuck with me?"

She flinched.

"Sorry." I rubbed my thumb across her hands. "I didn't mean it, I just—"

"Don't take out your anger with Vanessa on me. We are two completely different people. I can't even stand the color white."

"Your car's white, Isla."

"Because black gets too hot in LA and I don't like colorful cars," she pointed out like I should care. "Okay, how about we come up with a list of rules? Lines we can't cross during the next few months?"

I narrowed my eyes. "You would do that?"

"Jessie, do you really think I want you to shut me down? Do you think I want the world to look at my business, the one I've built from the ground up, and think we just sleep with clients' husbands?"

"I don't know? Do you?"

"The nonprofit was your life—this is mine."

"Touché." I knew I was pushing her, but I was just so . . . damn angry. Still. Over things I couldn't control, over things she helped set in motion.

Isla hung her head again. "You like control, I like control, though I'd like to point out that I at least don't have a stick up my ass. I'm more of the type of person who just likes to have a plan, whereas you like things to look a certain way." She stared at me. "Does it . . . bother you if I do this?"

She moved the magazines on the table, making it so they weren't straight but all over the place.

I almost broke out in hives.

"Okay, so that's a yes." She moved them back. "See? These are the things I should probably know—"

"No." Fear lodged in my throat at the idea of letting someone get close to me again only to betray me—only to make me realize that I was somehow lacking. "Engaged in name only."

"Like a regency novel," she said under her breath.

"Excuse me?"

"Regency. Historical romance." The smile on her face fell as she stood again. "So, no cease-fire, no rules, except what? Make sure that we hold hands and smile when we're in public, and don't get caught with your pants down?"

"Fine by me." I stood and stared at the door behind her, hoping she'd get the message.

She downed the rest of her wine and walked to the door, then turned around. "You do realize that a relationship means you give fifty percent, you meet in the middle, you compromise. I'm not asking for a spleen, I'm just asking for you to help me so I can help you."

She cringed.

I shook my head. "That's where you're wrong, Isla, the only thing I need from you is a ring on your finger and your word that you're going to fix what you broke. If you don't . . ." I shrugged.

"Ah, back to threats." I could have sworn tears filled her eyes, and I almost felt like a jackass for making her feel that way when I was just as guilty of nearly kissing her, of putting her in a bad place. The temptation had been too much, and fighting my growing attraction to her was almost as hard as hating her.

I still put the blame on her. On the yoga pants.

On the situation.

If we were keeping track.

She still ruined me.

And all I did was react to being with her in a trapped space with a working dick.

I missed her goodbye.

I only heard the click of the door.

And wanted to punch a hole through the wall when I looked out the window and saw her swipe at her cheeks.

# Chapter Fourteen

ISLA

Satan.

Satan.

Satan.

I threw a pillow against my bedroom door and scowled in the general direction of his stupid mansion with his white walls and good wine.

And nice wineglasses.

I could still feel the heaviness between my fingertips.

Angry. I was angry. Not lusting after his glassware!

What the hell was wrong with him anyway? I was saving his sorry ass. Granted mine was getting saved in the process, but could he at least try?

I almost felt sorry for Vanessa in that moment. Almost.

Then again, he'd basically put me in that same damn box. Could I understand the similar circumstances? Yes. But I wasn't manipulating him to keep him—I was trying to help him understand that people would see us and expect us to fail.

Failure was never an option.

I straightened my shoulders and went into the kitchen to grab a snack, only to nearly choke to death on a spoonful of peanut butter when a loud knock sounded at the door.

I shoved the spoon back in the jar and carried it with me.

I unlocked the dead bolt and opened the door a crack, then all the way when Jessie was standing there in a pair of low-slung sweats and a white tank top that didn't have a right to look so nice with his muscles, and build, and pecs, and—I choked again on the peanut butter and drool that came with it but managed to swallow.

"You gonna make it?" He smirked.

I hated his smirk more than I hated his body.

Because it made me react.

Hell, everything he did made me react and want to seek vengeance with a fiery purpose on his damned soul.

He made me want to fight for no reason other than my adrenaline pumped from simply staring at his perfect face and small dimple near the right side of his cheek. Where did that even come from? Had he always had that?

"Isla?" He waved a hand in front of me.

I shoved more peanut butter into my mouth because I didn't have words yet and I was still pissed off.

He glanced at the jar, eyes wide. "Why does it look like you added jelly to that already?"

I shrugged, mouth full. "I did."

"Of course you did."

"Saves time," I added. "And tastes amazing." And just because I knew it would gross him out and give me a reaction that wasn't disappointment or anger, I handed him a full spoon. "Give it a try, slugger, you may like it."

He stared at the spoon, the peanut butter was this giant glob with another glob of jelly on top of it. There was no part of it that looked even remotely gourmet.

He didn't take the spoon.

No, because this was Jessie sexy Beckett.

He grabbed my damn wrist, wrapped his fingers around it tightly then pulled my arm forward and opened his luscious mouth—the one that probably licked the tears of all the virgins he'd deflowered—and wrapped it around the spoon. His tongue came out next.

My eyes bulged a bit as he worked the spoon like he knew his way around a woman's body and wanted me to know he knew.

I flexed my legs.

I clenched.

I almost crossed.

And then he was done.

So I exhaled in relief.

"Good," he said, winking. "The ratio needs work."

He walked right by me into his property. Damn it.

"Well." I trailed after him. "We can't all be perfect."

He flinched at my obvious jab, then turned around. "Two hours a day."

I almost dropped the peanut butter. "Two hours a day you work out?"

"That too," he said seriously. "But I have a proposition. Until this is all over with, whenever that is, we spend two hours a day getting to know each other. I won't go into this the way I went into my last one."

"Oh? And how was that?"

"Blind." He said it so quickly I almost felt guilty for cursing him to hell a few minutes ago. "Colin warned me about his sister, but I was convinced I'd seen a different side of her, and well, I'm stubborn. I'd always wanted her and I was thrilled when the girl I'd always chased finally gave me the time of day."

It was more than I knew.

More than Blaire had told me when Colin explained their relationship.

He shifted on his feet and did a small circle like he didn't know what to do with his massive body. "It won't look good that I know nothing about you and you know nothing about me. If we want to sell it, I need to know everything, the good . . ." He licked his lips and turned, giving me his back. "The bad, the ugly . . ."

"I'm a freak," I admitted.

He froze and then looked over his shoulder. "Care to elaborate or do you want me to guess?" His smile was back.

I licked the peanut butter from my lips then smacked them together. "Guess."

"In bed?"

I snorted out a laugh. "That *would* be your first guess."

He tapped his chin, slowly approaching with a sexy-as-hell gait before stopping in front of me. "In the kitchen?"

"Nope."

"Shower."

"How are you a freak in the shower?"

He burst out laughing. "That's fair . . ." He circled and then stopped behind me, putting his hands on my shoulders. So silent. I wasn't sure what he was waiting for. "By the looks of the place I'd say you're a clean freak, but then so am I . . . not a thing out of place—"

"Is our two hours starting now?"

"Better now than never."

"Okay."

He guided me to the couch I'd had delivered from my apartment and then grabbed the blanket and put it over my legs.

Did he know I always used that blanket?

Why did I care that he cared?

Why was I still staring at the blanket like he'd just given me his firstborn?

"A freak . . ." He stared at my makeshift coffee table, eyebrows raised. "Well, I think I figured it out —you hate being late."

I gasped and quickly tried to hide my schedule for the week, but he had already grabbed it. "You do realize people don't use paper anymore, or highlighters really? You could just put everything in your phone?"

I snatched the papers away and held them to my chest. "I know, but what if I lose my phone?"

He gave me a blank stare and then smiled wide. "So this is your backup." He lifted his hands and made air quotes. "Just in case?"

"Your air quotes are insulting."

He did them again as he said, "So, this backup schedule, is it the only one? I mean what if your house burns down?"

My eyes widened in panic.

He grabbed my wrist. "Okay, I believe you, no need to make copies."

I was already itching, thinking of the worst.

"Isla"—he tilted my chin toward him—"I won't judge you if you do. And since you let me in on the secret, I'll even let you use the copier in the house, just don't sit on it butt-ass naked and leave evidence."

"Fun ruiner," I joked, suddenly feeling lighter than I had all night.

"Well, we did say rules needed to be established. I'll say that's rule number one."

"Rule two can be no walking around in socks without shoes, I hate socks, they seem unclean."

He stared me down. "What if they're clean socks I put on while looking for my shoes?"

"What if you wait to put on your gross socks until after you locate your shoes?"

"Ah, an answer for everything." He was so close to me I could see the flecks of gold in his clear blue eyes.

I shrugged and backed against the couch. "So, what are we going to do for another"—I checked my watch—"hour and forty-two minutes?"

His eyes dragged down my body before returning to my face. "I could think of a few things."

I gulped.

But he didn't act on anything and instead nodded to the TV. "We could binge-watch a show, I'll even let you make little structured discussion sheets with a highlighter . . ."

I smacked him on the leg as my eyes lit up.

"Oh God, I love that you're actually excited about taking notes."

"It's calming!"

"So why don't you color? It's the new thing! Coloring books, markers . . ."

"It's like coloring." I adjusted the blanket. "With labels."

His eyes narrowed. "You have a label maker, don't you?"

"It only makes sense, so I don't have to look inside my containers."

"Or drawers?" he said.

I didn't answer.

He moved so fast, one minute he was sitting next to me, the next he was in my bedroom, a look of extreme disappointment on his face. He shook his head and pointed to the label on the top drawer of my dresser. "Lingerie."

My face burned red.

He licked his lips. "What? You think you might forget it's the first drawer?"

I crossed my arms. "Really want to get into this, Mr. Black-and-White Everything—"

He held up his hands in surrender. "So how about that show?"

"I pick first?"

He walked with me back into the living room. I grabbed my laptop and popped it open.

"No TV?" He frowned.

I shrugged. "No need."

I didn't realize how close we'd have to sit.

Or how good he would smell.

Or how many sex scenes would be in the new *American Gods* show.

But there it was.

Sex.

Me.

A too-hot blanket.

And Jessie's massive body next to mine.

I fell asleep that way, against something warm.

And woke up with a blanket covering my body and a smile on my face.

# Chapter Fifteen

## JESSIE

Two weeks ago, if someone had told me that I'd be walking into Tiffany's ready to pick out a ring for my new fiancée, I would have laughed in their face and then gotten drunk at the nearest bar.

Marriage hadn't been good to me.

It had been a nasty little bastard I never wanted to face again.

And yet, there I was.

Hand in hand with possibly the most intimidating woman I'd ever met, pasting a fake smile on my face.

Fuck how history repeated itself.

"You don't have to look so excited," she said through clenched teeth, and then she winked and wrapped her arms around my neck and just hung there, her white blouse open enough for me to see her right breast and pale, silky-smooth skin. "I'll let you cop a feel if your smile reaches here." She tapped the side of my temple and grinned wider. "Come on, pumpkin, it will be just like junior high only this time the girl is letting you, and you aren't begging for a look at her boobs."

I wrapped my arms tightly around her waist. "What makes you think I had to beg?"

She scrunched up her nose. "I had you pegged as the creepy nerdy kid who stared at girls during lunchtime while playing with Star Trek action figures—am I that far off base?"

I leaned down and brushed my nose across her cheek as I whispered in her ear, "Try GI Joes."

Isla licked her lips and gripped my biceps. "They mentored you well."

I was smiling before I realized it as she clung to my bicep like she was getting ready to take a swing from it and shout to the world how big, bad, and strong I was. The longer I thought about it, the harder I smiled.

"There it is." She released my arm.

My smile fell.

Vanessa had never touched me because she wanted me—at least that's what I'd come to realize—she touched me because she wanted something from me.

There was a big difference in the way a woman touched you for her needs, or touched you for your own.

Isla touched me for me.

"Alright." Isla tapped her ear as someone got out of a car and took a picture of us. "You got your earpiece in?"

"I still don't understand why I need Colin to coach me through a fucking proposal, I know how to propose."

Isla covered her smile with her hand. "So what was your plan then? Let me guess, get down on one knee, say something like *I can't imagine my life without you?*"

I felt my face heat. "What's wrong with that?"

"Everything," she huffed as I opened the door for her and pressed my hand to the small of her back.

"How so?"

One of the managers weaved her way toward us, a tight bun pulled low on her head, her lipstick bright red, and her eyes lasered in on us with such intensity I almost saw dollar signs in her gaze. I'd called ahead to let them know we were coming, but beyond that, everything needed to look real, like we were just looking.

Isla turned and faced me, her eyes searching mine. "Because, Jessie, life is supposed to be shared, it's a partnership. Things don't work out when you feel the need to fully depend on that other person for your own happiness. The fact is, you should be able to imagine your life without the person you love—the difference is, you shouldn't want to. Get it?"

My jaw went slack as the manager clasped her hands in front of us. "I'm Janie, I'll be personally escorting you around our lovely store this evening. I hope you don't mind, but I've already prepared a few of our favorite pieces for your inspection."

I almost snorted at the word *inspection*.

What? Like we were buying a house?

After the first price tag, I imagined I could buy three houses, but it didn't matter, this was part of it. Besides, unless Isla fled the country, the ring was going to be returned.

Maybe I'd handcuff her every night to my bedpost just in case.

I squirmed at the thought.

Heat filled my veins, causing a bead of sweat to run down the back of my neck. I cleared my throat as Janie pulled out another ring.

"Shit, that's a lot of money," Colin said in my ear as I inspected the three-carat piece. It had a center princess-cut stone in a vintage two-prong band, but it felt too . . . normal.

And our situation was anything but normal.

"I like this," Isla said in that professional voice I was starting to hate. It seemed fake, like she was trying to please everyone else in the universe but herself.

"It's not her," I found myself saying without hesitation, and Janie and Isla shared a look.

"He's sweet," Janie said while Isla narrowed her eyes at me as if to say *What's the big deal? Just pick a ring out!*

"You think you know me so well . . ." Her voice held a teasing note, a challenge.

I crossed my arms. "I better since I'm sharing a life with you, isn't that what you said earlier?"

Her face flushed before she motioned to the rings. "Then pick."

The gauntlet was thrown.

I stared at the rings, everything was simple, elegant, unique, like the shiny façade she put on every single day in order to do her job.

But it wasn't her.

It was missing something.

Like life.

I exhaled and nodded to Janie. "I want something with a different color, antique, trendy, something that stands out, that wants to be heard."

Isla paled next to me.

I took her hand and squeezed it.

Janie smiled. "I think I have exactly what you're looking for."

She pulled out another set of rings, and before she even set it down, I pointed. "That one, right there."

Janie practically clapped her hands and started jumping. "The Soleste Pear, yellow diamond surrounded by white diamonds—one of our most unique rings. Though typically they only go up to a two carat, the one you've set your eye on is nearly four carats."

Isla looked ready to pass out.

"Four carats," I repeated out loud while Colin cursed in my ear like he was the one having to shell out a shit ton of money for a fake engagement.

But the moment felt . . . right, as I picked up the ring and faced Isla. Her hand shook as I slid the ring onto her finger. "Perfect fit."

Janie's sigh was loud enough to get the attention of the entire store.

Slowly, I bent down on one knee and held on to Isla's small hands. I had no idea why I was shaking right along with her.

Why I suddenly had no idea how to use the words floating around my brain, or why my tongue stopped working all at once.

Colin cleared his throat in my earpiece. "Tell her she's beautiful, she's the only woman you see and—"

"Isla." I ignored his protests about going rogue. "Share this life with me, not because I can't do it on my own—but because I can't imagine going another day without you by my side, without waking up next to you, touching you, laughing with you. I want you to belong to me, the way I already belong to you. Please say yes?"

Her eyes widened.

"Didn't think you had it in you." Colin sounded surprised.

Isla quickly gave her head a shake, rose to her feet, and pulled me in for a brief kiss before whispering against my lips, "Yes!"

Janie cheered as clapping and whistles sounded around the store. Isla leaned in and whispered in my ear, "Good job, Colin."

Rejection was swift.

I deflated a bit.

And swore in that moment I'd do anything so she'd never find out the truth.

It wasn't Colin saying those words. Prompting me.

They seemed to come from somewhere more terrifying.

More confusing.

A place that felt like my heart.

# Chapter Sixteen

ISLA

I toyed with the ring on my finger, twisting it around and around. It was soothing, the continuous movement, and yet every time my fingers touched the giant rock, I wanted to look down.

Fought the desire to stare at my left hand in awe.

Wayne had never bought me a ring. We were supposed to pick it out together. But he was always too busy.

I dreamed of having an actual Tiffany's experience, one where a gorgeous loyal man stood by my side, then fell to his knees with adoration and told me to pick whatever I wanted. It seemed so romantic to have someone take care of me like that, and now, now that I had it, I wanted to cry, because it wasn't real, none of this was, and for a fleeting moment, I closed my eyes and told myself it was, because it felt good to be treasured, desired.

The only person in my life who knew about my dreams was Blaire, which meant this was her first brilliant idea.

Encouraged by Colin.

Begrudgingly accepted by Jessie after a few minutes of begging on their end while I downed another cup of coffee.

When I woke up this morning, I had one plan.

Go to work, annoy the hell out of Jessie, have a relaxing yoga session, then go home and open a bottle of wine.

Instead, I was riding in a Tesla toward West Hollywood for a late bite to eat with Jessie so we could be "seen."

Colin and Blaire were meeting us there.

My nerves were already shot.

And my hand felt heavy.

"You're quiet," Jessie said as he parked at The Catch. I'd only ever eaten there once but was excited to fill the weird-feeling void in my stomach with something of substance.

I unbuckled my seat belt. "Sorry, just thinking."

"Bullshit," Jessie teased. "That's the look of a plotter right there, better get that planner out and highlight some things." He had the nerve to touch my cheek with his finger.

I smacked his hand away and tried not to smile. "No touching."

"I just spent over six figures on a ring, I think I should be at least allowed to touch your cheek."

I smiled over at him. "Imagine what you could have touched had you spent twice that?"

I was teasing.

I knew it.

He knew it.

Regardless, the air was suddenly sucked from the car as we stared at one another, breathing became more difficult as seconds of silence ticked by. Why? Why was he so impossible to resist?

Jessie was the first to regain his composure. "Just don't follow me into the bathroom or do any of your crazy PI shit, we're supposed to be in a loving relationship."

I snorted. "You even know what that looks like?"

It was a low blow, but he threw me off balance, made me feel panicked and out of control—something I would never get used to.

"This coming from the girl who's never even been married?" Jessie whistled as he slammed the door shut, leaving me in the car by myself.

I deserved that.

And then my door opened and he offered his hand.

I took it and stood. He jerked me to his chest, my head nearly knocked out his chin.

"Just leave crazy Isla in the car," he said.

I frowned. "What? Still worried about that perfect image of yours?"

He flinched.

It was slight.

It was enough.

"Are you worried I'll embarrass you?"

He didn't say anything.

He didn't have to.

"Alright, lover." I looped my arm in his. "Let's do this."

"Isla." His tone held just enough warning to make the hairs on the back of my arm stand on end.

I ignored them all.

Kept my head high, and walked right up to the door and waited.

He held it open.

Colin and Blaire waved at us from a table in the corner. Nobody paid me much attention, but Jessie? It was like setting a bomb off in the restaurant.

It was at least ten minutes before he finally stopped talking to his adoring fans and took a seat across from me. His smile was flat again, the crinkles at his eyes gone.

I hated his flat smile.

Even more when it was directed at me.

Cold. Lifeless.

I don't know what came over me, but I kicked him under the table.

His knee shot up, knocking over his water. "What the hell was that for?"

"I'm hungry," I said sweetly. "You made me wait."

"Eat bread!" He shoved the basket toward me.

I gasped.

Blaire let out a long sigh. "Isla doesn't eat bread."

Jessie's shocked expression wasn't at all helpful. "But . . . why?"

"Because"—I placed the napkin on my lap—"I don't like it."

Wrong thing to say.

Jessie stared. "I don't understand your anger."

"You don't need to understand, just accept it, and know that I get really hangry when I have to wait to get fed."

Jessie's eyes lit up a bit before he smirked at his menu. "Noted."

I rolled my eyes and then remembered we had to look in love, so I leaned forward, careful to show off the sparkle of my diamond ring. "So, Blaire, things all quiet online?"

Blaire lifted a shoulder. "The story was just leaked about your engagement, so I guess we'll see if phase one actually did anything before we move on to the next phase."

"Come again?" Jessie dropped his menu.

"Phase two?"

"Yeah, that one."

"Um." Blaire looked at me helpfully. "It's just . . . it's not enough you're engaged, people are going to speculate that she moved into your rental because she was getting ready to move into the main house. So, phase two, meaning you move in. Together."

I hung my head in my hands while Jessie said enough *Hell no*'s to make even the most secure woman want to jump off a cliff.

"That"—Jessie pointed his knife at Blaire—"is all speculation and assumption. What if we're waiting to move in! Saving ourselves!"

A couple glanced over at us.

"Please stop talking," I whispered. "People are staring, and the last thing they need to gossip about is me becoming a nun or Jessie not being able to get it up."

"How the hell does that translate to him not being able to get it up?" Colin said a little too loud.

I ducked my head behind a menu. "Because people exaggerate. They'll take the whole 'living separately' to mean second thoughts, problems in bed. Trust me, this is what we do for a living."

Blaire nodded her head in agreement.

"No." Jessie waved the knife in the air. "No, it's my sanctuary, I finally got my crazy ex out of that place and now you want this one to move in?" He pointed the tip at me. "No."

I grinned triumphantly.

Blaire nodded.

"She's not moving in," Jessie said in a stern voice. "That's final."

# Chapter Seventeen

My domain.

My home.

My inner sanctum.

I'd finally gotten it back from my ex-wife's greedy hands, finally embraced the single life.

Only to have Isla fucking Turner toss a throw pillow on my white leather couch.

It was red.

I hated it.

A red throw followed.

The color looked so out of place in my living room that I started getting anxious.

She was ruining everything.

Everything.

When she reached back into one of her suitcases, I put a stop to the madness, rushed over, and slammed it shut. "That's enough."

"That's two of my things."

"Exactly."

Her eyebrows knit together. "What about my clothes? Toothbrush? Unmentionables?"

"Put your pink underwear in the washer with my whites and suffer the consequences."

Her lips pressed together in a smirk. "Aw, Jessie, feeling a little bit uptight?"

I didn't respond. If I did I'd end up strangling the expression from her face or maybe just kissing it away and then locking her in the guest room. Forget the whole "two hours of conversation a day," I was tempted to kiss her senseless and send her packing back to her room.

"Why can't you just keep things inside the suitcase and take them out as you need them?"

Her green eyes narrowed. "Because I live here now, at least temporarily, and I don't want to live out of a suitcase."

"Try," I said through clenched teeth.

"You have no right to tell me what to do." She jerked her suitcase away from my hands and opened it up again.

I tried jerking it back, but she was too fast. She hurled it upside down and every damn thing came tumbling out onto my newly cleaned marble floors.

I groaned and covered my eyes, so much color. "Did you mean to blind me?"

"Do you even know your primary colors? Because it concerns me, it really does, that you only wear black, white, and maybe gray if you feel like getting frisky. Your walls match the state of your clothing, which matches your stellar personality." She grinned. "Maybe if you added a bit of spice to your life you wouldn't have—"

She didn't say it.

She didn't have to.

Wouldn't have lost Blaire to Colin?

Lost my wife in the beginning?

"Clean this shit up, I'm going to bed."

She hung her head. "Where's the guest room?"

"Pick one, pick all of them, just don't come into mine."

"Are we dealing with a real-life *West Wing* scenario here?" She laughed a bit.

My lips twitched but I didn't give in. "I'm just trying to be a good roommate. The last thing you want is to walk in on me doing something you can't unsee."

"Honey." Isla started piling things in her arms—oranges, reds, pinks, blues, I was dizzy trying to keep track. "I've seen it all."

And because I never backed down from a challenge, I pulled her into my arms and pressed myself against her. "I highly doubt that."

Her lips parted.

Her pulse was erratic.

I walked away.

Like an idiot with a swollen cock and a woman who hated me staring daggers at my back. It felt like déjà vu.

It felt like hell.

Ah, I nodded to myself.

Welcome to marriage!

# Chapter Eighteen

ISLA

Darkness swallowed up the house, making me feel small. Every shadow that crept along the wall jolted me awake, ready to grab my hair dryer and wreak havoc on the unlucky bastard stupid enough to crawl through my window. It always ended up being a tree, or security checking the premises, something I really wish Jessie had warned me about.

It always took me a while to get used to a new place. Jessie's house was gorgeous, but it was cold, lacking any sort of emotion or warmth, which left me more distressed than I normally would have been in an unfamiliar place.

I played with the ring, twisting it around my finger a few times as my stomach growled in protest. The clock said three a.m.

My stomach didn't believe it.

It needed to be fed.

And I'd been so wound up after the magical fake engagement and Colin's words coming through Jessie's mouth that I'd only managed to eat a few bites before tapping out and forcing a smile on my face as people whispered and pointed.

And much to my horror—took pictures.

I'd been out of the limelight so long that I forgot how invasive it could be, forgot how paranoid it made a person feel to be constantly watched, to see your face on social media when you hadn't given permission to take your picture in the first place.

I patted my stomach and tossed the white duvet from my legs. The ground was freezing thanks to Jessie's love of slate flooring in every guest room. He should have at least put a few rugs down to bring some warmth to the place.

I had to admit I loved that each room had its own fireplace.

If I ever had enough money to build my dream house, that was the first thing I was going to do. I loved the heat.

When I lived with Wayne in his Hollywood Hills home, he hadn't yet made it big, so everything was mortgaged to the hilt.

He never let me turn on the fireplaces because it would be an extra cost.

Apparently, I didn't deserve extra.

Then again, he thought the world revolved around him.

With a shudder at the distant memories, I slipped my feet into my tattered bunny slippers and made my way into the kitchen.

Not a speck of dirt.

Just the moon's reflection on the white granite, and so much stainless steel my eyes burned. I made a beeline for the pantry and rubbed my hands together as I took in fifteen boxes of never-opened cereal.

Just another weird quirk about Jessie.

He kept up appearances even when nobody would see it.

He forced poor cereal to go uneaten just in case someone came to his house and, God forbid, saw a pantry that wasn't stocked and wrongfully assumed he was bankrupt.

At least that was my assumption, since he didn't really hate cereal and at least took time to alphabetize it.

I took the first box and gave it a shake.

Empty.

As was the second.

Frowning, I looked underneath.

Sure enough, it was open from the bottom.

What kind of freaky cereal crimes was he committing under this roof?

I went down the line and prayed Fruity Pebbles wasn't empty.

It was.

But the Honey Nut was fair game and hadn't been mutilated by his backward ways. I opened the box like a normal cereal-fearing human, grabbed a bowl from the pantry, and filled it almost to the brim, licking my lips in anticipation. The light from the fridge had me wincing as I quickly grabbed his organic whole milk, rolled my eyes, and dumped it in the bowl.

Five trickles.

That's what I got.

Five. Damn. Trickles.

"That's it." I slammed the milk onto the counter. "The guy's an actual monster."

I couldn't eat half-dry cereal.

And I couldn't just run to the store.

I glared at the wall separating the kitchen from his bedroom—communicating my hateful thoughts through telepathy so he'd have bad dreams.

My controlling personality was having a hard time just giving up on the cereal—in fact, I was shaking with irritation from it.

Who puts a near-empty carton back in the fridge? Just drink the last gulp! Like a normal person!

But by all means, yes, give me hope for my midnight snack, the bastard!

A light flickered in his room.

Without thinking, I charged in. "Jessie, I know you're awake!"

"Son of a bitch!" A lamp fell in front of me, followed by Jessie jumping on one foot, in nothing but black boxer briefs that truly left nothing to the imagination. "Do you know what time it is?"

"I'm glad you asked!" I seethed. "It's midnight-snack time, and you screwed my midnight snack." It came out wrong.

He stopped hopping and leveled me with a glare. "I screwed your snack by what? My lack of participation? I'm sleeping! It's late!"

"Exactly!" I threw my hands up. "Don't you think I want to be sleeping too?"

His eyes narrowed. "Then do it, go!"

"But some monster"—I motioned to the kitchen—"decided not to buy more milk, and let's not even get started on the whole 'I only open cereal from the bottom of the box'!"

He had the audacity to look completely innocent. "So what? It's aesthetically pleasing, when you walk into the pantry it looks full, untarnished."

I gaped.

He got in bed and swept the covers back over it. "Now, if you don't mind, I'm going to go to sleep."

"But what about the milk?"

"I don't know, Isla, add water to the cereal? Just get out of my room, I have an early day tomorrow."

"We need house rules, a chore chart, something," I found myself saying. "Rules that don't completely ruin my sleep because your lazy ass doesn't know how to grocery shop."

He clenched his teeth, nodded, then shoved a pillow over his head. "There you go again with your charts and plans and highlighters." He let out a groan. "Good night, Isla."

"So that's a no?"

He flipped me off.

Fanning the flames of my rage even higher.

I marched back into the kitchen and stared down my cereal. There was no chance in hell I was sleeping now.

And if he wasn't going to establish some rules?

Well, that left me with free rein.

I started to whistle.

# Chapter Nineteen

I brushed my teeth so hard I was afraid my gums were bleeding, and with each stroke of the brush, I imagined Isla in nothing but silk shorts, a black, see-through, lacy tank top, and some slippers that had seen better days.

I spit into the sink and stared at my reflection.

Nope. Definitely not how I pictured my life going for the next few months.

I grabbed my phone, almost afraid to look at the news feed update. Blaire had already taken control of all the pings that went off when someone mentioned my name, and it was driving me crazy not knowing if people were buying my relationship with Isla or if they thought I'd actually lost my mind.

Maybe it would be better if I just told everyone I'd lost it.

Believable, at least, with Isla by my side.

The woman was too infuriating and sexy for words.

And somehow her perfume had magically kept itself locked in my room the entire night, meaning I'd woken up less than pleased to find my body ready to consummate my fake engagement against the nearest sturdy structure.

With a groan I threw on a pair of sweats and started my trek toward the coffeepot.

Five steps was all it took for my jaw to drop.

Six steps and I was dizzy. Seven steps . . . and I wasn't sure if I was having a heart attack or an anxiety attack or both.

Isla was perched on the counter—not a barstool, because that would be too normal—sipping her coffee from a bright-orange cup that in no way fit with the color scheme of my modern kitchen.

And the walls, well, the walls in the kitchen were no longer white, but a muted powder blue.

"What in the actual fuck did you do?" I roared, charging toward her.

She looked up, her cherry-red lips pressed together in a smug grin before she held out her orange cup. "Coffee?"

"Isla." My jaw clicked.

She shrugged. "I couldn't sleep. So after I went grocery shopping—"

"At three in the morning?" My voice rose an octave.

She patted me on the cheek twice. "Aw, you afraid someone's gonna kidnap me? Don't worry, I brought my Taser."

I snorted. "Almost feel sorry for the bastard that tries to take you."

Two white teeth bit down on the red. I licked my lips, and then she put her hands on her hips. I looked lower. The dress was a matching red, with a small cape going down the back.

"Follow me." She crooked her finger and opened up the fridge.

"I think I'm going to have a stroke," I said, panting slightly.

"Because I threw away all the bacon? Hey, we're about to say our vows, and I can't have you keeling over anytime soon. I replaced it with turkey bacon."

I started seeing spots. "And my beer? Where the hell is my beer?"

Isla had the audacity to smack my perfectly formed six-pack. "You were getting chunky."

"The hell I was!" I roared, pushing her to the side. Desperation took over as I scanned the contents of my fridge, no leftover takeout boxes, ribs, chicken, what was I supposed to eat? Kale?

I grabbed the kale and made a face.

"Say it with me," she whispered in my right ear. "Vegetable. Just sound it out."

I slammed the kale onto the counter and walked her backward toward the closed pantry door. "You may not want to go in there yet."

"Oh?" I reached for the knob.

"Yeah." Her cheeks paled a bit. "It's just, it might shock your system too much and I think smaller doses is a better choice."

"Can I get you in smaller doses?" I wasn't past begging. Hands-and-knees begging. Then again, that brought way too many erotic visions to my head, especially with that cherry-red cock-sucking lipstick.

"Sorry, I don't come in fun size."

"Ah, so that's why there is no fun." I tried moving her away, but she was a strong, yoga-doing pain in my ass.

"Move."

She rolled her eyes. "Fine, just don't say I didn't warn you."

I opened the door.

Nobody.

Nobody could have warned me.

Not even God.

It looked like an Asian grocery mart exploded inside my pantry—and not in a good, oh-look-Thai-food way.

In an I'm-going-to-be-eating-squid-and-eyeballs sort of way. With unmentionable canned items that didn't look dead yet.

"Isla," I barked. "You have two hours to get this shit out of here."

"But honey." She hugged me from behind, her breasts pressed against my back as her hands slid to my front. "Don't you want to learn about my culture too? It's important in a marriage to compromise. Besides, I know everything there is to know about you. Beer, hot dogs, extra cheese, cereal abuser . . . why not learn all about what makes me . . . special?"

"Too far." I twisted away from her. "This is insanity! Who's actually going to come into our pantry and look at the food?"

"Ah-hah!" She jutted her chin out. "And yet you mistreat cereal boxes!"

"It looks better!"

"So"—she crossed her arms—"my food looks better in here too."

I gripped my hair and tugged. "You're impossible!"

"I'm your soon-to-be wife."

"Same damn thing!"

She just grinned.

And I hated how that grin made me want to return the favor, made me want to kiss it away, punish, please.

I gripped the countertop. "I need to get ready, are we still on for later today, our two hours?"

Her face fell like she was upset I wasn't fighting with her. I knew it would be seconds before I kissed her if I stayed. I was torn between wanting to yell and wanting to strip her dress with my teeth and scrape them down her neck. "Wait, you're just dropping it?"

"One of us"—I tilted her chin toward me—"knows exactly what it's like to compromise, to give up everything for another person's happiness and suffer for it—so sure, I'll give in. I'm used to being the one giving in, except back then I was at least getting laid for it." I smirked at her angry gaze. "So, I'll tell you what, you can keep all of this shit in here, paint every wall in the fucking house, under one condition."

"I show you my boobs?" she countered in a weak voice.

"Everything." I leaned down until my lips almost brushed across her neck. "I want you to show me everything, and I want you to let me claim every single part of it . . ."

"Extortion." She winked. "I won't fall for it."

"And yet, something tells me you will."

Her eyes narrowed. "What? Why? Why would you say that?" I just snickered and walked off.

"Jessie!" Her heels clicked after me. "Jessie, I don't like that look."

"What look?" I called over my shoulder before saying under my breath, "Damn, she looks good in red."

# Chapter Twenty

ISLA

"So." Blaire eyed me wearily. "How was the first night with the man of your dreams?"

I slammed my hands down on the desk and sucked in a breath. "Sorry, I didn't get much sleep last night."

Abby spewed out her coffee.

Dirty little eavesdropper.

"Not for that reason," I called over my shoulder with an eye roll. "Trust me, that would have been better than discovering what I did."

Blaire leaned in, Abby put the call on hold, Penny wrapped her tail around my legs.

"So?" Blaire urged.

"The psychopath opens cereal from the bottom of the box." I made a motion with my hands while Blaire frowned. "Exactly! It's strange. That's what sociopaths do!"

"What? You looked it up online?"

"It's a hunch," I grumbled. "Besides, who the hell cares!"

"Jessie, clearly." Blaire grinned. "So did he say why?"

"It's pleasing to the eye." I almost growled. "It's weird, okay? And he didn't even think to get milk, so I poured three pathetic spurts of milk into my midnight snack and almost suffocated him in his sleep."

"Completely logical reaction," Abby said sarcastically.

That's the thing, though. I was the rational one.

I was the one who calculated, thought things out.

Jessie just brought out the worst in me. The need to verbally spar and physically strangle him over an empty box of Fruity Pebbles.

I'd never felt so out of control, and the minute I thought I had the upper hand he'd get that flicker in his eyes and I'd feel off balance again.

"Can't wait to see what happens tonight at the game." Blaire rubbed her hands together while I nearly passed out across my desk. "Hey, at least try to look excited, you know how awesome it's going to be watching the LA Rams from box seats?"

"So. Awesome." My mouth felt like a desert as I chugged more coffee. "So awesome that we're going to be in front of TV crews and thousands of fans, people who are waiting for Jessie to fail again, people prying into my life with the wrong assumptions."

"All you guys need to worry about is looking like you're in love." Blaire said it like it was easily done, but most of the time Jessie and I looked ready to kiss only during or after a heated argument.

"Right." I adjusted my blouse and reached for my black-rimmed reading glasses. "Shouldn't be too hard."

The door buzzed.

I jerked my head up. "That's our appointment with Danica."

"Let's do this." Blaire handed me a fresh bottle of water as we made our way to the front of the office to meet our new client.

The minute she saw us, she started shaking and then averted her eyes like she wasn't used to people noticing her. It was one of the first clues that something else was going on in the relationship, something bad, possible emotional or physical abuse. My heart sank.

I held out my hand. "I'm Isla, are you Danica? I know this is a very sensitive situation, but we need to get the facts, first from you, and then from our own research."

"And"—she lifted a shaky hand to her face to wipe a tear—"he'll never know?"

"Never," Blaire piped up and handed her a tissue.

I hated these situations, ones where the woman is so terrified of the guy she married that she can't even get help.

I nodded encouragingly. Brown hair fell across her bony shoulders, she was model thin with high cheekbones and long, jean-clad legs. If I didn't know any better I'd think she was still in college.

"Okay." Danica wiped another tear. "It all started a few weeks ago when I found a note in his jacket pocket, there were lipstick prints on the paper and a phone number attached. When I called it, it was just a generic voice mail. I ended the call and haven't done anything since."

Blaire took notes while I pulled Danica next to me and held her hand while she kept crying.

I hated what relationships did to people.

The way they destroyed souls that were meant to be united—ripping them apart in the end, ruining everything. The anger that once again burned so bright in my heart flared with each tear she shed.

How dare men think they have a right to cheat on a woman just because they're bored? Can't they keep it in their pants?

I was completely okay with people parting on good terms.

What wasn't I okay with?

Liars.

I hated liars.

And her husband sounded like he was guilty of just that if her story matched up with the recon mission I was going to need to do.

I kept listening as she told me about their two kids, and they even had a family dog that was dying of cancer.

"Seriously?" I muttered under my breath as I took in all the things in her life that were being affected by her bastard of a husband's selfish actions.

I underlined the word *bastard* about seventeen times before Blaire cleared her throat. I normally didn't take notes, so she probably saw the word and needed me to refocus.

I rallied. "It looks like we have everything we need, one of us will tail him after work and get pictures. We'll get the evidence, if there is any, and we'll do our best to make sure you have everything you need to make a clean break so you can take care of your children and—" I almost got choked up. "What's the dog's name?"

"Fluffer," she sobbed into her ratty Kleenex.

"She must be small."

"She's a Great Dane."

"Alright then." Blaire patted Danica's back, helped her to her feet, and offered her hand. Danica shook it and then gave us both tight hugs before walking out of the office.

"I so need wine after that one." Blaire sighed and collapsed back onto the couch. "Nothing seemed . . . off about her?"

"You mean other than naming her Great Dane Fluffer?" I yawned and then smiled a tired, weak smile. "Nah, she just seems upset, as she should be."

"You're probably right."

"Why?" I tilted my head. "You think she's lying?"

"I'm not sure, she just seemed . . ." Blaire chewed her lower lip. "It could just be because I'm gun-shy after the Vanessa thing."

I snorted. "That makes two of us."

"It's nothing. I'll start gathering info."

I nodded and checked my phone, and let out a little groan. "Four hours before the world's introduced to Jessie's next wife—next flame—next everything." I was nervous. Rightfully so.

We'd agreed that in order for people to believe us, we had to stay together for longer than a month.

Which led us to discussing six months.

And ended up agreeing on a year.

Of living together.

Sharing everything together.

Eating together.

Keeping up appearances.

But I was saving my business. I was doing the right thing.

Jessie, however.

I frowned.

Still confused about that man and why I was so fascinated by him one minute and ready to kill him the next.

My phone pinged with a calendar update.

Meeting with Danica rescheduled. She'll call and make arrangements later this week.

I sighed. No matter what Jessie's intentions, I was going to follow through with the farce, save my business, my reputation, and save that girl's marriage, or end it. People like Danica needed us, and I wasn't going to back down from this engagement just because I was afraid.

I gulped.

And shoved the fear away.

# Chapter Twenty-One

I wasn't ready.

Was anyone ever prepared to step into the limelight? I'd been at it for years and it still gave me anxiety. With the TV screens, the flashing lights, the applause? The constant judgment about my life when most people didn't even know the first thing about me? That was what was wrong with the celebrity lifestyle.

The judgment.

People were invited into your life through interviews and social media, and the minute they found a flaw, they pounced like rabid wolves.

Human.

They find out you're human.

And rather than rejoice in it.

They berate you for it.

They hate you for it.

They detest you for ruining the spell.

I clenched my fists on the wheel as I pulled my car up next to Colin's. The girls had ridden with him since I had a meeting at the gym we owned and thought I'd be late.

Colin knew it was a lie.

There was no meeting.

But I'd needed some time alone.

Some time to think about all the reasons I was doing this, willing to jump back into the very thing that had suffocated my last marriage. I'd married Vanessa out of love and quickly learned it was all a ruse, so we pretended for the media, just like I was doing now.

I'd even made a damn list comparing this situation and the last, where Vanessa slowly sucked the life out of me with this incessant need for us to be the perfect couple.

I didn't want to do that again.

I also didn't have a choice.

My chest felt tight as I got out of the car and waited for Isla to do the same. I expected her to be in the same red dress. Vanessa wouldn't have been caught dead in anything less than designer, especially when photographed.

But she wasn't in a dress.

Or gown.

She was in a Rams jersey with her face painted. Her hair was pulled into a high ponytail that made her look even prettier than before. She smiled wide and pulled out a foam finger, then charged toward me.

I opened my arms.

Not because it was expected.

But because her excitement was contagious.

I suddenly felt stupid in my nice, white button-down shirt and black slacks.

Her breasts pressed against my chest. I let out the air I'd been holding with such a whoosh that my entire body relaxed against her.

"What do you think?" She blinked up at me, smile wide, cherry-red lipstick glistening.

I gave my head a shake and whispered, "I think if I was on the opposing team I'd lose on purpose in order to have you tackle me."

"Jessie, are you saying you'd let me blitz your ass?"

I chuckled. "Well, maybe not my ass—"

Isla made a face and reached for my hand. "You know what I meant."

"And you know what I meant," I said under my breath as if I needed a reminder about our ultimatum this morning, letting her create chaos in my life for sex. It had been a stupid thing to say, but she'd made me angry.

Angry that she was right.

Angry that the first color I'd seen in my house hadn't actually caused anxiety like I'd originally felt, but excitement.

I'd take it to my grave.

The feeling had been so foreign I'd misdiagnosed it.

Isla froze as Blaire and Colin ran up in front of us and talked with security.

"You can do this." I found myself looking down at her. "All you have to do is watch the game and try not to slap me too many times in front of everyone."

"Promises, promises," she joked in a weak voice.

"Would it make you feel better if I handed you the staff schedules for the gym and a few highlighters? You can highlight the times?" I teased.

Her eyes actually lit up.

"Wow, forget chocolate for Valentine's Day, I'm sending you to the staff secretary to organize."

"Dream come true." Her voice was sad, and then she was smiling again. "And while that would make me feel better, I think people would assume I was ignoring you on purpose, and we don't want that."

She reached up and undid a few more buttons of my shirt and pulled it wide.

"Better?" I asked.

With a nod, her hands were back at her sides, and I felt the loss immediately. All it took was her cold fingers near my chest and I was ready to toss her over my shoulder and lock her in my bedroom.

Maybe it had just been too long since I'd had sex.

I was the problem.

Not Isla.

I sighed in frustration, gripped her hand with both of mine, and rubbed back and forth to warm her up. "Let's go."

She stared at my hands surrounding hers like she didn't know how to respond, and the last thing I wanted to do was explain I just liked touching her.

Taking care of her.

Because I'd never really been needed for anything until the charity.

Vanessa only wanted me for my fame, my money, my position.

Not for me.

I was more than all of that.

Colin turned back to us, his arm wrapped around Blaire. They gave us encouraging smiles like everything was going to go smoothly, but I knew that wasn't always the case.

The press could be relentless.

"Deep breaths," Isla said. I wasn't sure if it was for my benefit or hers, but we both seemed to inhale at the same time and brace ourselves as we followed Colin and Blaire into the private entrance. We didn't see any fans or press on our way to the box, but I knew that it wasn't about the walk to the box, it was about the cameras pointing in our direction between plays.

One of the attendants opened the door and ushered us inside.

It was just the four of us and a full staff, including a bartender, which was a nice touch if we were going to have to be smiling for the cameras.

Isla let out a little gasp. "We're so high!"

Her excitement was real.

The woman was pumped about how high we were? Imagine how excited she would be once the food came out and the game started.

We were just in time for the players to get announced. Isla's attention never wavered from the field as she and Blaire yelled with the rest of the crowd like their tiny voices helped.

Colin let out a laugh and then went to the bartender and grabbed us both drinks.

He held out a whiskey to me.

I stared at it, then looked over at Isla. "Why is she dancing in a circle?"

"Blaire told her we were playing the Seahawks, and she has a crush on Richard Sherman."

"Bullshit!" I shoved the whiskey away and glared at the cornerback already on the field. I wasn't sure if it was him, but I wanted him to feel my eyes.

"I was kidding!" Colin called.

Making me feel like an idiot.

I stomped back and glared.

He held out the whiskey again.

I hesitated.

Which I never did.

I always drank whiskey in public. Vanessa said it looked more refined, that beer appeared too white trash for our tastes.

So I'd suffered.

Never again.

I shook my head. "Nah, I'm grabbing a beer."

You'd think I'd just told him I was going vegan.

His mouth dropped open a bit before Blaire rushed over, grabbed the discarded whiskey, and clinked her glass with Colin's. "You boys ready for this?"

"Yeah." Colin smiled at me, a genuine smile that almost made me feel like he was proud of me, which was ridiculous. I shrugged it off and grabbed a beer for me and a glass of red for Isla, then found my seat next to her.

"Cheers." I clinked my bottle with her glass after handing it to her.

She grinned excitedly, then took a deep sip and moaned as she closed her eyes. "You know me well."

I'm sure she didn't mean to say it.

Just like my heart didn't mean to react to the words.

My body felt warm all over as her eyes met mine.

I cleared my throat and looked away while she returned her attention to the game.

I was all too aware of how close we were sitting, of how hard I was just brushing my hands against her body.

It was going to be a hell of a long four quarters.

# Chapter Twenty-Two

ISLA

I found myself watching the clock, wondering how many times Jessie would brush his leg against mine. So far I was at seven and we were only two minutes into the game.

Was he doing it on purpose?

His leg bounced up and down, up and down.

I finally gripped his right knee and stopped the bouncing, but kept my hand there. He stared at it. I could feel the heat of his skin against my fingers, my palms. Why did he have to be so sexy? Why did he have to feel so good?

His lips parted as he very slowly placed a hand on top of mine and then squeezed.

There was no release.

No return of my hand.

I wasn't sure if I liked it or if I wanted to run away screaming. Especially if a simple hand-holding had me wondering what else his hands could do, and his mouth, and his tongue. I shivered. I knew exactly what he was capable of as a kisser.

But those hands.

Those large hands.

I squeezed his fingers harder.

They were promising.

Very promising.

Mouth dry, I picked up my wine and downed it just as the Rams scored their first touchdown and the stadium went wild.

I picked up my foam finger and did a little fist pump, careful to keep my other hand on Jessie's.

My sudden movement must have caught him off guard because our hands moved, slipped into his lap.

He froze.

My eyebrows rose as my knuckles came into contact with either a freaking bat in his pants.

Or what was probably every woman's favorite part of Jessie Beckett.

Beckett had a bat.

The bat of Beckett.

Swing, batter, batter.

Oh hell.

Heat. So much heat emanating from his lap.

From . . . it.

I gulped again.

Jessie seemed frozen.

I tried to break the tension. "Football do that to you too?"

He didn't laugh.

His scowl was more pained than angry.

I stared at his lips, the way they parted, the way my own chest seemed to heave and pant all at once as I leaned in, and then pressed my hand backward. His eyes rolled back.

National television.

Bad idea.

All of it.

"You guys want a hot dog?" Colin yelled.

I jerked my hand away.

Jessie pressed a palm to the front of his pants and cursed.

I snickered behind my hand and whispered, "Jessie already got one."

"Hilarious." His lips twitched. "More like Polish sausage."

I scrunched up my nose. "I always add ketchup to mine and just swirl my tongue around the tip to—"

Jessie clamped a hand over my mouth. "Keep talking and your naked ass is going to be pressed against the glass while I fuck you."

Nobody had ever spoken to me like that before.

Excitement built up in my chest at the prospect.

Us together.

No.

That was what got us into this situation in the first place. With Jessie probably lusting after some hot cheerleader below, and me touching his penis and talking about hot dogs!

Ugh.

"Guys?" Colin asked again.

"Sure," I answered for both of us. "Two hot dogs."

"Load them up with ketchup," Jessie said without taking his eyes from mine. "Isla loves her ketchup."

I bit down on my bottom lip as he ran his tongue over his top lip and then tried to adjust himself again.

"Coming right up!" Colin yelled.

I snorted out a laugh while Jessie groaned again like it was the most painful experience of his life.

Colin handed me the food, Jessie grabbed his hot dog and shoved it in his mouth like he had no time for words or chewing.

I knew that type of behavior well.

I called it horny hunger.

Give your sex-deprived body something to chew on, otherwise you gnaw off your own arm or worse, sleep with the first person to hit on you at the bar and wake up to find out that he still lives with his mom and kisses her on the mouth.

Yeah, taking that one to my grave.

That was a long time ago, though.

Now, now I ate.

Poor Jessie.

Poor me.

I stared at my hot dog and wished it away, wished it was a Polish sausage, wished my situation with one of the hottest men alive was different.

With a sigh, I lifted the hot dog to my mouth at about the same time I saw myself on the big screen with a giant splotch of ketchup on my Rams jersey.

Right. Between. My. Breasts.

Granted, my shirt wasn't low, so it was on my shirt between my breasts, but it was still there.

And obvious.

Jessie turned to me, my mouth was still open. He grinned and took a bite out of the part facing him, then ran his finger down my shirt and licked the ketchup off.

I laughed and shook my head. "Best hot dog of your life?"

"I prefer a different kind of meal . . ." His eyes flickered down, and because I was horny hungry, because I hadn't yet eaten my hot dog and satisfied all hormonal cravings, I mauled him.

Maybe mauled was the wrong word, but suddenly my hot dog was midair and I was straddling the man and kissing him like I was trying to rescue the bite he'd just taken.

I was an animal.

He was turning me into an animal.

His hands gripped my ass as he deepened the kiss. I felt every part of him straining against me with such force that I wanted to move.

Insanity.

This is what insanity felt like.

Wanting to rub myself against him with a hot dog in my hand and ketchup on my shirt.

In front of the entire world.

"Guys," Blaire said through a haze of lust and almost dry humping. "Cameras are off you guys, good job. People were cheering and catcalling like crazy, can't doubt that kinda chemistry. You guys aren't drunk, are you?"

I pulled away as Jessie locked eyes with me and said in a gravelly voice, "Sober."

# Chapter Twenty-Three

## JESSIE

I would never look at a bottle of ketchup again without getting hard. It was a problem, since ketchup was everywhere.

Just like the taste of Isla on my tongue.

My mouth buzzed.

My body was irate.

And I didn't know where to put my hands.

At all.

Awkwardness washed over me as Isla slowly crawled out of my very disappointed lap and sat next to me, retrieving her hot dog and shoving the whole damn thing so far inside her mouth that I knew I'd be dreaming of the image until my death.

Either that or the image was going to somehow kill me.

I tried to get myself under control. Again. And then she had to go and grab another damn hot dog and do the same thing.

When she got up a third time, I gripped her by the wrist and very slowly said, "Chew."

"What?"

"Please." My voice was strained as I released her hand, and when she returned, she took small bites.

I almost wept with relief.

Halftime came and went.

I didn't move from my spot. I physically couldn't without showing Blaire and Colin why I was as stiff as a statue.

Isla toyed with the foam finger, and when the cameras dashed to us again, she hit me over the head with it. My reaction was anger and then irritation because I hadn't really been paying attention to anything but her.

I didn't even know the score.

I always knew the score.

I was an ex-NFL player.

We were two days in and the woman was already making me insane, changing things about myself I'd always known to be true. I always watched the game. Always. I ripped it apart, I memorized the plays, the routes, the different calls that should have been made by the offensive coordinators. I bled for football.

And I didn't know the score.

I grabbed her hand and kissed the back of it.

Not for the cameras.

For me.

Something broke free in that moment. Maybe more of the bondage that Vanessa had kept me under was starting to dissipate, but it felt good, it felt like . . . I could breathe easier.

All because I wasn't keeping score.

All because of a hot-dog-eating maniac who didn't play by my rules—or force me to play by hers.

"Still hungry?" I asked as I squeezed her hand.

"Starving." She shrugged like she was uncomfortable and then cleared her throat. "I, um, eat when I'm . . . at games."

"Most people eat at games." Was it my imagination or was she blushing?

"Right." She nodded and then pointed at the field. "It's too bad Seattle's beating the Rams."

"What?" I whipped my head back to the game. "When did they even score?"

"I think they were inspired by our kiss," Isla teased. "Either that or my hot-dog-eating skills are on point, because they've been scoring like crazy."

"Someone should," I grumbled and crossed my arms.

Isla leaned over and whispered, "Heard that."

"Oh, you were meant to," I fired right back.

And just like that, the tension crackled, increased, and burst in front of my eyes until all I saw was her.

Two and a half quarters of hell down.

One and a half more to go.

# Chapter Twenty-Four

ISLA

I watched the game.

But wasn't paying attention to anything other than Jessie's movements.

His knee bounced up and down again like he either had to pee or was ready to do something crazy.

I didn't blame him.

The room felt too small.

The air too hot.

My clothes too tight.

And the food had only made things somehow worse.

"Hey, guys." Blaire and Colin were still here? Blaire's voice sounded louder as she made her way toward us. "We're going to go grab some merchandise, you want anything?"

"No," we said in unison, like we planned it.

She looked between us with a frown, then shrugged. "Alright, we'll be back in a bit, the lines are probably crazy, so who knows . . ."

The door shut.

I looked around us.

The staff was gone.

The bartender wasn't there anymore.

The food was left on the tables.

We were completely alone.

But visible from every angle except against the back wall, thanks to the giant window to the front and sides of our booth.

I slumped back in my seat just as Jessie's hand crept onto my right thigh and then retreated like he had second thoughts.

My chest heaved as I looked at him from the corner of my eye. His gaze was on the field.

But his presence was completely with me. I felt him, like I could read his thoughts, like I knew exactly what he would rather be doing.

Me.

Sex would ruin things.

I couldn't give him that kind of control over my body—men like Jessie were greedy. They'd ask for more, they'd use promises to get it.

And then they'd get bored.

A time-out was called.

And the cameras panned to us again.

I quickly bounced onto Jessie's lap, thinking it would look playful and fun, only to realize he still had a huge problem.

Huge.

Problem.

"Fuck!" His hands came to my waist, fingers digging into my skin. "A warning next time before you break my dick off."

"Sorry." I wiggled my ass to get comfortable and grinned at him as he pulled my legs across the arms of the chair.

He clenched his teeth. "Move that ass again and I'm spanking it on national TV."

I moved.

He spanked hard.

I moved again.

Rachel Van Dyken

And I'm sure parents everywhere covered their children's eyes as the camera quickly panned away from our little PG-13 show.

"Cameras are gone," he whispered as his hand stayed on my ass like it belonged there. I could have sworn I felt him grow beneath me, strain to reach me.

"I know."

"You don't have to stay on my lap."

"I've made a new friend, it's rude to just abandon him."

His eyebrows shot up. "Oh, have you?"

I nodded. "I'm friendly."

"Very." He swore loudly and then wiped his face with his free hand. "You have no idea how much."

"Does this count as our two hours?" I tried changing the subject in order to keep myself from jumping him.

He tilted his head. "Do you want it to?"

"No," I gulped, surprising myself and him at the same time, if I read the look on his face right.

"Me either," he rasped.

I pressed my hand against his chest. "This would be a really bad idea."

"What?" He gripped my hips harder. "Kissing your fiancé again?"

I grinned. "Nice justification there."

"I would justify every damn thing in the world for another taste of you."

He really shouldn't say things like that to me.

To someone starving for that look in his eyes. Even if he only meant sex, his look matched those words.

They were dangerous.

So. Dangerous.

To someone who was cheated on.

To someone who still looked in the mirror and wondered what they were missing.

120

To someone like me.

I kissed him first.

His lips molded around mine as he cupped my face with his hands. I didn't care about the TV screens, the cameras, this was for me.

Jessie was for me.

His tongue slid past my lower lip on a groan.

I pulled back and slid off his lap, then grabbed him by the shirt, tugging him up the stairs and toward the back of the box.

I made it maybe three feet before he gripped me by the waist and slammed my body against the wall. His hands went from my waist up to my breasts then down again like he couldn't decide where he wanted to place them. His mouth never left mine as his thumbs grazed the bare skin on my stomach, my shirt rose higher and higher. I reached between us, tugging him against me with his belt. I undid it and let it fall to the ground, even as my mind reminded me this wasn't smart.

Bad idea, bad idea.

My body wasn't listening.

My heart was pretending it wasn't happening.

And my blood was pounding so hard I was sure that he could hear it roaring through my veins.

"I've never wanted someone so desperately." There he went again with the words, the words he didn't mean, the ones he didn't know I needed. I tugged his pants down at about the same time his mouth met my neck, and I lost all sense of time and just felt tongue, teeth, lips, sucking.

My knees buckled, he caught me with one hand while I gripped his length and felt him pulse beneath my fingers.

It had been too long.

So long.

Damn, everything was long.

Huge.

His kiss deepened on another moan from me as I moved my hand. His body jerked in response like he wasn't used to women touching him, pleasing him, which in turn pleased me, made me want to drop to my knees and make him feel good the way he was making me feel good.

So I did.

I slid down the wall.

His half-lidded gaze was the type of lazy, sexy gaze that every woman wants, but none of us really get. It was fantasy.

The entire situation wasn't real.

But this I could make this real.

Every touch.

Every lick.

"Isla," he said just as I leaned in. "You don't need to do this, this isn't—"

I shut him up as he slammed a hand against the wall behind me, and when I pulled back I could have sworn I heard him utter, "Only you, I've never let anyone . . ."

And then he stopped talking.

# Chapter Twenty-Five

## JESSIE

I stared at my reflection in the bathroom mirror, my skin had a rosy hue, my breaths were still coming out short.

I blacked out from lack of oxygen.

From kissing.

From thinking I could survive off her lips.

And when oxygen isn't present, you say and do things you shouldn't, like allowing her to drop to her knees in front of me.

Like letting her suck me dry until I saw stars and hallucinated while my soul took a vacation and floated above my body.

Her mouth.

Her tongue.

Her.

Just. Her.

Vanessa had never touched me like that, and when I asked why, she said it was demeaning, yet anything went when it came to her having sex outside of our marriage.

I never told anyone.

Because guys like me didn't complain about their own wives finding them disgusting.

It was my secret to keep.

That I was used in my own marriage for sex only when it was convenient for her—only when whoever she was sleeping with wasn't putting out. I'd gotten myself tested and never looked back.

Dry spell didn't even begin to cover it.

More like dry years.

She wanted sex, she used me.

So I withheld.

I stared back into the mirror—my life with Vanessa had been so fucked up and I didn't even realize how bad until I was out from underneath it.

A knock sounded at the door. I washed my hands and opened it to see Colin giving me a funny look.

"What?" I tried to look casual while my eyes searched for Isla. She was back in her seat with popcorn in her lap. For being so small the woman could really put away her food.

"Did anything happen"—he motioned to the room—"in here while we were gone?"

"No," I said quickly and patted him on the shoulder as I made my way to Isla. The minute I sat she handed me popcorn without a word.

It was like nothing even happened.

Confused, I watched the game with her, held her hand, talked to Colin and Blaire as my confusion grew, and when she got in my car after the game, all hell broke loose.

"Two hours start the minute we get to the house," she announced, "and all I want to know is why."

"Why?" Dread pooled in my stomach. I played dumb. "Why what?"

"Why you made me think that was your first, and if my assumption's correct, why your bitch of an ex-wife never touched you like that. Why we let her live without sniping her. And why she's so stupid."

I laughed.

It felt so damn good. "Know many snipers, pumpkin?"

Her answer was a shrug.

Note to self.

Never piss her off.

# Chapter Twenty-Six

ISLA

Jessie's expression was more pained than angry when we finally settled onto the couch with a bottle of wine and two glasses.

He checked his watch as if he was going to start a timer, which yesterday would have made me laugh or roll my eyes. But today? After tasting him, after doing something that I didn't normally do—hadn't really ever fully done if I was being completely honest—it stung.

I didn't want him keeping track of the minutes.

I wanted him counting them down, coveting each one.

He ran his hands through his thick, dark hair, mussing it up before turning to me and grimacing. "It's not really something I talk about."

"Really?" I said in a deadpan voice. "I'm surprised that you don't gush all your secrets to Colin over wine and then sob into the nut bowl, do men not do this? Astonishing!"

"The nut bowl?"

"Mixed nuts, the ones at the bars." I sighed. "I'm a good listener, I promise, plus I kind of feel like you owe me an explanation for that bomb."

"More like I owe you." His face transformed into a grin.

"Don't keep track, you'll only ever be in debt."

He coughed out a laugh. "Does this whole pillow-talk conversation mean you're going to stop painting my walls?"

I was momentarily stunned by his deep laugh but quickly recovered. "I don't know, are you actually going to buy milk?"

"That depends, are you going to turn my pantry into an Asian market?"

I grinned, my aunt would be proud. "You'll change your tune after I start cooking."

Bachelors. So. Easy. His face lit up like a Christmas tree at the idea of cooking, I could practically see his mind working.

"You win," he finally said.

"I always do."

He narrowed his eyes, shook his head, and then poured me a glass of wine and one for himself. "If you were Colin or anyone else I'd just say she was a manipulative witch that I didn't want touching me, I'd say I didn't want her whore mouth anywhere near my cock."

I nodded. That's what I expected. But something in his expression told me it was more. "I'm not Colin, or anyone else."

"No," he exhaled. "You're not."

"Fiancée." I showed him my ring.

It made him smile at least, even though it was small, maybe even more like a grimace. I tried not to look deflated.

"The truth." He wasn't looking at me, he stared into his wine and exhaled again. "The truth is I don't think she was ever really attracted to me as a man. She was attracted to my money, my title, my fame." His voice lowered. "There was nothing else I had that she wanted." He tilted the wine back. "God, it sounds worse saying it out loud than it did in my head. No man ever likes hearing from a beautiful woman that he lacks in areas that matter, that a woman as attractive as Vanessa didn't want him."

"Vanessa"—I said that woman's name with venom—"is the ugliest person I have ever known. Ugliest." I had to say it twice. I was ready to kick her ass and I wasn't the fighter of the group, that all went to Blaire. But Jessie's expression was so . . . devastated.

I'd never seen a man so willing to share insecurity.

So confident in every area of his life except one.

A big one. One that mattered, especially in a relationship.

"And I want to throw my stiletto at her Botox-injected face." I gritted my teeth. "Honestly, she saved you by not touching you in that way, hell, she could have ruined blow jobs forever for you! Can you imagine?"

"That would be a travesty." He finally looked at me, his eyes locked on with an intensity I'd never experienced before.

"Yes." I squirmed in the chair. "World-ending."

"Catastrophic."

I grinned. "Her loss, Jessie."

"You're not just saying that because you're my fiancée?" he probed, his eyes searching mine in a way that made my knees weak, even though I was sitting down.

"I'm saying that because it's true. Your relationship ending was the best thing that could have happened to you. And you know it. What's better is that you never let her lips touch you."

He winced.

"What?"

"There's more . . ."

"More?" Did we need another bottle of wine? What could he possibly mean, more?

He eyed the wine like he was contemplating chugging the whole bottle before he faced me again and said, "A year."

"A year?"

"No sex for a year, not with her, not with anybody else." He exhaled and then shrugged. "I couldn't touch her, couldn't even look at her some days."

"You're not the only one." I took a drink of wine. "I still can't look at her, and she never cheated on me, just made my eye twitch and gave Blaire hives."

"I think she has that effect on most people," Jessie joked, pouring himself more wine and taking a huge gulp.

"So today . . ." I just had to probe, didn't I? "That was your first, uh, sexual encounter since—"

"Yup."

"Oh."

"You can wipe that grin off your face now, I'm right here." He filled my glass while I kept smiling. "Oh hell, what do you want? An award? A high five? Do I need to tell you how good it was? How I felt my balls tighten so fast and hard that I almost passed out on top of you? Or that watching you drop to your knees was one of the most arousing things I've ever seen in my life? That it turned me on to see your tongue touch me? The warmth of your mouth—I don't think I'll ever get over or forget. Yes, Isla, to all those things. You did all those things. And I'm probably not going to sleep for a year because of it."

My heart skipped a beat, stuttered to a stop, and then pounded as he talked. I opened my mouth to speak but had no words. So I just stared at him.

He stared back.

And that's how we sat for a few minutes in each other's company, drinking wine, stealing glances. My mind whirled, and my body wanted.

I felt his intensity.

I could feel it sizzle in the air, touch it with my fingertips.

It was insane.

"So," I finally choked out, "should we keep watching *American Gods*?"

He cleared his throat and checked his damn watch.

My heart deflated a bit.

"I'm stealing time," he whispered.

"What was that?" My head whipped in his direction so fast a flash of pain hit my neck.

"Time," he said again with that same confident voice that oozed sexuality and made me want to lean closer just so I could feel the words hit my face. "I'm going to borrow from the day we made the agreement to get married, we never had our two hours that day. Technically they're owed to me, and I'm adding them to today."

"Is that your way of saying you want more hours?"

"Yeah."

"You could have just asked."

"You like rules." He smiled. "And I like control, right? Both of us have our things . . . if I asked you for more time, if I went over today without explanation you would wonder, you'd analyze, you wouldn't sleep, and you'd have to write it into your little calendar and then wreck yourself planning for the next day." He grinned. "I'm just helping you out."

"That's nice." Sweet, thoughtful, wonderful. Stoppppp . . .

"I'm a nice guy." His eyes fell to my mouth again. I licked my lips and nodded my head in agreement.

"Should you grab your laptop?"

"Oh." I jumped to my feet. "Yeah, I'll just be right back."

I slammed my hand against my head once I made it to the guest room, grabbed my laptop, and rushed back out to the living room. Jessie had refilled my wineglass and turned down all the lights.

What's worse.

He grabbed a blanket.

Didn't he know I was already burning up?

I smiled and set the laptop up.

He put the blanket over me.

Sweet. Fresh. Hell.

I was going to end up leaving a sweat print against his leather, and I knew that wouldn't go over smoothly.

He wrapped an arm around me and pulled me close.

So hot.

Burning up.

I yawned.

The last thing I remembered was a kiss to my forehead, but I must have imagined it, because when I woke up, I was in my bed with the blanket tucked up to my chin, and a smile on my face.

# Chapter Twenty-Seven

## JESSIE

Watching her sleep was only creepy if she woke up. I tried to take my eyes away from her face—but with her sleeping and her claws tucked underneath the blanket, it was probably the only chance I was going to get to really study her face, the place where her eyes meet her nose, the way her chin juts out just enough to show her sharp jawline, only adding to the sassiness I'd come to realize was just part of her personality. She inhaled deeply and turned on her side, pressing a hand to my chest and grabbing hold of my shirt.

The feeling that came with that hold.

With that touch.

Was entirely foreign.

I couldn't categorize it, and that left me panicked in a way I wasn't prepared for. It wasn't sexual, it wasn't lustful, it wasn't even love, it was something much more dangerous.

Trust.

It was a touch that said you'll protect me, you'll keep me safe, don't hurt me, and I was the last guy she should be touching like that. With the past that I had, with the present demons I was fighting while trying to find myself again and destroy the very woman I blamed for taking everything from me.

It wasn't her.

But her business was the tool that threw my life into the very chaos I'd always been so afraid of.

I was still spinning.

Still running.

Still trying to find my footing, and she made it so much worse—there was nothing calming or serene about Isla, she was as collected as she was fiery, a complete contradiction on a daily basis.

I had no way to categorize her.

And it bothered me.

Because my entire life I'd been able to categorize people.

Colin? Best friend, brother from another mother, loyal to a fault, and would kick my ass without thinking.

Blaire. She'd been the one who got away, the one I compared everyone to, the one who always came out on top. And then after seeing her again, the only feeling I'd ever really had for her had been desperation—I'd wanted someone to want me, and I knew she could.

But I'd never wanted her in that way, not really.

I'd just wanted an escape from my hell.

Which brings me to Vanessa.

Fucking. Vanessa.

She'd been the trophy I was so obsessed with obtaining. But up close, I saw the scratches, the flaws, the manipulations, the need to be the best at everything, to beat everyone. The world revolved around her and she didn't have a place in her life for those who didn't agree.

My OCD had gotten worse with her, not better.

Because I'd tried to control her as much as she controlled me, she helped me justify my need for perfection, she fed it, made me think it was normal to panic over having dirty floors, normal to yell at a waiter for spilling red wine on the pristine white table.

She made me feel normal for those feelings.

When deep down I knew it just made me an insecure jackass who cared way too much about what people thought of him.

I reached out and ran my fingers through Isla's hair. It felt like silk. I wrapped a few pieces around my fingers, tugging them as I leaned down and pressed a kiss to her forehead.

Maybe my view of perfection was wrong—had been wrong all along.

It wasn't the perfect house.

The perfect wife.

It wasn't the perfect life or career.

It was moments like this, with a woman I would never understand or deserve, lying on my lap asleep, and me wishing I could hold on to the seconds a little bit longer.

Keep the moment for me and only me.

It was the moments that looked like chaos but felt like peace.

Perfection wasn't my world.

Perfection was hers.

# Chapter Twenty-Eight

ISLA

Breakfast was torture.

I typically did a bowl of oatmeal with my coffee, then, if I was still hungry, made an egg with my sweet Asian chili sauce, the only way to have eggs. But this morning was different.

I was in his kitchen.

Eating.

Cooking.

Sure, I'd painted his walls and raised hell, but things had shifted enough that I felt awkward.

I should have known it wouldn't last long.

The awkwardness.

Our clashing personalities wouldn't allow it.

So when I finally made it into the kitchen and plugged my ears because the Ninja blender was so loud, I knew I was in for a rude awakening.

The man didn't do breakfast.

And he also didn't clothe himself in the mornings.

No, I was greeted by two overly large pecs.

A six-pack that looked more like an eight if you actually stared hard enough.

The V women drool over whenever they watch Ryan Gosling movies.

And triceps that looked like they deserved their own zip code.

Who the hell works out their triceps that hard?

I gulped and nervously tucked my hair behind my ears as my heels clicked against the slate. "Morning."

Jessie looked up and grinned.

It was a smile I could get used to, damn him. It was so much easier when he was being a creepy stalker jackass with binoculars. I almost rolled my eyes when he poured part of the gross green contents into his glass, only to have some spill onto that perfect chest when he took a long gulp.

It would be rude not to tell him.

Just like it would be rude not to volunteer to lick it off.

I kept my hands pinned at my sides.

The man made me crazy.

In all the worst ways.

I hated protein shakes.

"Made you one." He grabbed another glass and poured while my stomach clenched with anxiety. It was green! I didn't even see the label! I was into labels. He knows this! I at least wanted to know what I was drinking so I could decide for myself, but he made me breakfast—I winced—in his own jock way.

It was sweet.

I took the glass with a shaky hand and sniffed.

"Did you just sniff?"

"No," I lied.

He leaned his massive body against the counter. "Liar, I saw your nose move. What? Don't trust me not to poison you?"

"Actually I was more worried about what I was drinking, but poison brings this to a whole new level."

"Arsenic typically does." He moved and braced his hands on the counter. "Come on, just one sip."

"But"—I looked into the glass and made a face—"it's green."

"And the licorice you and Blaire always eat is red. Coffee's black, especially yours . . ."

I narrowed my eyes. "See all that with your binoculars, did you?"

He winked and eyed the front of my open blouse. "I saw a lot of things with those binoculars."

"Pig."

"Stop deflecting." He moved around the island, put one finger under the glass, and started moving it toward my lips. "I promise, this is my gift in life."

"Making people choke?" I said sweetly.

"Didn't choke last night, did you?"

My face went hot. "N-no."

"Drink." We were chest to chest. I wasn't breathing, was I breathing? "I promise, you'll not only like it, you'll ask for more."

"Doubtful," I said in a breathy voice.

He shrugged and fired right back, "Trust me."

I hated that I did.

I hated that when I looked into his eyes I saw no maliciousness, just . . . kindness. Ugh, he needed to revert to his jackass ways fast before I fell head over heels and begged him to impregnate me with the next NFL star.

I needed logic.

Order.

My aunt.

I needed to visit my aunt.

She'd know what to do.

She practically balanced other people's chi by just existing!

I didn't plug my nose even though I wanted to. I tilted my head back and drank, then swallowed.

"So?" He looked so proud of himself I wanted to dump the shake over his head. Whatever the hell it was—it was good.

"It's . . ." I shrugged. "Drinkable."

"Drinkable," he repeated. "If it was white like a vanilla shake you'd say it was the best thing to pass those lips of yours."

"Not the best thing," I said without thinking, causing the sexual tension to skyrocket so fast my vision blurred.

His body moved toward mine. He pulled the glass from my hand and set it on the counter, his arms moved, and I was pinned against the granite. "Oh yeah?"

I licked my lips, still somehow tasting him there, greedy for more. I leaned in, he met me halfway.

The doorbell rang, jolting us away from each other.

"Expecting company?" I laughed nervously.

He pushed off the counter and ran his hands through his hair, then made his way to the door, jerking it open so hard I thought it was going to splinter in his right hand.

"Sir." One of the guards I'd seen the other night was talking in hushed tones. He eyed me and nodded, kept talking to Jessie, then hung his head and left.

Jessie kicked the wall with his bare foot at least three times, then slammed the door, opened it, and slammed it again.

I jumped as he kicked the door again then slumped to the ground in a hunched position.

"Jessie?"

"Not now, Isla." His voice was barely a whisper.

I made my way to him and knelt down only to have him hold up his hand for me to stop. Hurt, I backed away.

"Vanessa must have seen the show last night."

I flinched at the words, because yes, it had been a show, but both of us knew there was more hanging in the balance than that, we were completely blurring the lines. And he was an equal participant in that.

"And?" I prodded.

He stood and faced me. "You fucking said this would go away? Let's get engaged, you said, let's get in the spotlight, show our love!" His voice rose until I was backing away from this man I didn't know, this angry, out-of-control man. "She must have gotten pissed that people were switching sides, because she just dropped a bomb . . ."

I was afraid to ask.

"She said we separated because I asked her for an abortion. Yup, said my career was more important, it's all over the news."

"But it's not true!" I could kill that woman. "She was the one who got the abortion without telling you."

Jessie narrowed his gaze on me. "Specu-fucking-lation. Isn't that what you said? People would rather root for my downfall than my success, and she's just made sure I'm never coming back." He wiped his face. "Shit."

My first reaction was to cry.

My second was to get even.

Head held high, I walked to him. "I'm a PI, this is what I do, Jessie. I'll get her confession, I'll expose her lie." I crossed my arms. "All you gotta do is let me." Anxiety filled my chest at the thought of more work, but if I didn't do this, we'd lose everything. Everything.

"You're the reason I'm in this situation."

"So let me continue to help you out of it," I fired back. "We're already getting married, what's a little espionage on top of that?"

"You're going to spy on her and your ex? The one you hate? The one who would recognize you in a heartbeat if you got too close? Not to mention Vanessa?"

I shrugged. "I'm a professional, of course I'm not going to spy as me when necessary, but with Vanessa, why not spy out in public? She's already suspicious."

His eyes narrowed. "You're serious?"

"Engaged by day." I flashed him my ring. "Spy by night." I held up my hand like I was swearing an oath. "What do you say?"

He stood and crossed his arms, staring me down before saying, "You should have been an army general."

I grinned. "Thank you."

"Wasn't a compliment."

"Yeah it was."

He snorted and then opened his mouth, his face looked sad, repentant, but I kept my emotions on lockdown, I didn't want his apology. I'd already seen how quick he could turn against me.

Our two hours. Those were ours.

But that wasn't life.

And this wasn't reality.

"I'm going to go visit my aunt and then head to work. I'll text you later and we can have a powwow and make a game plan with Blaire, alright?"

He frowned. "Look, Isla, I'm—"

"See ya." I flashed a smile I didn't feel and fled the house. I drove across town to Aunt Betsy's retirement home.

When I pulled in, I was fighting tears.

By the time I made it to her apartment, they were streaming down my face. I knocked on the door.

She jerked it open. "You bring coffee?"

"No." I sucked my tears back in.

She shrugged. "Take off your shoes."

I tossed them to the side and walked to the living room, where she had a pot of tea and two cups already on the table. "Sit."

The plastic on the couch made a comforting noise as I sat and faced her. She grabbed the plastic-covered remote and clicked down the volume. "Why are you crying?"

I shrugged. "It's a long story."

"Does it have anything to do with that *man*?"

The way she said *man* almost sounded like a curse.

"Uh, yeah." I was wearing my ring on my left hand. She'd be hurt if she thought I got engaged without her—then again, her favorite show was *TMZ*, so she probably already knew. "We're kind of engaged."

She sniffed. "And you did not tell your Aunt Betsy you were making sex with him because?"

"We aren't 'making sex.'" I used Jessie's dumb air quotes.

She slapped my hands down. "You engaged, Isla! Of course you are making the sex! That is what you do! You lay down, you put your legs high into the air, and—"

"Ohhhh, Goo-Poh, we had the sex talk years ago."

"I refresh your memory!" She seemed so excited about it that I almost felt bad.

"Don't need help in that area." I pressed a hand to her thigh. "But thank you."

"Remember not to talk about the moon at night."

"Goo-Poh." Did I mention she was a bit . . . superstitious?

"And no talking about money."

I sighed.

"Does he sleep on the left or the right?"

I had no clue! I guessed. "Left?"

She muttered something in Chinese and spat on the floor.

"You've never acted like this with my other boyfriends."

"Pah, those other boyfriends were boys, not men. This man has muscles that could make any woman turn her head." She grinned shamelessly. "Our ladies spent days talking about that man's muscles, the men asked him what he drank for sperm count. He said he didn't have to!"

I burst out laughing.

"Isla, are you hearing? He doesn't have to! Because his sperm count is so high he simply lives his life in the great blessed way a man should! He will reproduce like a rabbit!"

Great. Visual.

"Actually, that's not why I'm here."

"It's not a Tuesday." She nodded solemnly. "When you texted, I worried he hurt you during a sexual act. Kids these days, they go too fast, the injuries from dog—"

"Goo-Poh!"

"It is too deep?" She used her hands.

I closed my eyes.

"Don't be such a prude," she harrumphed. "If he tries that, you simply add a bit of an arch to accept his blessing into your womb."

"Got it. Accept his blessing." I was leaving this room scarred. Changed. With horrible visuals of her closed eyes and hand movements.

"It's not real," I finally admitted. "The relationship. We're doing it because we were caught in a bad position that would affect my business and his reputation. Nothing was happening between us when we got engaged." She scoffed like she didn't believe me. "But it looked bad."

"It looked bad because something almost happened," she pointed out. "The press saw something—it reported what it saw, what everyone saw who clicked on the YouTube video."

There was a video? "What do you mean?"

"Guilt." She threw her hands up. "And a shiver."

"A shiver," I repeated. "As in I was shivering?"

"Oh, not that kind of shiver, the kind where the body reacts in such a powerful way it pulses, it moves. Both of you, you were pulsing, your auras were glowing. Oh, something was about to happen, just think—you could be pregnant by now!"

"Joyful day," I said in a deadpan voice. Pregnant by a guy who doesn't love me. Every girl's dream!

She smacked the back of my head. "Don't mock the blessing."

"Sorry." I held up my hands. "I just needed some advice, things are . . . complicated." She sighed like she knew exactly what that meant. "And I think I'm falling for him, but today—"

"Say no more." She patted my knee. "Let me get my tonics."

"No!" I jumped to my feet. "I don't need tonics or oils, your love teas. I just need advice."

"No." She went to her cupboard and clasped her hands, then cracked her neck. "You need my tea. It was passed down four generations."

I loved her. I did. But tea wasn't going to fix the growing attraction I had for him, and the way he shut me down earlier was proof that he wasn't on that page. Embarrassment washed over me. I'd literally sucked him, touched him, I'd done things I'd never even done with Wayne because I never wanted to.

And I was still enemy number one.

Apparently, sex changes nothing.

Still hated.

"Here." Goo-Poh handed me a small pouch of tea leaves. "Just use two. If you use more than two, there's no telling how much it will affect him."

"Goo-Poh!" I gasped. "I'm not drugging him!"

"Do you want him or not?"

I chewed my lower lip. Was I really considering this craziness? Yes, I wanted him. Yes. I was finally admitting I wanted more of him, more of his talk, more of his kisses, more of everything.

But I wanted it to be real.

Not brought on by her horny tea.

"Thanks." I was about to tuck it in my purse, but I frowned. "It's labeled *Headache Tea*?"

Betsy just shrugged. "I have to hide the good stuff."

"Right." I leaned in and kissed her cheek. "Thank you. I'll give this to him." Over my dead body. "And I'll think about what you said."

"Yes." She pressed her hands against my cheeks. "You accept his blessing," she just had to add. "Wide."

"Yup!" I backed away slowly. "As wide as I can go!"

"That's my girl." She was way too excited about my sex life. I left her apartment not feeling any better about our situation but determined to make it right.

# Chapter Twenty-Nine

"What crawled up your ass and died?" Colin did his next set of cleans and dropped the barbell, giving me a scowl as I bent over and started my set.

I heaved the bar up and dropped. "Everything."

"Huh." He watched me complete my set, then walked over and faced me, his eyes probing, searching. Damn him. "Because last time I saw you, you looked . . . what's the word I'm thinking of? Oh, there it is, satisfied."

I gritted my teeth.

"Content." He shrugged. "Spent."

"That's enough," I growled.

"And now defensive." He held his hands up. "Just saying, is the honeymoon already over?"

"Hilarious, since it hasn't even started," I griped, adding another ten pounds to each side. Isla had texted me about an hour ago asking to meet after work, and already I was feeling irritated.

Not at her.

It was all self-inflicted.

I'd snapped.

Projected.

Blamed.

I'd done all the things I hated doing.

And it was directed at her because she was available, close, making me feel vulnerable, making me want, making me fucking terrified.

"I think she's good for you," Colin said, interrupting my thoughts as I started my second set.

"Oh?" I finished my last five and dropped the bar. "Why the hell would you say that?"

Colin stared me down, waited a few seconds, and said, "You don't even realize it, do you?"

"Realize what?" I wiped my face with my towel and tossed it to the ground.

He punched me lightly on the shoulder and winked. "You're wearing a red shirt."

That was it.

That was all he said.

I moved my attention to the mirror.

And there it was.

Plain as day.

A shirt I didn't even realize I'd grabbed out of my dresser rather than my closet and put on when I was pissed and ready to start my workout.

Not black.

Not white.

Not gray.

Red.

Fucking red.

Like her dress.

Like her lips.

Like I imagined her nipples would be.

I closed my eyes and hung my head.

"Don't sweat it." Colin came back and tossed me a dry towel. "Baby steps, just try not to keep all this sexual frustration pent up for too much longer, you don't want to end up biting her tongue, knocking a tooth out, or, God forbid, impaling the poor woman."

"One. Time," I gritted out.

"Impaler, impaler!" He cupped his mouth and kept chanting.

I chucked my towel at his face and tried to hide my smile. "One time, and I was young."

"Exactly, you had your small stature on your side."

I rolled my eyes and lifted. "Don't know what you're talking about, I've always been huge."

"Attaboy," Colin whooped. "Just be careful, the last thing I need is you hurting Isla and keeping me from sex because she needs a good cryfest with her best friend, *Outlander*, and a pint of ice cream."

I grunted. "Noted."

"I'm serious, Jessie."

"Me too."

And oddly enough.

I meant it.

# Chapter Thirty

ISLA

Jessie picked up one of my black duffel bags and started rummaging inside. "Duct tape, night-vision goggles, Tasers, a paintball gun? Why the hell do you need a paintball gun?"

I wrenched the gun away from him and placed it back in the bag. "You'd be surprised."

He pointed to one of the briefcases I kept for special clients. "What's that for?"

"That's my baby."

"You keep a baby in a briefcase. Nice."

I rolled my eyes, went over to my pride and joy, and typed in the code. "No, this baby goes with me in order to see if a baby's possible." The suitcase opened and Jessie peered in, his eyebrows shooting to his hairline. "Impressive, right?"

"Isn't this what *Dateline* uses to shame hotels into cleaning better?"

"Exactly." I picked up my black light and did a little jig. "But I use it to find sperm."

"Ah, from PI to a sperm hunter, should have known."

"Easy there." I pointed it at his crotch. "Any confessions?"

"Yeah, I haven't jacked off today, so you aren't going to find shit on me."

"Jacking off doesn't produce shit, poor baby." I patted him on the shoulder. "Missed that in health class, did you?"

He glared and jerked the black light out of my hands, then pointed it at me. "And you? Anything you'd like to confess?"

I held my arms out. "Clean."

The lights weren't off, so he wouldn't be able to use it anyway, but he must have trusted me enough to set it down and keep searching through our gear. "Cameras, car jacks, ninja stars? Is that really necessary? When will you ever need a ninja star?"

Blaire walked into the office with Colin. "Summer of 2016 threw a ninja star at a perp's calf, took him down in one fell swoop right along with the pictures he stole from our office. Lives saved. Badge earned."

I gave her a high five while Colin and Jessie stared at one another in confusion. Jessie spoke first. "Who *are* you people?"

"The best," I said with pride. "So if anyone's going to take down your skank of an ex-wife, it's going to be us." Mainly me. I was done with her messing with his life, and I was done taking the blame for her inability to tell the truth.

I grabbed the paintball gun and pulled the trigger. It fired into Jessie's thigh.

"What the hell!" he roared, stumbling backward. "Why are you shooting me?"

I winced. "We don't store them loaded, sorry, accident?"

"Accident, my ass." He rubbed his thigh. "I'm getting a welt!"

"Don't be such a baby."

He narrowed his eyes. "Be honest, did you shoot me on purpose?"

"Nope." I shrugged. "But had I known it was loaded, you betcha."

"Relationships," Colin said cheerfully. "It's like Christmas every day."

"Hear, hear," Blaire said awkwardly.

"Not married yet," Jessie just had to say as he pried the gun from my hands and set it back in the duffel bag. "So what's your brilliant plan?"

"Divide and conquer." I grinned. "We're two days away from the Academy Awards, Wayne's up for Best Director and Best Picture. We camp out in Hollywood at their hotel, follow them, get Vanessa drunk enough and pissed enough to confess."

"And how exactly"—Jessie crossed his arms in doubt—"are we going to accomplish all of that?"

"Bait." I grinned wide and held out my hand. "You get to be bait." He took it, and I whispered, "Welcome to Dirty Exes."

"May the force be with you," Colin muttered under his breath.

# Chapter Thirty-One

Well. At least I could admit one thing.

Since my fake engagement to Isla, life certainly wasn't boring, not even a little bit. My point was proved when I adjusted the earpiece in my right ear then reached for my coffee.

I'd been at the Hollywood Hilton on several occasions.

And I'd never been bugged on any of them.

Let alone trying to set up my ex-wife to make her look like the villain she was.

"Are we sure about this?" I said under my breath.

"Positive." Blaire's voice came over the earpiece loud and clear. "The staff is going to send her out by the pool to relax after her massage, a drink will be brought to her table with a note that compliments her and points her gaze to you."

I shuddered. "Great."

"Hey, that's what bait does! You reel them in, and then we pounce."

"Why isn't Isla bait?"

"She's bait's date!" Blaire laughed. I heard Colin snicker, which made me roll my eyes.

"Shhh, she's coming."

I waited for another snarky remark and got nothing, apparently they were all business when they needed to be.

My body rippled with tension as I saw her figure across the pool. She snapped her fingers at one of the towel attendants as he laid everything down to her specifics. My body felt like it had something crawling all over it when she gripped his forearm, leaned up, and whispered in his ear.

His eyes went wide and then he slowly nodded his head.

She blew him a kiss.

My balls retracted a bit when she sat and stared in my direction with her dark sunglasses on and a glass of white wine in hand. From the outside she was perfection. Not a hair out of place. Blood-red lipstick against pale skin, honey highlights in her typically frosty blonde hair, and legs for days.

Anyone would look at her and do a double take.

All I wanted to do was toss her in the pool and hold her under until she admitted that she was a lying, cheating bitch.

A tremor of anxiety slammed into my chest when the attendant returned with a bottle of water and a shot of whiskey. She frowned, looked at the whiskey, and then the card next to it.

Her eyes darted around the pool then locked on to mine.

It hurt like hell to force that smile, to seem interested when I wanted to puke, when the last time she was with me I felt so emotionally confused, abused, that my worth got lost in the definition of us.

"Stay calm." It was Isla's voice.

I felt my body relax.

"There you go," she said in that same voice. "Remember, this isn't real, you don't belong to her—she has no right to even touch you. But you're going to let her assume she does. You have to make her wonder."

"Right," I said, more to myself than anything. "Did I mention I failed drama class?"

Isla laughed. It felt good to hear her laugh.

I relaxed even more just as Vanessa rounded the corner and pulled up a chair so close that when she bent over, my mouth almost touched cleavage. "Hey there, stranger."

"Vanessa." I kept my voice soft, smooth.

She dropped the card onto the table. "You probably shouldn't be sending a drink when you're in such a committed relationship."

I leaned back. I knew how to play her game. "And you probably shouldn't accept a drink from your ex-husband when you're in such a loving one, right?"

Her chin lifted a bit. "Wayne is fantastic."

Isla gagged in my ear.

"Oh, I bet he gives you things I never did." Like sex and at least twenty different STDs.

Her eyes narrowed. "Why are you here?"

I leaned back to put some much needed distance between me and her Chanel perfume. "Can't a man enjoy a drink by the pool?"

"At the same hotel I'm staying at?"

I just shrugged.

"Jessie." She placed a hand on my thigh, and it took every ounce of strength I had not to react and shove her chair into the pool. "It's over between us, sweetie."

Oh God, I could strangle her for using that voice, the one she reserved for small children and old people.

I gave her the most humble smile I could, one that looked regretful, possibly . . . sad, and then shrugged. "I know that."

Her eyes softened. Had I blinked I would have missed it.

"There you are!" Isla rounded the corner looking hot as hell in a white bikini top with a white sarong around her hips. All I saw was skin—everywhere—a woman in nothing but a bikini, see-through sarong, and red heels.

Give a man a warning next time!

I gaped.

Vanessa cleared her throat.

I ignored her, I couldn't pull my eyes away from Isla.

Isla leaned down and pressed her left hand, the one with the rock on it, on my cheek, then kissed me full on the mouth, turning only briefly to wink at Vanessa. "Thanks for keeping my man company."

"Funny"—Vanessa clenched her hands onto the chair—"since he was my man when you started screwing him."

"Now, Vanessa," Isla said in a soothing voice, "we both know that isn't true. Besides, wasn't it Blaire that you threw at your own husband in hopes he would stumble and fall? Proving infidelity?"

Vanessa gritted her teeth. "Does it really matter?"

"The truth always does," Isla said sweetly.

"You wouldn't know the truth if it slapped you in the face." Vanessa shoved past Isla hard enough for Isla to get pushed against me.

"That went well." I sighed and ran my hands through my hair.

"I know!" Isla seemed a little too excited that my ex didn't confess a thing and that she had seemed more pissed than I'd seen her in a while. "I can't believe she reacted so quickly!"

"Were we at the same meeting?" I looked around. "She said it didn't matter and called us liars."

"Nope." Isla leaned forward and patted my cheek once. "She got a bit vulnerable, and she doubted some choices, it was in her eyes, then I swept in and she got jealous, then pissed off. It's the perfect combination. She'll be thinking about nothing else all day, and she's bound to do something stupid. It will get worse before it gets better, but I know just how to push her off the edge. It's in the job description, or the contract, then again you never signed one, so . . ."

"Because you're the reason I'm here," I confessed in frustration.

Isla took a sip of water and then stared me down. "One day, Jessie, I hope one day you'll stop blaming what you can't control for why your life is out of control."

I jolted at her words as they hit their mark, making my body stiffen with shame and anger. "Maybe one day you'll stop hiding behind your schedules and highlighters to live life without a plan."

Her face fell.

"Um," said Blaire, still in my ear. I grabbed the earpiece and tugged it out, throwing it onto the table. Suddenly exhausted.

"Our rooms are ready," Isla finally said.

"Isla—"

"Always with the apologies." She smiled sadly. "This one's on me, though, I'm sorry for being too honest too soon, and I'm sorry it forced you to do the same."

I stood and wrapped an arm around her shoulders. "I don't wake up wanting to hurt you."

Isla laughed. "Yes you do! You wake up every morning wanting to destroy my business!"

"No I don't," I said honestly. "Lately I've been waking up with an aching cock and visions of red, but that's probably not something we should discuss with you wearing only a patch of clothing on your body."

Isla shivered. I felt her body react with desire so poignant the air shifted between us as we walked.

"Good job, guys." Blaire said. She and Colin were waiting in the lobby with all our suitcases. "Room keys, our suites are connected, try to keep it down."

"Shouldn't we be saying that to you?" I said.

Blaire just gave me a knowing smile and waved us off. "Don't forget dinner tonight, we've got reservations next to their table."

"Can't wait," I said under my breath, my skin still crawling with the need to take a long hot shower.

I glanced at my room key and froze.

Isla grabbed her bag before I could grab it for her. "What's wrong?"

"Same room?"

"Engaged." She held up her finger and then smiled. It wasn't a real smile, it was a fake one, the one I hated because it meant I'd been a complete dick and caused her to shut down when it came to us.

It was the last thing I wanted.

I trusted her even though I didn't want to.

I wanted to believe she could fix this.

I just didn't know how.

And it frustrated me that she was right, that my blame was misplaced, but it made me feel better if I could point a finger at someone else rather than look in the mirror in defeat.

"Let's go." She nodded to the elevators.

I followed her in silence, the elevator music was an instrumental version of "SexyBack," by Justin Timberlake. Classy stuff. We finally made it to one of the executive suites. Isla immediately went into the bathroom and started a shower.

Guess I was going to have to wait until she was done.

It was torture imagining her rubbing soap up and down her body, and me pulling the string of her bikini with my teeth while watching water cascade down her belly, streaming between her legs.

I gripped the edge of the couch just as she rounded the corner. "Shower's ready for you."

"Aren't you?" I pointed at the shower. "Aren't you, um, going to wash up?" I could see her nipples through her white top. I didn't have the power to look away, I really was a dick, wasn't I?

She shrugged. "I have some work to do and a bottle of wine calling my name, take your time. Plus you looked uncomfortable." She whispered the last part. She could probably sense my discomfort at being near Vanessa, my need to wash away the past so desperately that I was itching. The fact that she got me on that level made me feel even worse for my mood swings.

"Thanks." It came out so guttural, so low, I almost winced.

Her smile was sad. "Anytime, Jessie."

My name on her lips didn't sound angry.

It sounded like it belonged there.

I rubbed my chest again and coughed. Maybe I was getting sick. Because this tightness refused to go away. I went into the bathroom and jumped in the shower. Perfect temperature.

I let the water pelt my skin until I was numb.

And then I turned it hotter.

I was probably pink from the water abuse, but I didn't care. I felt a million times better as I stepped out of the shower and rubbed my body with the lush white towel.

"Listen," I overheard Isla say in a calm voice. "I'm sure there's no cause for concern. One of my colleagues, Abby, is great at hacking, and she's gone into every single file on his computer and found nothing. Next week we'll start the second phase, but for right now, we really have nothing to go on other than your feelings, Danica."

Danica.

Danica.

Danica.

Why did that sound . . .

Oh shit. Shit. Shit. Shit.

Shame washed over me again until I almost went to the toilet and puked. What the hell had I been thinking? I hadn't. I just wanted to destroy.

Isla ended the call and ran her hands through her hair just as I stepped out of the steam-filled bathroom. "Everything okay?"

"Yeah." She frowned at her computer screen. "I just don't have a good feeling about this client, there isn't really any evidence that her husband's cheating."

"Drop her," I said too quickly.

"You think?" She tilted her head. "I mean we've never had to do that before, but something's not adding up."

I shrugged. "I say go with your gut, and if your gut says she's not being honest, you can terminate your contract."

Isla chewed her lower lip. "You're right. It does say in our contract that within the first thirty days either party can terminate and the client will get half their deposit back."

"Deposit?" I asked curiously. "Just how much do you girls charge?"

Isla's smile lit up. "Enough."

"Isla . . ."

"Why don't you take a look at the contract and let me know?"

I coughed again and rubbed my chest.

"Are you getting sick?"

"Men don't get sick."

She rolled her eyes. "That doesn't surprise me."

I rubbed my temples as a pulsing headache started to make itself known. "I'm probably just dehydrated." I pointed to the computer. "You really don't mind if I take a look?"

"All my other files are password protected, so have at it, big strong man who doesn't get sick."

I grinned at that and took her laptop as she stretched her arms overhead and motioned back to the bathroom. "My turn, you use up all the hot water?"

"On purpose." I smiled over the computer.

"What purpose would that be?"

"To hear you scream," I said with a smirk.

"Aw, how cute, is that because it's the only way you can make me scream?"

My eyes narrowed. "You do like research, only one way to find out."

And there they were again.

Nipples.

Two. Ripe for the plucking, begging to be sucked.

She swallowed slowly and made her way to the bathroom. My headache jumped about a billion times harder in my head, pounding everywhere. It was the stress. "Hey, Isla, do you have any Tylenol?"

"Purse!" she called.

"Thanks!" I set the laptop down and grabbed her white Louis Vuitton purse and started rummaging through it only to find a small plastic bag labeled *Headache Tea*.

Huh, tea did sound good.

I went over to the kitchen area and put on a kettle.

# Chapter Thirty-Two

ISLA

I felt like a new woman after that shower. Not because of the heat or the privacy, but because the shower had been a few desperate minutes that I was able to put my armor on and ignore the way the towel looked like it was ready to fall from Jessie's waist at any minute.

I stared at that damn towel more than I stared at his six-pack.

That's really saying something.

Maybe because I knew what the towel was packing.

And it was magnificent.

Songs should be written about that man's package.

I'd know every word.

And cheerfully sing it at the top of my lungs.

I regained my focus.

My control.

I thought of my notes.

I thought about my clients and my appointments for the week, including this weekend with Jessie and his ex.

Focus.

Regain control.

Make a plan.

I had a plan.

Stick to the plan, Isla.

I put on one of the hotel bathrobes and slipped on their fluffy white slippers, then opened the door to see Jessie in a low-slung pair of sweats with my laptop in his lap.

"You're brilliant." He said it without looking up. "Fucking brilliant."

I was too stunned to speak. And for some unfortunate reason, my throat closed up so tight I was afraid I was going to burst into tears.

"The clauses you put in your contract, the way you run your business, there's no way you guys could ever really be sued, it's ironclad. If your contracts look like this . . ." He whistled. "God save anyone who tries to take you down."

He finally looked up at me, his eyes soft.

Was it wrong to want to run into his arms and straddle his lap?

I went with a simple "Thank you. That means a lot."

"I mean it," he said seriously, his eyes locking on to mine.

The tension swirled, it danced between us, it made my heart beat a bit faster while my body pulsed with awareness.

"I know you do."

He winked and lifted a mug to his lips. "This is really good, by the way."

I frowned. "We have tea?"

"Oh sorry, I hope it's okay, but I found this headache tea in your bag and thought it sounded better than Tylenol."

My lungs seized. "O-oh, that's . . . just fine!"

My smile was so fake it was painful. I walked over to my purse and nearly passed out when I noticed almost every single ounce of the tea gone. I picked up the bag but didn't see a dosage.

"I, uh . . ." I swiped my phone from the charger. "I'm going to make a quick phone call, my aunt, she's not . . . well."

"Really?" He looked suspicious. "A few days ago she grabbed my ass."

161

"Hah-hah, that's Goo-Poh, always . . . grabbing things."

A puzzled expression crossed his face as he drank more tea. Not good. I rushed into the bathroom, slammed the door, and dialed her number.

She answered on a yawn. "Isla? Is that you?"

"He drank the tea!" I hissed into the phone.

"Your blessing is coming!" She sounded freaking overjoyed.

"No!" I started sweating. "The blessing needs to stay . . . inside his body, Goo-Poh!"

Another yawn. "But if it is his time, why not be accepting of the gifts of our ancestors? Did you know that when your father—"

"Goo-Poh!"

"I was going to say he was born very strong from that tea, everyone says so."

I rolled my eyes. Yes, I knew the stories. Strong as an ox. Blessed by the universe. Salt would not melt him. I'd heard it all. And yes, he was a tall man, but nothing like Jessie.

"How much did he drink?" she asked.

"Well, he took the bag and dumped almost all of it into the damn hot water. How much did you think he drank?"

She started mumbling.

"What are you doing? Goo-Poh? Hello?"

"Praying," she whispered. "He will be ready for you soon."

"I don't want him ready for me soon!"

"Oh, Isla." She laughed so hard I had to pull the phone away from my ear. "You do not have a choice. Even now his body is readying itself to give. You must now ready yourself to accept." Why did I even call her?

"Thanks." For nothing.

"Oh, you're so welcome. Now, I know your parents wouldn't approve, but you must bless the family by being bountiful with children, so you lift those legs, Isla, lift them like you've never lifted before."

"Lifting." I sighed. "Love you, Goo-Poh."

I hung up the phone to more prayers and chants.

Great. So she had prayers and chants and tea. There was no way I was leaving this hotel room without getting pregnant, was there?

I slid the phone into my robe pocket and cracked the door open. Jessie didn't look any different, in fact he looked . . . relaxed.

I opened the door wider, my eyes narrowing as I took a few steps toward him. His hands were flying over the computer keyboard like it was his, not mine.

"Jessie?"

"Hmm?" He didn't look up.

"How's the, uh, headache?" And penis, how's that? Hard? Painful? Dying a slow, choking death inside your sweat pants? "You feel any . . . different?"

"I feel great." His eyes didn't meet mine. "Maybe a bit tired, but it's a relaxed tired. I don't know what the hell was in that tea but I feel . . . alive."

Oh, sweet ancestors. I was going to murder Goo-Poh!

"That's . . . just . . . good for you, Jessie." I patted him on the shoulder. He grabbed my fingertips and let out a little moan. Uh-oh.

"Your skin," he whispered. "It's so damn soft." He clenched my fingers in his as his head fell back. "By the way, I hope you don't mind, but I altered a few of the things in your business plan, it was open. The trajectory for the next ten years is off with all the clientele you're getting, and I noticed you were going to hire two more PIs, but I think you need to hire at least five. I added a few notes, you can delete them, but—"

My heart thundered against my rib cage. "You . . . you took notes for me?"

He kissed my hand. "Yeah, like I said, if I overstepped—"

"Notes," I repeated. "You typed out notes."

"I highlighted them in different colors too," he just had to freaking add.

Rachel Van Dyken

I was ready to maul him right there, ready to shove my computer onto the floor and accept my blessing, alright.

Wide.

The doorbell to our suite rang.

"Shit!" Jessie rubbed his eyes. "Is it already time for dinner?"

My entire body revolted.

No.

No dinner.

He took notes!

In different colors!

I was ready to lick from navel to chin, and I was tealess.

Jessie released my hand and stood, clearly not noticing the way my chest rose and fell, or the way I had to clench my thighs together to keep myself from doing something stupid.

So stupid.

I really needed to stop wanting him.

My body and brain did not want distance between us. My heart said, He took notes! My body went, Damn, his ass looks good in those sweats.

And my brain said it hurt too much to think of all the reasons we couldn't at least have him one more time.

Inside us.

Accept your blessing.

Hah!

Thanks, Goo-Poh. She was probably on her hands and knees chanting right now, that's why I was feeling funny.

And maybe the tea made him more likely to do something nice?

I made a mental note to ask him later.

Colin and Blaire piled into our room dressed for a fancy dinner while I was still in a bathrobe. "Give me like five minutes!"

"Jessie, man, you too?" Colin shook his head. "What were you guys doing anyway?"

"Working," Jessie answered for me. "Sorry, I got distracted, I was looking at her business plan, and the contracts." His face lit up. "It was impressive, sucked me in a bit, to be honest."

Blaire's eyes widened in my direction.

I waved her off, meaning *Drop it.*

Which in Blaire's world meant *Please pursue him like a bank robber, use aggression if necessary.*

"Well, Isla really is the brains behind this whole operation, I'm glad you're helping her out, that's not really my thing, I'm more of the muscle than the brains."

Lies. All lies. She helped me write the whole thing!

She winked.

I prayed for patience and disappeared into the bathroom. A hard knock came on the door, I pulled it open a crack. Jessie stood on the other side with clothes in hand. "Sorry, I just noticed you brought your dress in here."

"No, come in, what's up?"

He gave his head a slow shake and then pressed a hand to his chest. "Sorry, my heart just feels like it's going to beat out of my chest."

Shit, was that a side effect? Racing heart!

"Let's get you some wine tonight," I said helpfully. "That should calm you down."

"Yeah . . . okay."

"Did you need to use the bathroom?"

"No. Yes." He took a deep breath. "I just need to make sure my hair isn't a mess and brush my teeth."

"Do both." I kicked the door wide. "I just have to shimmy into this dress and brush my hair and I'm done."

"Great." He sidestepped me and hung up his suit.

The shirt was a light blue.

It was gorgeous.

And his pants were a dark gray.

I tried not to stare as he stripped, then I quickly turned around and dropped my bathrobe and grabbed my white strapless cocktail dress. It was simple. Classy.

I stepped into it and pulled it up just in time to feel Jessie's hands at my hips as he slowly moved his fingers to my zipper and pulled up.

Without me asking.

He just. Knew.

He really was getting harder and harder to hate.

When he was finished, his hands lingered on my shoulders. I could feel the heat from his chest. The temptation to lean back was so strong I held my breath. Slowly, he ran his hands down my arms and backed away.

I hated the loss of those hands.

That heat.

His body.

The tea was seriously messing with my mind.

When I turned around he was already dressed and brushing his teeth. It was such a normal thing to see him doing, it almost made him look approachable, human.

When he wasn't any of those things.

He was a football legend who had more money than most Hollywood actors and who just happened to want to end me. At least I was going to cling to that threat even if he was being nicer, because if I acknowledged things were changing, I really would shove him up against the sink and lick him.

Why was he suddenly taking notes?

Was it to really bring me down?

Or was he finally seeing he could trust me?

My head spun with the possibilities as I brushed out my hair and wrapped it in a low, messy bun at the nape of my neck.

"Ready?" He was watching me with such intensity I wanted to lock the door and see what the tea was made of.

Instead I nodded and said, "Ready."

Disappointment flashed across his face so briefly I almost missed it. "You look beautiful." He kissed my cheek, then opened the bathroom door.

Colin and Blaire were watching TV.

"Finally." Colin tossed the remote. "Let's go to the stakeout."

"It's not a stakeout," Blaire grumbled. "It's a dinner."

"Spy dinner," he corrected.

Jessie grinned and wrapped an arm around me. I tucked my body into his and let myself believe it was real when it wasn't.

# Chapter Thirty-Three

My body felt heavy.

Everything looked brighter, I kept blinking my eyes as I rubbed small circles on the back of Isla's hand. I didn't want to let it go. Her skin felt so good in that spot beneath her thumb. I could stay there forever.

I smiled at the stupid-as-hell thought.

Stay on her thumb? Really?

I chuckled.

I sounded high.

Isla elbowed me.

"What?"

Her eyes narrowed. "Are you sure you're okay to go to dinner?"

"Headache's gone." I smiled even harder. "I feel . . ." The elevator jolted, causing her to grab my shoulders. I winced as my hard-as-nails cock grazed the front of my pants. "I feel . . ."

She looked worried. "You feel what?"

"Hot," I finally answered. "And"—I leaned in—"what perfume are you wearing?"

"What I always wear." She laughed awkwardly as the elevator doors opened. I had her walking slightly in front of me so nobody took a picture of my raging hard-on as we passed filled tables.

I pulled out her chair, nearly harming myself in the process, then sat next to her and quickly put my napkin in my lap.

"Alright." Blaire was all business. "Vanessa and Wayne have reservations at six, the plan is to feed her curiosity, jealousy, her need to be in the spotlight. She'll most likely know people are watching us and will walk over to face you, to create a scene."

"Scene," I repeated slowly, liking the way it felt on my lips and confused why the word felt funny. "Got it."

Blaire frowned at Isla, then at me. "Are you feeling alright?"

"Great." I reached for the bread basket, suddenly starving, and grabbed a piece of hot bread, then took a huge bite and moaned.

Isla coughed next to me.

I opened my eyes. "Sorry, I didn't realize how hungry I was."

Isla started fanning her face. "Hah, well, it's been a hard day."

"So hard," I grumbled. "Harder than nails."

Isla gripped my thigh with her hand and dug her nails in. It did nothing to alleviate the ache, if anything my dick twitched in the direction of her fingers. Every blood cell in my body rushed south.

I moved my hips a bit.

Her hand slid toward the napkin as she covered my lap, but not before grazing her knuckles against me.

I kicked the table with my knee and knocked over my own water.

"Jessie?" Colin leaned forward. "Your eyes are like pinpoints, are you sure you're up to doing this right now?"

I would do her right now.

So hard. Next to that bread basket.

She'd be screaming my name for days.

I ached in a way I'd never experienced before, like I was ready to spill into my pants, every time they brushed against me, my hips had this insane need to pump.

I'd never felt so . . . fucking aroused in my entire life.

I was ready to rub one out under the table. Desperate.

Insane.

I eyed Isla, she patted her mouth with her napkin and hid a smile behind it.

And then choked on a laugh as I moved again.

Laughing.

She was. Laughing.

I pinched her side.

She yelped, then stared back at her menu. When Colin and Blaire looked away I whispered in her ear, "What the hell was in that tea?"

Her throat moved as she swallowed and whispered, "Oh, leaves. You know . . ."

"Leaves," I gritted out. "Fucking leaves don't make me want to rip that dress from your body and thrust into you without warning. Leaves don't make me think of pumping into you a million different ways only to do it again and again. I am minutes away from taking you on the table, and you say *leaves*?"

Isla's face flushed as her eyes darted around the table. Both Blaire and Colin were in deep discussion over the menu.

"They were special . . . Chinese herb leaves."

"You drugged me!" I hissed.

"Shhh!" she hissed back, her blood-red lips spread into a smile. "You said you were grabbing Tylenol, but no, you just had to grab tea!"

"Why the hell did you label it Headache Tea if I wasn't supposed to use it for my headache?" I whispered, my lips touching her ear, wanting to stay there, kiss down her neck. Damn it, I'd never been so horny in my entire life.

Ever.

Including that time in junior high when I first discovered I had a dick.

I held back a moan as she whispered in my ear, "Look, it was just an accident, I visited my aunt, she gave me tea—"

"Clearly you weren't using it for a headache," I grumbled.

"It was mislabeled." She cringed.

"Hey, guys," Colin interrupted, "looks like our girl's a no-show, or gonna be a few minutes late . . ."

Jessie's eyes met mine. "Why don't we call it a night, it's been a hard day, just like Isla said."

Her eyes widened. Oh yeah, you're trapped now. With me. In a room.

I was going to seek my vengeance.

In the best way possible.

"But—" Isla protested.

"Jessie's right." Blaire nodded seriously. "Plus we have a really difficult morning since Vanessa's hell-bent on being seen by everyone at the pre-parties."

"Exactly," I agreed cheerfully, giving Isla my hand.

She had no choice but to toss her napkin and stand. I turned my back to my friends.

"Don't worry," Colin called out, "I'll just charge the bread basket to the room."

"Thanks, man!" I called back, not even caring he was smirking like he knew exactly where I was headed—and what I was going to be doing.

I pressed the elevator button.

It opened.

"Get in," I whispered in her ear.

Isla shivered and took a few steps into the elevator.

I didn't wait for the doors to close.

171

I attacked her from behind, my mouth on her neck as she arched against me, my hands cupping her breasts, squeezing, feeling her nipples strain against the thin fabric. "This is coming off."

"Yes," she breathed, lifting her leg high enough for me to run a free hand up her thigh, and spin her around. My cock ached harder when her body was pressed against mine. I pinned her arms above her head and plunged my tongue into her mouth as I grazed her hips and tugged at her lacy thong.

The elevator doors whooshed closed.

Isla tried to break away from me.

"Not a chance in hell," I muttered. "I don't care who sees, let them all see, this is mine." I squeezed her ass so hard she whimpered, just as the elevator stopped and the doors opened again.

Someone cleared their throat.

I glanced over my shoulder to see none other than her ex staring back at us with wide eyes.

"Something bothering you?" I snapped.

He shut his mouth, then smirked. "Enjoy her, I know I did."

I lunged for him just as the doors closed, leaving him outside. The bastard almost ran out of there, probably because he knew I would actually kick his ass into Sunday.

Isla grabbed my head with her hands and pulled my mouth back to hers. I dragged my teeth along her bottom lip and moaned when she started unbuttoning my shirt.

"Did you drink the tea too?" I asked between heated kisses.

"Don't need tea," she confessed.

I locked eyes with her. "Me either. Been wanting this for—"

"Shut up." She kissed me again.

We stumbled back against the elevator door, it opened seconds later. Down the hall, I waved my key card over the door's sensor and we pushed into our dark room.

I ripped off my shirt.

She kicked her shoes into the air and shimmied out of her thong.

It was so hot.

Her need being as great as mine.

When she turned, I unzipped her dress and let it fall to the floor. She stepped out of it and faced me completely naked.

"Thank God for tea," I muttered as I dropped my pants and finally freed myself.

Her eyes widened again like she forgot how big I was.

And my cock grew because the greedy bastard did what cocks do—get cocky.

I leaped for her, digging my hands into her hair, pulling it free from the band that kept me from wrapping its silky tendrils around my fingers. Her mouth opened, accepting me, my tongue, as I slid it by hers, tasted her, sucked on her, and begged the universe to let me stay in her.

I picked her up and dumped her onto the bed then hooked her knees over my shoulders. "I'm desperate for you." I felt sweat collect on my upper lip. "So believe me when I say I'll make this good for you later tonight, but right now, I think my heart may actually stop if I can't get inside you." I gritted my teeth as I grazed her entrance. "I'm clean."

"On the"—her eyes rolled back as I inched farther—"Pill."

"Good." I thrust forward and saw black spots as she moved with me, clung to me like her body wasn't ever going to let me go. With each greedy movement I was more and more crazed, her heat, the way she clawed at my back, tugged my hair, sent me over the edge, and when her eyes locked on me and then on us together, my balls drew up so tight I knew I was going to burst before I had time to warn her, to tell her that it wasn't normally this out of control, that I wanted to please her first, but couldn't imagine waiting another second.

Her walls tightened and then I was losing myself.
I was clawing at her body like a crazed man.
I was.
For the first time in my life.
Out.
Of.
Control.
And I never wanted to go back.

# Chapter Thirty-Four

ISLA

Jessie's lips dragged across my neck over and over again with heated kisses that had me moaning his name before I could even open my eyes. The tea had clearly done a number on him—postsex he nearly passed out. I almost called Goo-Poh again but knew she'd probably spout something else about blessings and pregnancies, plus just how exactly was I going to lead into that particular conversation? *Hey, Goo-Poh, sorry to call again but the man I accidentally drugged passed out with his hands cupping my breasts and I'm kind of stuck? Is this normal?*

No. Not normal.

Nothing about lying in bed with Jessie Beckett was normal.

I'd fallen asleep soon after with a smile on my face.

Only to be woken up by this.

His mouth.

I smiled wide as his kisses lowered to my stomach, and then I felt his hands on my ass as he spread my legs wide and whispered against the inside of my right thigh, "Morning."

"Morning," I croaked back as he used his mouth to show me just how good the morning was about to be. I gripped his head and pulled him away. "Kiss me."

"Hmm, thought I was . . ." He chuckled against my mouth.

I dug my fingers into his hair as his tongue slid past my lower lip. Jessie kissed like he had a PhD in knowing a woman's mouth. He kissed like it was a game that he never lost—only winning with that mouth. Tremors pulsed through my body as he flipped onto his back and pulled me on top of him.

I was exposed.

Topless.

And his grin was so smug it was a tie between wanting to kiss him and punch him.

"So . . . the tea wore off?" I asked curiously as he put his hands behind his head and watched me, like I wasn't naked on top of him with a very large part of his body pressed against me. It was hell not to move against him.

One inch, if I moved just one inch.

"Completely." He grinned. "Something wrong, Isla?"

I gulped and tried not to squirm as my body got hotter and hotter. How dare he turn me on then stare at me! "No, nothing, I'm . . . fantastic."

My blood roared *Liar* as I tried to even my breathing.

"Hmm." He still didn't move his hands, just stared at my breasts, licked his lips like he could still taste me on them, and then met my gaze. "That's nice."

I gritted my teeth. "I should go get ready."

"No."

"No?"

He shook his head. "You're not going anywhere."

"I'm not?" It came out breathless, my body felt heavy with need the longer he stared at me with that half-lidded gaze, licking his lips like he was going to feast on me again.

His lips twitched. "You drugged me."

I glared. What was he getting at? "You drugged yourself, genius."

"What the hell were you doing with sex tea?"

"Sex tea?" I rolled my eyes. "I don't know, Jessie! Maybe I was going to steam some, put it in your oatmeal, then trap you in a sauna!"

His eyes widened. "What sort of psychopath would do that?"

"I was kidding!"

"I orgasmed in my sleep." He bit down on his lower lip and then reached out and flicked my nipple. "To a vision of this."

I sucked in a breath as his hands moved to my hips and gripped them, pressing me harder against him, making my body downright tremble.

"I woke up hard at least a dozen times last night to find you sleeping." His knuckles grazed my chin. "Painful doesn't even begin to describe the last few hours wanting you so damn much."

I gulped.

"So"—he grinned—"your punishment for the drugging, and don't worry, we'll get back to the reasons you had that tea in the first place . . ." He sighed, and then put his hands behind his head again.

"My punishment?" I repeated. "You never said."

"I'm more of an action sort of guy," he said before positioning himself and thrusting into me without any sort of warning, just his hard length pressing inside me like I'd been wanting for the last ten minutes.

And if I was honest.

The minute we finished last night.

More.

I'd wanted more.

He pulled out, my eyes snapped open. "What's going on?"

"Nothing." He slid back in.

I gasped as he flipped me onto my back and then retreated again just as I was about to scream his name and tell him how amazing he was.

"Jessie." I said his name like a curse.

"Yes?" He braced his body over mine, his smile smug, his intentions clearly bad.

"Stop stopping!"

"Is this what you want?" He filled me so hard and fast I saw stars. I gripped his biceps and tried to focus on his face as he leaned down and parted my lips with his tongue. "I want to punish you, but it seems punishing you"—he slowed his movements—"means I'm punishing myself." I couldn't get enough of that man's tongue as it coaxed more and more moans out of me. "You feel perfect."

It was sweet.

He was being sweet.

I almost wished he had said something dirty.

Something about how I was ready for him. How good it felt to be inside me.

Instead, he said I was perfect.

Me.

Tears filled my eyes before I could tell my emotions to stop reacting, and when he locked eyes with me, it wasn't with punishment or teasing, it was with admiration and a little bit of respect.

He looked at me the way every woman wants to be looked at.

With awe.

Then he kissed me.

Breaking eye contact as his thrusts increased, he braced my head with his hands, controlling the kiss, controlling the pace, taking the control from my hands in a way that wasn't controlling at all.

But to a girl like me? Complete surrender.

I let myself get lost in his kiss, in his movements, in the way he filled me up completely.

His hands moved to mine.

They tangled.

Our palms pressed against each other as his forehead touched mine. We locked eyes again, no words were said.

I didn't want to look away.

I was afraid if I did, the moment would shatter.

His lips brushed my forehead as he slid a hand between our bodies, touching me, releasing me, beckoning more surrender, taking more control.

I moaned his name, then saw two of him for a few brief seconds as our bodies moved in perfect sync, as my mouth sought his.

I kissed him deep, hard.

He growled against my mouth, lips parted, breathing the same air.

"Don't want to stop," he said.

"Then don't." I would beg on my hands and knees.

He chuckled against my mouth. "I can't last forever."

"I thought athletes were known for their virility?"

"Isla?"

"Hmm?"

"Shut up." He kissed me harder, digging his hands into my hair, twisting it around his fingers like he wanted to hold on. He tugged the pieces hard with one last thrust, sending me over the edge as he gripped the headboard and filled me harder.

My body arched up off the bed as I screamed his name.

I didn't even realize I was closing my eyes until I opened them to see him staring at me with that same look on his face, and then he was kissing me again, his mouth never leaving mine.

And I wondered if that's what the other half of the world felt like.

The happy ones.

The ones in relationships.

Because I'd never experienced sex in that way before.

With a man who once promised to destroy me.

But in that same voice, he cried out my name like it was the only word he ever wanted to pass his lips.

I wrapped my legs around his waist, my arms around his neck as he slowly sat up and took me with him. "I've never wanted to call in sick so much my entire life."

"Call in sick?" I laughed. "What are you talking about?"

"Oh, I'm a PI now. I have an ex to catch and an ex to beat the shit out of. Tell me he was bad in bed, tell me he didn't touch you like I did—"

"He was selfish. Enough said."

"I was selfish last night," Jessie admitted.

"Right, but you were also drugged."

Jessie pulled me in for another kiss. "I didn't need drugs to convince me that you would be perfect—I just needed them as an excuse to strip you down."

"Oh yeah?"

"Isla?"

"Hmm?"

"Today . . . wear red."

# Chapter Thirty-Five

*JESSIE*

The elevator was quiet.

I couldn't stop touching her.

The tea had completely worn off. I could tell because I wasn't walking around the hotel trying to hide the baseball bat in my pants. Then again, it's not like I wasn't still sporting something.

My hands grazed her arm so many times she had to know it was on purpose.

She wore red.

Red.

A color that would normally make my eyes burn was doing something else entirely. The dress hugged every curve, it was simple, elegant.

It was Isla.

She'd even curled her straight dark hair just enough to make me want to reach out and touch it. We were already running late to meet Colin and Blaire, so it was near impossible to grab her.

To run my hands down her ass.

To blurt out that I wanted her again.

I had no excuses this time, though.

No tea to lean back on.

And for once in my life I was curious where I stood with a woman, and maybe a bit anxious. Was I just a quick screw for her? Or was it more? Did I still want to destroy her? The anger that I'd always put front and center was now more of a lazy, simmering irritation with a heavy, sickening dose of fear.

Fear that I was jumping into something too soon.

Fear that she saw me the way my ex did.

My thoughts were causing another headache, and this time I couldn't drug myself with some weird Chinese medicine.

Which is the only admission I got from Isla when I asked again this morning.

I cleared my throat to say something to her, to tell her that I wanted to hit the button to our floor and hide away in the room. To tell her to screw it, that I didn't even care anymore about Vanessa.

But the truth was.

I still cared.

People don't change overnight.

But I wanted to know how.

I was out of control last night.

And it felt good.

She was wearing red.

And I couldn't stop staring.

Maybe change wasn't so bad?

"Hey!" Blaire and Colin were waiting near the elevators. Blaire pulled Isla in for a quick hug while Colin gave me a once-over. It took him less than three seconds to smirk.

It took me less than two to flip him off without the girls seeing.

"Good morning, Jessie," he said in a cheerful voice. "Sleep well? In your bed? Upstairs? In the room you're sharing with Isla?"

Blaire looked between us.

Isla's cheeks heated. "We did, thanks, too bad Jessie wasn't feeling so well."

"You got sick?" Blaire sounded skeptical.

"It was hard"—Isla just had to say *hard*—"on him."

I looked toward the ceiling and mumbled a curse.

"I hate it when things are hard." Colin nodded solemnly. "Maybe next time you're dealing with a situation of hardness"—oh God, someone shut him the hell up!—"which you clearly were last evening, you just get a little help from . . . a friend." He looked to Isla.

"Colin," I said in a warning tone.

"After all"—he just wouldn't stop!—"I get by with a little help from my friends."

Blaire covered her laugh with a cough and then hit Colin on the chest.

He winked. "Alright, so now that you're all . . . better, and by better I mean you've gotten laid and aren't as cranky as you've been the past few weeks, let's get started."

Isla turned about ten shades of red.

"Are we doing this?" I rubbed my hands together and tried to deflect from my sex life and my best friend's ability to read my smug expression, and the fact that I couldn't stop stealing glances at Isla.

"Absolutely." Blaire pulled out her phone and frowned. "Hold on a sec, Isla, did you answer Danica's email?"

Isla stiffened next to me. "Yeah, I even called her, something seems off about her situation. Abby said everything was clean except for some weird cash transfer into their joint account for a large sum of money."

"How large?"

"Shouldn't we be focusing on Vanessa?" I interrupted, as a sick feeling washed over me. Shit. Shit. Shit. I sent myself a reminder text while Isla and Blaire kept talking.

"Ten grand." Isla sighed. "Large enough that it's suspicious."

"Is that typical?" Colin just had to ask.

Fuck me.

"Sometimes," Blaire answered before Isla could. "If they're trying to move money around or pin something on the other person. It just feels strange, especially since it was wired the day she called for a consult."

I started breaking out in a sweat.

"Huh." Colin eyed me and then the girls. "Alright, we can save the world another day, let's focus on getting Vanessa's confession before Jessie gets too horny again."

I groaned. "I accidentally drank tea, alright?"

"Boner tea?" Colin laughed. "Is that what it was?"

I glared at Isla. "Tell them."

"He had a headache." She snickered behind her hand. "And my Goo-Poh is a bit"—her eyes glazed over, and I hoped to God it was because she was thinking about what happened after the tea, what was still happening every time we touched—"helpful in the area of tonics and teas. She thinks of herself as a doctor."

I rolled my eyes. "That lady would be a menace in a hospital, mislabeling every damn thing," I grumbled, still thinking about the way the tea made me slur my words and how my body felt on fire next to Isla's. The thing is, though, after the tea wore off, I still felt it, the pull to her. The need to touch her was so intense I had to look away and at Colin instead.

"Other than asking what the hell a Goo-Poh is, I guess the lingering question is . . ." Colin grinned as we started walking toward the pool. "Why'd you have that kind of tea on hand, Isla?"

"Exactly my point," I said.

We stopped walking and stared at her.

She gulped and looked to Blaire. But Blaire held her hands up. "Oh no, I'm not covering your ass, I wanna hear why you had the tea too."

"I, um . . ." Isla's face matched her dress. "My Goo-Poh is insane, alright, guys? Jessie's met her, she grabbed his ass! She heard me complaining about cohabitating with this charming thing over here"—she shoved a finger into my chest—"and said murder was too messy."

"Smart woman," Colin muttered.

"So"—Isla nervously licked her lips—"she told me to seduce him instead, said to, er, accept his blessing."

My jaw nearly dropped.

Colin's expression matched mine.

"And just to be clear, when you say *blessing*," I said with the air quotes she hated, "you mean my"—I looked downward—"blessing."

"Praise." Colin lifted a hand in the air while Isla covered her face. "I think we should invite this Goo-Poh to Thanksgiving."

"No!" Isla and I said simultaneously.

"Hey, she's nice!" Isla reprimanded me.

"She sells illegal drugs masquerading as tea leaves!" I yelled, gaining a few odd stares from hotel guests. "Okay, let's just drop it, I drank the tea, I lived—"

"Through a very hard time." Colin was dead to me.

"Yes," I said through clenched teeth. "So let's focus on psycho Vanessa, not the blessings."

"Of your package," Colin added with a thumbs-up.

"Sometimes I wonder why we're friends," I muttered while Colin wrapped an arm around Blaire and kept walking.

Isla hung back with me, her face still red.

I tried joking. "Would it be too much to ask you to say something like *God bless us, every one* next time we—"

"Finish that sentence and I'm asking Goo-Poh for tea that makes your blessing go soft."

"Ouch." I winced.

"And we wouldn't want it to be permanent."

"You wouldn't . . ." I added with a cocky grin.

She rolled her eyes but I didn't miss the small smile on her lips. It was enough to hope that maybe it wasn't over, whatever this thing was between us.

A gust of hot air hit me square in the face as I followed everyone outside to the pool area. Vanessa was perched at the corner in a white bathing suit that I used to think looked sexy as hell on her.

Because I'd loved white.

Now I thought it looked cheap, like she was trying too hard to get noticed.

She sipped on a mimosa while Wayne chewed a cigar next to her.

They looked like snobs.

I almost gagged.

"And there she is," Blaire said under her breath as we found a table and sat. "Let's order some breakfast and see if we can bait her to come over here, I've already been recording our conversation—"

"Thank God!" Colin burst out laughing. "So I can replay all the blessed parts?"

Isla groaned.

Blaire winked at him. "Yes, so if she says anything incriminating we'll get it on tape. But she has to be angry enough to react, you know?"

"Got it." I reached for a glass of water as the waiter approached. We ordered, I glanced at my phone. I couldn't just text and fix my other problem.

I needed to call it off.

I just couldn't do it in front of Isla. What the hell had I been thinking?

My anger had blinded everything.

And now, now I was stuck wondering where I stood with the one woman I wasn't supposed to actually fall for.

But was.

While the one that I wanted out of my life forever continued to dig her claws into me any way she could.

Life wasn't fair.

And was getting worse by the second as a shadowed figure approached and said in that perfectly breathless voice, "Hey, Jessie."

# Chapter Thirty-Six

ISLA

I wasn't a violent person.

I was calm.

Controlled.

Serene.

I was going to pull every hair extension from her head and set it on fire.

I accidentally dug my nails into Jessie's arm, causing him to wince. Either that or that was his "Vanessa smile."

I hated it.

I hated her.

I hated that she'd touched him.

I hated that she'd wrecked him.

I hated that a part of him would always be hers.

I hated so damn much.

And I didn't know what to do with the hate, because it was such a foreign feeling. The last time I felt this angry was when Wayne cheated on me, then admitted it and asked if we could get back together.

Yeah, because that sounded like the perfect life plan! He even had the nerve to say this was expected with men in his position and that I shouldn't berate him for being attracted to multiple women.

At.

A.

Time.

God, he was such an asshole.

Vanessa flicked her eyes in my direction, then glanced back at Jessie. "It feels like you're stalking me."

Jessie smirked. "The world doesn't revolve around you. I know how disappointing that may be, but I'm actually here with my friends."

She glared at Blaire first, then raised her eyebrows at her brother. "Ah, the traitor."

Colin's nostrils flared. "I see you're spending the trust fund with accelerated speed."

She rolled her eyes and touched her lips—ah, she'd just gotten them done, and by done I mean overdone. I was no stranger to Botox or getting a little help in the lip area, but she looked like you could toss her against a window and she'd stick. "I don't need it anymore. I have Wayne."

She turned her venomous glare toward me. "You know Wayne, right? Ex-fiancé? Successful director? The best lay I've had. Ever."

If she was trying to hurt Jessie, he didn't show it.

I, however, burst out laughing and then sobered. "Oh, I'm sorry, I thought it was a joke. Yes, Very Exciting Wayne, you know, when he can get it up without the little blue pill."

Her face paled.

"But you know all about that, right?"

She crossed her arms. "Anyway." We were getting dismissed.

The waiter brought our drinks.

Blaire's panic was evident.

Vanessa wasn't going to confess anything.

Damn it, we needed to get her drunk.

I reached for the mimosa just as she put on her sunglasses, and had no time to react as Blaire grabbed the drink and laughed. "Isla! You know you can't drink when you're pregnant!"

Jessie choked on his next sip.

My stomach dropped. "Uh, right, er, I just, it's so new that I, um . . . forgot."

Jessie patted my hand. "I just can't believe it."

"Me. Either." I sent a seething glare to Blaire before forcing a smile at Vanessa. "It wasn't planned, but hey, we're already engaged, so . . ." I shrugged and leaned toward Jessie. He captured my mouth with a hungry kiss that felt just as real as this morning and last night. I grabbed ahold of his shirt and tugged.

When we parted, we were both out of breath.

"And now I know how babies are made," Colin joked while Vanessa's lips twitched like she was about to burst into tears.

"You guys," Blaire said in her all-business voice, "are going to be the perfect little family. Aren't they, Vanessa?"

"You bitch!" Vanessa spat out, teeth clenched. "What, your life wasn't good enough? You had to steal mine!"

"Hey, you're the one who had an abortion without talking to your man first."

"I did what was necessary!" she said in a hushed voice. "For my career and for Jessie."

"You are such a coldhearted bitch." Jessie stood, towering over her. "And you had no right to do that. I was your husband."

"It's my body."

"Don't say it's about your body when we both know it had everything to do with your career, not mine, yours. You were selfish then, you're somehow more selfish now. And if you ever defame my character again, I'm going to sue the hell out of you."

Vanessa snorted. "Oh Jessie, you can't sue me for telling the truth."

"Yeah." Blaire held up her iPhone to show it was recording. "Actually he can, since you've been lying."

I could see Vanessa's wheels turning. Like she was seconds away from creating a scene by jumping across the table and grabbing the phone, so I stood. "Vanessa, you already have everything, you have a director boyfriend, and you're going to the Academy Awards tomorrow night. Let Jessie go."

She swallowed and stared at the ground.

"Let. Him. Go." I said it with more purpose as I put a hand on her arm and waited for her to jerk away.

She didn't answer.

She just shrugged me off.

And walked away.

But when she got back to the chair, she was wiping underneath her eyes. Wayne didn't even notice.

Jessie exhaled next to me. "So, we got rid of one problem only to have a brand new one."

"Huh?"

"Apparently we're expecting." He didn't look amused.

"That wasn't my fault!" I said defensively. "And you know Vanessa can't say anything now!"

"Not Vanessa I'm worried about." Jessie made a face then nodded toward the waiter. "He heard, I guarantee it's going to get leaked."

And because the universe was out to screw us, Blaire's phone beeped, she looked at it, then hid it under her napkin and said with fake enthusiasm, "Congrats! You're having twins."

Jessie groaned and collapsed into his seat.

"Relax, guys." Colin reached for his mimosa. "I'm sure her Goo-Poh has a tea for that."

"So. Helpful," Jessie said through clenched teeth while I panicked.

"Goo-Poh!" I sprang to my feet. "She's going to die!"

"What?" Jessie stood. "Why would she die?"

190

"All she's ever wanted from me is children!"

"I'm sure it's not that bad." Jessie put a hand on me.

"She used to pray it over me when I was six!" I said with a half scream. "When all the normal girls went to school with thoughts about prom, my Goo-Poh was at home lighting candles of fertility!"

Jessie hid his smile behind his hand.

"Don't you dare laugh." I pointed at him. "You're going with me."

"Going?"

"To explain to Goo-Poh that I most definitely did not accept your blessing wide and—"

Colin snorted with laughter.

I covered my face with my hands. "I'm so screwed, this is so bad, isn't it? This is like a monumental screw-up!"

"At least you guys are already engaged," Blaire pointed out.

"Yes, thank God, we're already engaged before I bring a fake set of twins into the world!"

Jessie took a step back from me.

"Don't attract attention," Blaire said through clenched teeth.

I sat back down and reached for Colin's mimosa, then put it back. "Damn it!"

"I've never seen you so . . ." Blaire looked like she was searching for a word. "Chaotic, I kind of like it."

"This, this was not the plan." I tapped the table with my fingernails. "Our plan was simple, get engaged, make everyone believe in the fairy tale, then quietly separate a few months after it died down. A baby is permanent, splitting while pregnant will not bode well for either of us. It makes Jessie look like he abandoned me, and it makes Dirty Exes look bad."

"So . . ." Blaire leaned in. "You stay together."

"But—"

"What's the worst that could happen?" she asked softly.

Jessie had been quiet next to me. I elbowed him, but he only chuckled and said, "Oh well, I'm sure she has a list."

I did have a list.

Never mind him.

"Dismemberment, poisoning, painting my walls, plotting my demise via Chinese food, yelling, so much yelling." Of course he would add that. "Need I go on?"

"I did not try to dismember you!"

"It really is only a matter of time," Jessie said seriously.

"I can't believe this. Or you!" I jutted a finger at his chest and dug in. "You, you aren't supposed to sit there and smile, I need you to freak out. I need you to do the rational adult thing and freak the hell out and then fix it."

"But that's what you're doing."

"I'm not freaking out." I sucked in another sharp breath. Why was it so hard to breathe? Things were spiraling. This was not how it was supposed to happen.

"You are." Jessie leaned in. "And as much as I want to freak out on the outside, I can't, because people are watching. So put your napkin back in your lap, lean over and kiss me, and we'll find a way to fix it later."

I nodded, not trusting my voice.

"But first," he said with a sigh, "it seems like we may need to make a visit to the retirement home."

"Wear a cup," Colin said helpfully.

# Chapter Thirty-Seven

"Now remember," Isla said for the fifth time, "this is more war zone than retirement home. And stay away from Stanley."

"Stanley?" I repeated. "Who the hell is Stanley?"

"Just give him a wide berth." Why was she shaking? And why was a man named Stanley suddenly after me? "He's just as crazy as Goo-Poh, and they're constantly fighting over position."

I think every future erection just died. "Sexual position?"

Isla jerked her head in my direction before reaching for the entry doors. "No, you ass! Why is everything about sex!"

"You're the one that said *position*! What was I supposed to think?"

She reached for the door, but I opened it for her. "Trust me, sex would be better than the territorial war they have going on. They fight over the annual Christmas party, Thanksgiving is a nightmare, and don't even get me started on Easter."

"Easter?"

"Shhh!" Isla cupped a hand over my mouth. "Not too loud, his hearing aid is always on high, you can't breathe without him hearing about it. And if he corners you, there won't be an escape without him telling you a two-hour story about the one time Goo-Poh forgot to decorate her door."

"You're shitting me."

"To this day, he puts a paper cross on her door every week to remind her of her failures."

Stunned, I could only stare at Isla and wonder what the hell sort of retirement home I'd walked into. Last time I'd only been aiming to get at her—this time, it felt like I'd stamped my passport and taken a ride on the crazy train.

We walked arm in arm down the hall, people waved, she smiled brightly. And then she quickly shoved me to the right so hard I rammed my head against the wall.

"Kiss me."

"What the—"

Her mouth collided with mine so fast I had to hang on to her for support, and then all I was thinking about was the kiss.

And her soft body.

And the fact that even after Stanley walked by with a look of disgust on his face, I could still get an erection.

It was a win-win.

She pulled back and looked over her shoulder. My mouth followed her, aching for more, needing her taste, wanting to cover her body with mine and plunge into her like this morning.

"Oh good." She pulled back and grabbed my hand. "Stanley's also nominated himself the Night's Watch."

"Like *Game of Thrones*?"

"Yup, he's a huge fan of Jon Snow, and he's been known to wander the halls saying, 'Winter is coming' whenever Goo-Poh walks past. Naturally she retaliates with a Chinese curse. I think they secretly like each other but both are too stubborn to make the first move."

"Why make the first move when you can live in a perpetual state of sexual tension? Sounds like a great way to live the rest of your days," I muttered.

Isla grinned up at me. "Know a thing or two about sexual tension?"

"I almost mounted you next to the bread basket last night—so that's a strong yes."

She blushed that pretty pink. I wanted to kiss it away from her face, was about to, when she stopped in front of a door.

Sure enough, there was a paper cross taped to it. She ripped it off and knocked twice.

It jolted open.

"Goo-Poh!" She was doing a really bad job of selling the excitement.

Goo-Poh looked away from her and to me. "You drink the tea?"

"By accident," I said through clenched teeth. "I had a headache."

"Hah." She motioned for us to come in. "Works every time."

Son of a bitch.

Isla mouthed *"Sorry"* to me as we walked in.

I don't think many things could have prepared me for what I walked into, and by the time the door shut behind me, I knew it was the beginning of the end.

Everything was wrapped in plastic.

Like Goo-Poh was a Chinese Dexter just ready to murder me and wrap my body up. I gripped Isla's hand, but she just walked over to the couch, sat down, and began pouring fucking tea like I wasn't about to get murdered by her aunt.

I sat next to her, and Goo-Poh sat on her right.

Isla looked at her as she poured, and stopped when Goo-Poh pressed two fingers to the table.

Isla nodded.

I wondered what the hell I was missing in the exchange, and hoped to God it wasn't sign language for *Yes, carry on with the killings.*

"So." Goo-Poh sat back against the plastic couch with her tea. "You've impregnated my niece."

"About that—"

"This moment"—Goo-Poh grinned so wide I was afraid her face was going to crack—"I have prayed to the ancestors since she was born. I have told her every day that your duty to your family is to bring honor with more family. And the only way to do that is on your back."

I choked on the tea Isla had handed me.

"With your legs in the air like so." She flicked her wrist into the air. "To receive." Was I supposed to say something back like *You're welcome?* Or *It was a great time, thanks for the boner tea?*

"Uh," I gulped and then smiled. "Well, as you know, I care about Isla very much."

It wasn't a lie.

But Isla would assume it was.

Her face fell slightly.

"But you need to know . . ." Shit, I was going to give her aunt a heart attack, her eyes were assessing as she locked on to mine and waited, her lips parted.

Was it hot in here?

I tugged at my shirt and cleared my throat as Goo-Poh tilted her head ever so slightly, like she was bracing herself for war or a great disappointment.

"That we . . ." I couldn't do it, I couldn't say it. "Couldn't be more happy to be having a baby." I spread my arms wide. Shit, I was going to hell.

The words just rushed out before I could stop them.

Isla pinned me with a glare I'm sure she learned from Goo-Poh, and I chugged the rest of the tea and prayed for the apocalypse.

She was happy! Her face. I didn't want her to clutch her chest and say Isla brought shame upon the family!

"Oh." Goo-Poh smiled wider and then stopped smiling. "You sure you did it right? Because sometimes these pregnancies, they don't stick, you need to do it often and well." She stood. "Here, let me just find a few things."

She went to a cupboard.

I peered around Isla.

The cupboard was floor-to-ceiling.

Everything had a label.

Even the kitchen drawers had labels.

"So, I take it you learned how to label from her?" I whispered to Isla.

She chucked the plastic-covered remote at me. "What the actual hell!"

"I'm not going to be responsible for killing your Goo-Poh! You can't just drop that kind of bomb on an eighty-year-old woman!"

"You can! You will!" she whispered harshly. "You just get up and say, *Hey, I don't have swimmers!* Or *My swimmers can't make it.*"

"My swimmers damn well make it every time and you fucking know it!"

"Can this not," she hissed, "be about your penis, just for once? Can this be about not getting deeper into the shit we created?"

"I'm not making this about my penis, you're making it about my penis! And we're in shit because Blaire opened her big fat mouth!"

"Don't bring Blaire into this—"

"Here we are!" Goo-Poh was back.

With a bag.

A giant bag full of smaller bags.

Oh God, I was leaving with drugs.

"Now"—she dumped them onto the table—"everything is labeled wrong, so you'll need a code." She pulled a highlighted sheet of paper from her pocket.

Isla covered her face with her hands.

"Blue is the nickname, pink is the real contents. Easy!"

"And you do this with the wrong labels because?"

She scoffed. "It's not like a man to pick up a plastic bag that says *Erection* and go, *I should make that tea right now!*" She laughed.

I didn't.

"Though it's not wise to drink all the tea." She winked.

"Noted," I said tersely. "I'll be sure to be more careful next time."

I was setting that bag on fire.

Goo-Poh sat with her hands in her lap. "Now that's taken care of, where am I planning the wedding?"

"Oh, Goo-Poh." Isla looked uncomfortable. "Remember it's not real, this marriage isn't—"

Goo-Poh spat on the floor, then raised a hand and said something in Chinese. "Young lady, you will not bring shame on the family. You will marry this nice young man with his big muscles. You will have many babies. You will have a fertile womb. And you will do it next week, during the even days."

It was my turn to panic.

We'd never planned on going through with it, but she was so excited, beaming actually, and to backtrack now? Admit we lied? Admit everything after seeing her excitement? I didn't know what to say, what to do.

"Now, we should discuss the meal."

I struggled for words.

I had none.

Isla looked at me for help but I'd already screwed us, hadn't I?

"The, um, meal," Isla gulped. "Naturally you'll be in charge of everything."

Goo-Poh patted Isla's thigh. "Good girl." She grabbed Isla's face with both hands. "Now we eat, you look too skinny."

And with that, she got up and walked into the small kitchen.

"Yesterday I was too fat." Isla slumped. "What are we going to do?"

I said the only thing I knew we could do.

"Eat."

# Chapter Thirty-Eight

ISLA

I was surprised I wasn't hyperventilating. Nothing was going as planned. We'd had a plan and not just deviated from it, but gone over a hundred miles an hour in the opposite direction.

Blaire just had to open her big mouth.

Granted, at least we got Vanessa's confession.

But now I wasn't just getting married to Jessie Beckett—and soon—I was giving my Goo-Poh free rein for the prewedding meal, and I wasn't even allowed to drink because I was pregnant.

I touched my stomach.

"It happens." Goo-Poh motioned to my hand. "When the blessing is beginning to grow."

I quickly dropped my hand while Jessie's face paled next to me.

The problem was that we'd had sex while my aunt prayed.

Yes, I was on the Pill.

But I wasn't stupid, I knew that things could still slip through.

Powerful things.

Things from that giant delicious man who kept trying to eat his rice with chopsticks even though he was worse than a toddler.

I finally took pity on him and grabbed him a fork.

"Thanks," he muttered.

"Naturally we will invite the whole family," Goo-Poh said between bites. "I think the community center would be a lovely place, it can house the most people.

"For a wedding?" Jessie interjected.

"No, no, for the reception after the ceremony. The wedding, of course, will be a combination of your traditions and ours." She grinned at Jessie. "Though there is one that I refuse to back down from."

"Only one?" Jessie said in a shocked voice. I elbowed him in the ribs.

"The delivery of the bridal bed." Goo-Poh clapped her hands together. "It is one of the most important parts of the premarriage ceremony, it must take place on an even month and date, and since next month is March we must do it this month. Tomorrow is the eighteenth, that means we are at a two and eighteen, both lucky numbers. We will deliver the bed at six a.m."

"We?" Jessie choked on a piece of rice.

"I am considered a wise woman, I will be present for the delivery and blessing." She grinned to herself. "And that means we must have the wedding exactly ten days later. I know a good church and can get us a good deal on Chinese invitations, none of that boring white and flowers, we want something sacred. They will be red."

"Wouldn't want it any other way," Jessie said under his breath, making my heart beat a bit faster as he reached across and squeezed my hand.

"See?" Goo-Poh pointed to our joined hands. "Already you are glowing with excitement!"

"I'm glowing with something," I said through clenched teeth while Jessie squeezed my hand tighter.

"Oh!" Goo-Poh touched her face with her hands. "How could I forget? You need your rest. Have your man take you home and you sleep. When you wake up don't forget to drink more tea, it will make your bones strong!"

"Isn't that milk?" Jessie said out of the corner of his mouth.

I glared and then kissed Goo-Poh on both cheeks. It was rare to show that much emotion, but she'd practically raised me, and since I was only half Chinese, I told myself it was okay to forgo some of the more crazy beliefs, like the one that said we do not hug or touch or encourage.

We feed our children.

They grow and have families.

Then they feed their families.

Our world revolved around blessings and eating.

But touching? Not so much.

Jessie bent down and kissed Goo-Poh's hand.

She shivered and then brought the same hand to his face and whispered in the most serious voice I'd ever heard, "You give me boys. Yes?"

"Yes," Jessie replied right away. The man didn't have a choice, it seemed, better he start researching how to do it than say, *We'll see* and risk her wrath.

She slapped his cheek lightly twice. "Good man. I'm tired now, so are you. I'll call you with more details about the bed."

Jessie opened the door to find Stanley standing on the other side with a paper cross and tape midair.

"Were you about to knock?" Jessie asked.

"Knock?" Stanley sniffed. "I wouldn't touch this woman's door with a ten-foot pole."

"And yet you do, Stanley, at least twice a day just to check." I gave him a smile and grabbed Jessie just as Goo-Poh started spouting curses in Chinese.

We left with Stanley holding up the paper cross in front of his face like Goo-Poh was a vampire.

I was surprised he didn't toss garlic.

By the time we made it to the car I was exhausted.

"So . . ." Jessie smirked at me. "Bridal bed? Do I want to know?"

I groaned into my hands.

# Chapter Thirty-Nine

JESSIE

I was at a complete loss.

For once in my life, I had no plan other than try to survive the next day without ending up front-page news, going to prison, or losing my mind as Isla showed me a side of her I wasn't quite prepared for.

Baking.

She was a baker.

And not the clean-up-your-mess sort of baker.

But the kind where flour filled every crevice of my house.

The only way I even saw it was because I had blue walls, but that was beside the point.

The point?

I went to take a shower with every intention of coming back into the living room, pouring her a big glass of red wine, putting on a movie, and possibly getting lucky.

But when I walked out?

It was the exact opposite of what I expected.

Chaos.

Complete and utter chaos.

Isla had covered her red dress with an apron—a lot of good it did her with all the flour on her cheeks. She was rolling out something with such aggression I almost felt sorry for the dough.

Something that smelled sweet was cooking in the oven. She pulled the dough up and started pounding it with her fist, giving me a little jolt.

My eyes fell to every dirty dish.

Every inch of space that was taken up with something gooey, sticky, that didn't belong.

The things that had no place.

A bomb had exploded in my kitchen.

And she just kept going, pounding, yelling things in a language I didn't understand.

Anxiety squeezed my chest as I mentally calculated how many hours it would take me to clean the house. My erratic paranoid thoughts wondered if she was tracking flour with her shoes, if she would clean her dishes or leave a mess.

My mind was everywhere.

And then she swiped her right hand underneath her eyes as a tear fell into whatever the hell she was making, and my heart stilled.

More yelling followed as she pounded the bread.

A warm sensation gripped my chest, replacing the anxiety as I pulled out my phone, scrolled through some slow music, stopped on "Only," by Shashi Pratap Singh, and pressed "Play."

She looked up as I approached, and then back down like she was ashamed.

I walked behind her and wrapped my arms around her waist, then twirled her in my arms and started dancing.

Her eyes flickered to mine with uncertainty. "I know you're pissed, I'll fix it, I just need some time, and I'll clean up my mess. I just needed to get lost in something so I could think and—"

"Isla?"

"Hmm?"

"Shut up." I covered her mouth with mine before she could protest, then wrapped my arms around her, our bodies danced, our tongues did the same as I comforted her in the only way I wanted.

I forced the world away.

And concentrated on her.

The minute I stopped thinking about myself, my own anxiety, the mess, I relaxed and enjoyed the moment.

I embraced the chaos surrounding me.

And just let go.

She moaned against my mouth then broke off. "I feel like any minute you're going to yell at me for this disaster, or for getting us caught in this horrible position, and I'm really sorry about your car."

I flinched. "What did you do to my car?"

She smirked. "Gotcha."

"Oh, you think that's funny?" I reached for her before she could pull away and punished her with another kiss, then lifted her onto the counter. Flour caked her ass and then my hands as I tugged the apron off and scooted her dress up. I gripped her hips, making flour handprints on her skin.

I liked the way it looked.

The way it felt.

To see my handprints on her body.

Mine.

"What are you doing?" She looked so innocent then, with her hair pulled back in a low bun, flour caking her cheeks and pretty red dress, and the few tears that you could still see streaked down her face. God, I wanted to eat her up. I didn't want to let her go. And it scared the shit out of me. "Two hours, how could you forget?"

"Oh?" She grinned wickedly. "And what are we going to do with our two hours tonight?"

"Actually"—I made a face—"I didn't get two hours last night. Being drugged cancels out any sense of time—especially since I wasn't aware time existed in your arms."

I didn't mean to say it out loud.

Her lips parted.

I captured them again, one by one, taking my time sucking as I cupped her face, pushed open her knees, and walked between her thighs. Her heels hooked behind my ass as I laid her down next to whatever she'd been attempting to bake.

Our eyes locked.

Hers were hesitant.

Mine only saw her.

So when I shoved everything off the counter and it crashed to the floor, I could see her surprise, I could feel her desire and shock.

And I wanted to be the man to do that to her every fucking time.

I opened my mouth to tell her.

To tell her something was changing.

To tell her that it was me.

That it was her with me.

But she didn't let me, she pulled my shirt over my head and hungrily devoured my mouth until it was hard to breathe. I tried again to speak when she shoved my sweats down with her gorgeous stilettos, and then I was tossing them to the ground while she inched her skirt up higher.

"No underwear," I breathed out and nearly lost consciousness as she wiggled closer to me and shook her head.

"Were you like this at Goo-Poh's?" Why was my voice so strained? She nodded slowly.

"Shit." I braced myself on either side of her, then climbed onto the counter, my knees spreading more flour everywhere while her hair made a snow angel with the rest of it. "You're gorgeous."

"I have flour in my ears."

I chuckled and blew in her ear, then kissed it and whispered, "Like I said, gorgeous."

She moaned when I tugged her ear with my teeth.

And then she was clawing at me as I thrust into her. Flour went flying like dust as her body moved against the island.

I'd owned this house since my first marriage.

I'd never once had sex anywhere but the bed.

I suddenly wanted to burn my bed and set up camp in every other available space, as long as I had a flour-covered Isla.

Our mouths met with each crazed thrust, my body was so tight, so ready for her, ready to explode, and I could tell she felt the same, like she was on the edge of sanity just waiting for me to push her off.

Waiting for me to jump with her.

"Never want this to stop." The words rushed out. "I think I like you better on a bed of flour than one of expensive sheets."

Isla moaned. "Me too. I like you like this." She placed a crazed kiss on my mouth and then her flour-caked hand was running down my cheek slowly as dust filled the air around us.

I moved deeper, I felt her constrict around me as the walls surrounding my heart crumbled further, as something like freedom took over and replaced the bondage that had been my comfort.

Our mouths clanged together as I pumped faster.

And then she was there, I could feel it in the way she pulsed, released me, and shook in my arms. I didn't want it to end. Every selfish part of me cried out with my release, only to beg for more seconds later.

I refused to acknowledge my feelings in that moment.

Because I was afraid that hers weren't the same.

Afraid I'd pushed the good away.

Made her leery of my intentions.
"I don't want to destroy you," I whispered against her mouth.
She sucked in an unsteady breath.
I just want to keep you.
That I kept for myself.
When I should have shared it with the one woman capable of giving me what I needed.

# Chapter Forty

"You've got to be kidding me." I laughed as Jessie picked up the Magic Eraser and showed me the proper way to clean a cupboard. "It's like magic!"

"It's the single best invention of all time." He grinned and tossed it at me.

I was going to buy stock in those suckers.

We were both still covered in flour, but at least the dishes were done, the bread was in, and I think most of the flour was removed from the kitchen, though if I knew Jessie at all, he was probably going to do a second cleaning just to make sure.

I didn't want to push him too far.

The hottest thing I'd ever seen was watching that man toss my dough to the ground and climb up on the counter. I would fan myself for years over that vision of him in flour.

I shivered.

"Shower." He directed me to the master bath, not the bathroom I normally used. Something had shifted between us, I wasn't sure if it was all the marriage talk, baby talk, or maybe just the simple fact that for now, we were stuck together.

He turned on the shower and grabbed another towel. He pulled off his sweats and walked over to me, then unzipped my dress, careful to pull my hair away from the zipper as he dropped the dress to the floor.

His eyes raked over me before he hung his head. "Damn."

Flour covered his abs. I reached out and wiped some from one of the ridges and shrugged. "Not so bad yourself."

He gripped my hand and pulled me into the large tiled walk-in shower. Water fell from the ceiling like a waterfall. I could live in that shower and be happy the rest of my life. I held my hands out wide and laughed.

"Ah, she likes getting dirty but being clean is better?" His mouth worked mine again before he started rubbing soap down my chest, arms, legs. I watched him wash me and nearly passed out when he reached between my legs.

"You have the best shower in the world," I said, my eyes not leaving his.

He moved the soap up my inner thigh. "I'd say you give it a vast improvement by standing there."

"Charmer."

"Always, I just try to play hard to get."

"Oh, so that's why you're such a jackass?"

"Of course." He laughed. "It makes you appreciate my kindness so much more, doesn't it?"

"Bastard."

"You don't mean it." He winked and then ran his hands through his hair before grabbing some shampoo, squeezing it into his hands, and motioning for me to turn around. "Let's just hope this doesn't make your hair fall out. On the bright side, you'd still be pretty with no hair, so I think we're safe."

His compliments were constant. Fast. Like he'd been keeping them all inside and finally felt the freedom to share them.

I gulped around the giant knot in my throat.

Not real. Not real.

But God, I wanted it to be, so bad.

I'd never had this.

The easy camaraderie that comes with knowing someone from the inside out, the flaws, the good, the bad, the ugly, and still wanting to joke with them and take showers with them. Still wanting them despite the bad, because in the end you complete each other. You make each other better.

A hollow ache expanded through my chest.

Because this would end.

I knew it.

Good things always did.

And when it did.

I was going to be devastated.

His hands worked against my skull and then he was washing the shampoo out and adding conditioner. I moaned when he started massaging my temples, and almost asked if I could take a nap with him doing just that when he was finished showering.

He quickly washed himself and then turned off the shower.

The towels were warm, fluffy, luxurious.

If this was how the other half lived, I wanted in.

I yawned behind my hand and was immediately scooped into his arms and placed in his bed.

His. Bed.

I didn't show my panic.

Jessie picked up one of his white shirts and tugged it over my head, then grabbed a brush.

Why was he grabbing a brush?

Tears filled my eyes as he slowly brushed my hair out, careful to get every tangle. I thought we were done.

He grabbed a blow dryer. And like a pro, dried my hair.

I was so shocked I wasn't sure how to respond.

We didn't speak.

He didn't seem agitated or bothered, just pulled the covers over my legs and kissed me on the forehead. "Sleep."

"But—"

"Don't do the thing."

"What thing?"

"The thing where you write down everything about today then highlight the good parts, the confusing parts, the annoying parts, messy parts." He grinned. "Isla, if today I was able to survive an explosion in my kitchen, you can handle not doing the thing and just letting this, whatever it is, be."

I fell a little farther.

Harder.

He leaned forward and kissed my mouth then walked out of the room.

It wasn't until I was almost asleep that I realized why everything had been so normal.

Jessie wasn't a psycho control freak because he was a psycho control freak and loved the color white.

He'd just reverted to what he could control when his wife didn't allow him to take care of her.

To love her.

He controlled what he knew he could.

I hated her more.

Wanted to destroy her.

Because she'd done something worse than rejecting his love.

She'd broken his spirit.

And damn her if she thought I wasn't going to do everything in my power to give it back.

# Chapter Forty-One

She was asleep in minutes.

My back was against the wall. I inched down, hanging my head. What the hell was I doing?

I wanted her to stay.

I wanted . . . God, I wanted it to be real.

I wanted to tuck her in bed at night. Kiss her as she fell asleep.

I was losing my mind.

Or maybe I was finally making sense. Whatever it was, this feeling of satisfaction and excitement in my chest, I didn't want to let it go.

Hands shaking, I grabbed my phone and sent Danica another text. That was five texts and three phone calls.

All of which she'd ignored.

She'd signed a damn NDA, so she wouldn't go to the press, but I never said anything about going to Isla about it.

Shit.

Why did it feel like whenever I got close to something good I messed it up?

Because that's what Isla was. Good. So damn good.

Every little quirk about her made me want her more, rather than send me running for the hills.

I actually liked her messy side more than her controlling side. What shocked me most? That I was able to have sex without cleaning the kitchen before.

I chuckled to myself and shook my head. Things were changing. Now that Vanessa was out of the picture, I was going to change.

I had no choice but to move forward.

I just hoped Isla would join me for the ride.

# Chapter Forty-Two

ISLA

Goo-Poh was calling at four a.m.

I was going to murder her.

Jessie was asleep next to me, so warm, so big.

I snuggled next to him then answered. "What?"

"Are you still sleeping?"

"All the normal people are sleeping!"

"I've been up for hours!"

I rest my case.

"So, the delivery will be made in the next two hours, be ready and awake, I'll be there as soon as I grab the food. And I know we did away with chickens years ago, but I still bought five for you to set free in your yard. We'll have them pass beneath the bed, and if the rooster is first you will have a boy!"

I was already holding the phone away from my ear in horror.

"Goo-Poh!" I hissed. "Listen to me, do NOT bring chickens into Jessie's home!"

"It is as much your home as it is his."

I gritted my teeth. "This is a chicken-free zone, and no roosters! The bed is already a bit much, but I know you've done this for every girl in our family, so I'm allowing it."

She sniffed.

"Are you crying?"

"I chose the most beautiful red sheets!"

I covered my mouth with my hands when I looked at Jessie's stark white sheets, white duvet, gray walls. Yeah, he was going to shit a brick.

"Great, sheets are great, just no chickens!"

"But—"

"Goo-Poh! No chickens!"

"Fine," she huffed. "Do you have any spare children that can jump around on the bed before the marriage?"

My mind immediately went to Blaire and Colin. "Yeah, I think I can rustle up a few children."

They should be so lucky to have to stay out of this.

"Oh good, this will mean you will have many children."

"Great, Goo-Poh, love you."

She hung up.

Typical.

Jessie's gravelly voice stirred me. "Chickens?"

I groaned. "Go back to sleep."

"She's not bringing chickens, right?"

I sighed.

"Your hesitation isn't comforting me." He groaned and flipped onto his back then pulled me to his side.

Like it was normal.

Like next week I was walking down the aisle for real.

Like this was our reality.

When both of us were just living without discussing the ramifications of our actions.

I was too afraid to be the first to say something.

Too afraid he'd agree with me.

Too afraid of my own logic—mixed with his.

I was petrified that he'd finally realize that this wasn't him, that rushing into something like this was so out of character it was only a matter of time before he said the dreaded "We need to talk." And it would break me.

I tried to straighten my spine, readying my heart for the initial break. Warning my chest it would hurt.

Badly.

"Stop thinking." Jessie kissed my head. "Just . . . breathe, Isla."

Funny, because I'd been holding my breath.

I exhaled.

"I'll be here in the morning," he whispered so lightly I almost missed it.

Tears welled in my eyes as I clutched him like a lifeline.

He'd gone from my greatest threat.

To my hero.

All within the span of a week.

The easy friendship we'd been trying for before all the drama with Vanessa was back.

With more feelings involved.

And I didn't know what to do with them except keep breathing and know that when Jessie made a promise.

He kept it.

# Chapter Forty-Three

I was on my third cup of coffee when the doorbell rang. I don't know what exactly I was expecting, but it wasn't a bed two times the size of the one I already owned.

Goo-Poh was firing off instructions to the poor men carrying it and, by the looks of it, doing a mental calculation of all the things she was going to change about my house.

I was going to break out in hives before the day was done.

"Where is my niece?" Goo-Poh leveled me with a glare. "We must prepare the foods."

"Food?" I repeated dumbly as Colin and Blaire walked into the house, matching looks of horror on both their faces. Yeah, welcome to life with Goo-Poh.

She waved me off. "The foods, the foods! The ones that I present on a platter, you will both sit on the bed and eat the foods. I can't believe she said no to the chickens."

I was going to reward Isla for that later.

She walked out of the bedroom in a pair of skinny jeans and a white top, something that almost disappointed me, I was so used to seeing her in color.

Goo-Poh handed Isla two bags.

I walked over and peeked inside.

Red sheets.

Blood red.

I smirked.

Her pale skin against those sheets?

I could like the bridal bed very much.

"Is that a dragon?" Colin pointed to one of the bedposts the guys were bringing in. On each post was a gold dragon wrapped around a pole, creepily setting their eyes on the bed, on whatever happened on the surface. The headboard had the same ornate dragon design, one on each side, with their talons joined.

It belonged in a museum, that bed.

"For protection." Goo-Poh beamed.

"Don't you already have a dragon, Jessie?" Colin winked and then pointed at my dick.

I flipped him off before Goo-Poh turned back around.

"Oh, but these are larger dragons," Goo-Poh said, not missing a beat.

"Wouldn't bet on it," Isla said sweetly while Goo-Poh muttered something under her breath.

It was just the comment I needed as I pulled her into my arms and pressed a kiss to her open mouth. She wrapped her arms around my neck only to be pulled away by Goo-Poh.

"Come, the women make the foods." She eyed Blaire. "You too, you help us make the foods or you can't eat."

I've never seen Blaire move so fast.

Leaving me and Colin staring as the movers tried to assemble the bed in my second master suite.

"So." Colin rocked back on his heels. "You're sure selling it really well."

I frowned in confusion and then cleared my throat. "Yeah."

"Anything you want to tell me about the lines you keep crossing? The sex? The constant touching and kissing? You can't keep your eyes off her, man."

To prove his point, my gaze had already found hers from across the room.

I jerked my head away and stared at the floor. "I like her."

"What was that?" Colin cupped his ear. "I didn't quite hear you."

I shoved him. "Don't be an immature jackass. I like her. I care about her, I'm falling for her chaos . . . I'm . . . drowning in it."

"Good drowning?"

I nodded.

"Man!" Colin slapped me on the back. "I'm happy for you, this is good. You should at least be smiling right now?"

I rolled my eyes. "I promised to ruin her life, Colin. Repeatedly. And then I went and . . . tried to do just that only to realize that she's real, everything about her is legitimate, she even let me see her books. Who does that?"

"Someone who trusts you," Colin said slowly. "So what's the deal?"

"It's not real." I glanced over my shoulder to make sure she wasn't back already. "There's an expiration date."

Colin crossed his arms and leaned against the wall. "So, get a Sharpie and cross that shit out. It's your life, it's time you took back control and started living it."

"Took back control," I repeated. "I think I'd rather just give it up."

I'd never seen my best friend so shocked.

"Please don't cry," I muttered when he pulled me in for a hug and then slapped me on the back like I'd just won the championship.

"I'm damn proud." He grinned wide. "Maybe now with all this Vanessa stuff behind you, you can finally be free."

Free.

I just had one more loose end to tie up.

And then I would tell her everything.

# Chapter Forty-Four

ISLA

Thankfully, the food didn't take long. By the time Blaire and I made finishing touches, Goo-Poh had already blessed the bed and the room. She came back to grab the platter of various foods: an even number of tangerines and oranges, pomegranates, dates, dried lotus seeds, and several other things. All the items had a purpose, and Goo-Poh took their arrangement very seriously. She walked back into the bedroom and laid the platter on the bed.

I followed her in with Jessie by my side, Colin and Blaire close behind.

"That's it." Goo-Poh clasped her hands together. "Now, neither of you are allowed on this bed together until the wedding next week."

Colin wheezed behind us.

Yeah, left that part out.

"If you must sleep on the bed and lack self-control"—she pointed at Jessie—"a boy must be with you in order to restore balance, no one side should ever be empty. Those are the rules for balance, it will bring bad luck if the bed has only one person sitting on it, especially if it's the groom without the bride."

"Shit, am I the boy?" Colin muttered out loud.

"Oh, and we need children to be present in the room or on the bed." She grinned. "This helps bring good luck and happiness into the marriage! The more laughter the better!"

Jessie and I stepped aside, earning glares from both Colin and Blaire.

"Go play, kids!" I said in my most enthusiastic voice as Jessie gave me a high five.

Goo-Poh looked heavenward and then sighed. "If that's the best we can do."

Colin actually looked offended.

She kissed my cheek. "Eat all of the food, it's healthy for your reproductive system. I'm tired now, I leave." She waved goodbye.

Jessie and I rushed to the bed and grabbed the food just as Colin and Blaire started stealing pieces.

We both sat next to them. I sighed.

"Hey, it could be worse," I pointed out. "She could have brought chickens."

A scratching noise sounded near the closet. I clearly spoke too soon.

"What's that noise?" Colin asked.

"It's coming from the closet." Jessie reached for the handle at about the same time I yelled no.

Four chickens and a rooster rushed toward us.

We all jumped onto the bed as they dove underneath.

The door to the bedroom swung open. "You will have healthy boys!" Goo-Poh retrieved the rooster and walked out again.

Leaving us with four chickens.

Birdseed under the bed.

And four very gobsmacked adults.

"Congrats, guys—"

"Don't." Jessie held up his hand while Blaire and I burst out laughing. Soon Jessie and Colin joined in.

# Chapter Forty-Five

The glaring brass bed with its loud red sheets would normally send someone like me into a perpetual state of anxiety. Hell, it would send any sane person toward the bottom of a bottle of Jack.

Instead, every time I walked by that room, I smiled.

Every. Damn. Time.

The door was closed.

Apparently Goo-Poh didn't want to tempt us to use the bed too soon, that would of course cause us not to have fortune in life.

Or sons.

I smiled to myself and made my way into the kitchen. I'd needed to run a few errands, mainly to the pet store, where I dropped off four chickens.

I was on my way back to the house when Isla texted me a grocery list, and it wasn't until I walked into the kitchen, bags in hand, that it hit me.

What I was doing.

What we were doing.

I almost backed up a step.

Almost turned and ran.

The scene was surreal.

Undeniably sexy and terrifying all mixed up in one.

She was wearing leggings and a crop top, grilling vegetables on the stove and dumping in an insane amount of some sort of sauce while she hummed to herself.

This, this is what I never had with Vanessa.

Never.

We ordered takeout.

Hell, I didn't even know the stove actually worked until Isla moved in and started using it.

I was surprised the oven turned on.

And more surprised how much I liked seeing her standing there, even if she was humming off key.

"Hey there." I cleared my throat and approached.

She glanced up and winked. "I'm making my version of stir-fry."

"And what makes your version so special?"

"My special sauce." She scrunched up her nose and pointed the wooden spoon at me. "And no, I'm not telling you what's in it, that completely takes the special part away."

I laughed. "Yeah, I guess it does."

"So"—she kept stirring—"today went well."

I gave her a blank stare. "Isla, your Goo-Poh brought live chickens into our house. A bed with etched dragons. Fire-engine red sheets. And birdseed. If that's a good day I'd hate to see the bad ones."

She giggled. "So we may have to move."

She realized her error the minute I did.

Tense silence fell between us.

She cleared her throat.

"Don't do that," I whispered as she forced a smile my way.

"What?"

"That smile, I hate it."

"Wow, thanks . . ." she said tersely.

225

"Isla." I walked up and tilted her chin toward me. "I want a real smile, a good one."

She glared.

"Don't pretend . . . not in our house, not with me."

Her eyes widened at my use of *our*. But I meant it. I needed her to know that. It wasn't mine, not anymore. She gulped. "But isn't that what we're doing? Pretending?"

The question hung between us as I searched her eyes for answers, waiting to see if she felt anything beyond the awareness buzzing around us. If she felt the same way I did. Wanting to change the *mine* to *ours*.

"I don't know," I finally said, probing a bit. "Are you?"

She tried to look away.

I didn't let her.

I gripped her face with both of my hands. "What do you want, Isla?"

"It's not that easy."

I grinned and then brushed a kiss across her lips. "I'll make it easy for you."

"Oh? Just like that?"

"Watch and learn, baby." I jogged into my office and grabbed a few highlighters, pens, and a pad of paper. "Pros." I wrote it out in black ink. "Cons."

She smirked. "Jessie, what are you doing?"

"Making you hot." I drew a line down the middle. "Drawing you a chart."

"It's like you know all of my weaknesses."

I stripped out of my shirt and tossed it to the ground. "Better?"

"What chart?" she joked.

I leaned over the island and started writing. "Pros, Jessie Beckett."

"Oh God, you didn't really just write your name as a pro, did you?"

"And highlighted it in pink." I nodded. "Sure did."

"You're unbelievable."

"Exactly. See? Pro." I chuckled under my breath and moved to the con side. "Moving too fast." She sucked in a breath. I looked up again. "I'm going to put down the good and the bad, that's fair, right?"

A slow nod from Isla was all I got.

"Pro." I went back to the column. "Already moved in."

"True." She walked around the island and joined me. "And moving twice within a year is really stressful, let alone a month."

"I would hate to stress you out," I mused, focusing on her parted lips and the way they beckoned me to taste.

"Okay." She quickly looked away and tucked her hair behind her ears. "So what's the next con?"

I cleared my throat and very slowly wrote the word *trust*.

She eyed the word like a disease.

I highlighted it in yellow. "You don't trust me, you want to, you don't."

"It's not you," she said in a small voice. "It's men in general, powerful men, beautiful men who could have anyone they want. Men who are used to getting everything, men who want for nothing. Men who would take my heart and crush it without thinking about the tenderness a heart like mine needs."

It was the most I'd ever gotten out of her.

"Isla." My voice lowered. "I hate to look more arrogant . . . but I know exactly what to do with your heart."

A little gasp fell from her lips. "Oh yeah?"

"Yeah," I answered. "I don't want to hold your heart, Isla . . . I don't even want to own it . . ." I brushed a kiss across her lips. "I just want you to share it with me."

Tears filled her eyes. "You aren't supposed to say things like that to me."

"Why?" I reached for her hand.

She squeezed my fingers tight. "Because this is all going to come crashing down on us, we're getting lost in something that's not real, and in the end, someone's going to get hurt."

I hated that we shared the same fears, hated that she made complete sense. It was insane, and yet I wanted the insanity. I didn't want the perfect engagement to the perfect woman, with the perfect allotment of time between every monumental thing in our lives.

"So we're back to trust." I fought like hell to keep the annoying thought from popping up in my head, the one that said she had a valid reason not to trust me, but I wasn't that same man.

I didn't want to be.

She released my hand and went over to the stove.

I grabbed two plates and offered them to her.

We worked in silence.

Her hands shook as she dished out her secret sauce and vegetables, and when the shaking increased, I finally just took the food from her hands and spun her around to face me.

She stared straight ahead at my chest.

"Playing it safe doesn't guarantee you don't get hurt."

"It's better than living dangerously," she argued.

I captured her bottom lip then whispered against her mouth, "Hate to break it to you, but you were living dangerously the minute you proposed."

She gasped. "I did not propose!"

"You did. I mean I did the one with the ring, but you're the one that started this, Miss I-Don't-Live-Dangerously." Had her there.

She glared.

I kissed her mouth again.

She didn't respond, still glaring.

And then I wrapped my arms around her and backed her up against the counter. "Admit it, you don't hate me."

She gave in, sighing against my body. "I'm having a hard time conjuring up anything but lust and need. You've been shirtless for at least eleven minutes."

"Keeping time?"

"It's been a good eleven minutes." She grinned.

"And if I take off my jeans?"

She reached for the front button and slid her hand inside. "I think my enthusiasm matches yours."

"And you think you play it safe. How cute."

She squeezed me. Hard.

I flinched and then chuckled as I reached for a breast and said, "Two can play that game."

"Tit for tat." She released me and then climbed me like a fucking tree, wrapping her legs around my waist as her tongue slid past the barrier of my lips.

God, this woman.

This. Woman.

I dug my fingers into her ass, walked her over to the closest guest room, and opened the door.

"Jessie!" she hissed. "It's bad fortune!"

"It's a bridal bed. You're my bride. Now strip."

"I swear if we find any more chickens . . ."

"Only cocks in here, sweetheart." I laughed and then nearly tripped as she threw a pillow at my face.

It smelled like her.

Sweet.

Her shirt was gone.

Leggings stripped.

Nothing but a thong and a smile.

I crooked my finger.

She pounced first, launching herself in my direction so fast that I had to brace myself against the wall.

229

We never made it to the bed.

I was inside her before I could count to three.

And she was screaming my name before I could breathe out a four.

I never wanted to leave that room.

My chest ached when I thought of all of the times I'd put up with a wife who loved herself more than she loved me, and now I knew what it felt like to be part of a team.

To want someone so badly.

And know without a doubt it's returned tenfold.

I love you.

I said it in my head.

I meant it from the heart.

But it was too soon. Although we'd technically met a year ago, I had only really gotten to know her in less than two weeks.

It was because I was a man starved.

A man who'd been living a life of gray and was finally introduced to red—Isla.

I never wanted to go back.

She lit me up from the inside out, coaxed a slow burn of desire that refused to extinguish.

She was fucking mine.

She just didn't know it yet.

# Chapter Forty-Six

ISLA

It was almost impossible to concentrate on work. Jessie's words, his promises, the way he held me the night before. All of it played like a bad rom com in my head until my temples pounded.

I analyzed.

I didn't want to.

It was in my nature.

I looked at every angle.

And all I did was go in circles over and over again.

"Isla?" Blaire snapped her fingers in front of my face. I straightened and forced a smile. "You've been staring at your computer screen for twenty minutes."

"I'm researching," I lied.

"It's black. The screen." Her eyebrows shot up. "So unless you're researching black computer screens and why they exist, you're daydreaming."

I rolled my eyes. "I'm just . . . tired."

"From all the Jessie sex?"

Abby tilted her chair backward and eyed us. "Jessie sex?"

"Phone's ringing!" I yelled.

Luckily the phone rang at the perfect time.

"This isn't done!" Abby called back to me.

I laid my head on the desk. "Why is he so hot? Why?"

"There, there." Blaire patted my head and then took the chair next to me. "Well, it's probably because he's out to get you. He's being hot on purpose, damn him."

"Shut up."

"Hey, you're the one marrying and sleeping with the enemy . . . in a dragon bed. But we won't discuss all the reasons that's weird, we don't have enough time."

I groaned and lifted my head. "It's a bridal bed."

"Yeah . . . that makes it worse. Let's just call it the dragon bed."

I reached for my cold cup of coffee. "Seriously, it's like the minute he smirks at me—and you know the smirk—"

"Honey, your Goo-Poh even knows the smirk. A nun would know that smirk. Hell, my blind grandma would know the smirk by feel alone."

"Not helping."

Blaire grinned. "It's just in his nature to be hotter than ninety percent of the male population, don't hold it against him."

"He needs more flaws."

"He eats cereal from the bottom up—that counts as at least ten flaws in my book. Who the hell massacres a box of Lucky Charms because it looks prettier?"

I nodded in agreement. "But he's just so . . . big and muscly. Blaire, last night I counted at least five muscles near a rib. A RIB!"

"And you were counting his muscles while he slept because?"

"Leave me alone! If I want to count muscles instead of sheep I'll count muscles!"

She leaned back and nodded. "Woman has a point."

"Besides, he said things, and then I couldn't sleep, and . . . the things were nice, they weren't typical Jessie things."

"So he wasn't being an asshole?"

"NO!" I threw my hands into the air in exasperation. "But it would be so much easier if he could revert back to that before I—"

I cleared my throat and looked away.

"Before you . . ." Blaire prodded. "Or since you've already?"

"What's that supposed to mean?"

"You like him . . . you're well on your way to falling in love with the guy, plus I know you. I've never once seen you do casual sex. It's not in your nature."

She got me there.

I even made Wayne wait until we were engaged.

See? I had major personality flaws! Why was Jessie giving me the smirk?

"Isla." Blaire grabbed my hand. "Stop overthinking this, because honestly it's not going to make a lot of sense. There is absolutely nothing logical about moving in with a guy, fake marrying him, and claiming to have his twins. There's just not. You aren't going to rationalize crazy, it's impossible."

I frowned. "Then how do I deal with it? I have to put everything in its box so I know how to deal."

"Or," Blaire said slowly, "you can just take it one day at a time and stop thinking about tomorrow."

"Easy for you to say."

"Easy to say, not easy to execute."

I sighed, blowing a breath from my lips as I eyed my phone. "Should I text him?"

"Oh hell," Blaire whispered. "I don't know, do you think he'll circle yes or no if you send him a boyfriend request meme?"

I narrowed my eyes at her.

"Adulting. You should try it." She winked and stood. "Now if you'll excuse me, I'm off to find myself a cheater."

"Danica?" I guessed.

"Oh yeah." She saluted. "I hope you don't mind, but she wanted to have lunch with us, apparently she has something to confess. At any rate, I knew you were busy with Jessie's muscles so I'm taking one for the team."

I frowned. "Blaire, I can go."

"Nope, you just sit there and stare at the black computer screen while thinking about Jessie's six-pack, way better use of your time, and if you get the sudden urge to do some work you can go through the client profiles for the next two weeks. We're booked solid and we need to pick the fastest cases first."

I sighed. "Got it."

She grabbed her keys and left.

I stared at the screen like a lovesick idiot.

Then grabbed my phone.

A text popped up.

**Jessie:** Don't overanalyze the next sentence.

I smiled at my phone.

**Jessie:** I miss you.

I'd tried so hard to keep my heart protected, so damn hard.

And with one simple text he had me wanting to sprint to wherever he was and kiss him on the mouth and rip his clothes off.

I texted him instead.

**Me:** I miss you too.

His reply was immediate.

**Jessie:** Lunch?

Me: Time and place?

Again immediate, I loved it.

Jessie: Seedy pub where we can get burgers, I'll text you the address, want me to send a car for you?

I frowned at my phone.

Me: Why would you send me a car?

Jessie: So you don't have to walk or drive or do anything except sit and think about all the wild sex we're going to have tonight.

I cleared my throat and fanned myself before I replied.

Me: Deal.

I felt giddy.
Like this was a real date.
Maybe everything was going to be okay.
Maybe Blaire was right.
Maybe it was time to take the plunge and stop rationalizing about all the reasons why—and focus on the why not?

# Chapter Forty-Seven

## JESSIE

I sent off another text to Danica, explicitly telling her that the deal was off, and that under no circumstances was she allowed to have contact with Blaire or Isla again. I'd been in a low place when I hired her. The press was having a field day with my failed marriage and all the lies Vanessa and I had told to keep up our perfect façade. Speculation continued about my lying about our perfect relationship, and I just . . . I lost it. Fixing the situation had been my only goal, and I had been obsessed with it.

*"Sign it," I'd ordered in a low, irritated voice, exhausted from seeing my face on so many tabloids, and my ex-wife giving so many interviews about our private relationship.*

*Danica blinked at the paper and scribbled her name across the dotted line.*

*I exhaled in relief, this would fix everything. "Any questions?"*

*She gave her head a shake. "Nope, I think I got it. You sure I won't get caught?"*

*"They won't see through it, if that's what you're asking, and by the time they do figure something out, you'll already have the info I need." The information that would sabotage Dirty Exes and show me to be the innocent party.*

*She shook my hand.*

My body trembled with rage. At myself. With horror at what I'd been willing to do in order to take them down.

If she did sue, it wouldn't be done quietly.

I was too afraid of screwing things up again and landing on national television.

I took a sip of water and grinned when the town car pulled up and that gorgeous woman stuck one heeled foot onto the pavement, then another. The driver offered his hand.

She tipped him.

Of course she would.

It was Isla.

Her white wrap dress was paired with red heels that had me dying to get her back home. I was going to demand she keep those heels on the whole time.

I waved her over when she walked in.

And because I missed her.

Because I couldn't help it.

I stood and pressed a searing kiss to her mouth in hello.

She returned the kiss with equal enthusiasm and wrapped her arms around my neck. I moaned into her mouth before breaking away.

Her blush was gorgeous. "Sorry, long morning."

"Long morning without enough kissing," I agreed.

I pulled out her chair and handed her the wine list.

"Wow, I get wine *and* a juicy hamburger?"

"Play your cards right and I may even get you an ice-cream sundae."
I winked.

She lowered the wine list and reached her hand across the table.
At first I thought she was going for her water, but she kept moving. I
gripped her fingertips and immediately a pulse of heat sizzled between
our palms.

"I'm sorry," she whispered.

"What are you sorry about? I mean other than the chickens."

She bit her lower lip like she was thinking and then pursed her lips.
"I'm sorry for last night."

"We had sex four times last night. Please don't be sorry," I joked,
trying to lighten the mood.

She released my hand and smacked my arm. "That's not what I'm
talking about. I guess I'm just sorry about not trusting you."

I held my breath.

"I do," she said in a small voice. "I'm trying. I want to. I . . . trust
you."

I almost jumped out of my seat and threw a fist into the air, instead
I went with "Thank you."

My first mistake was being too engrossed with Isla to check my
surroundings.

My second mistake was thinking that I could get away with a lunch
date without being noticed.

"Hey." A woman with a low-cut crop top walked up to our table
and started jumping up and down. "You're Jessie Beckett!"

"I am."

Isla pulled her hands away from me.

"And you!" She turned to Isla, shocking the hell out of me. "How
dare you!"

"Excuse me?" Isla looked between me and the girl.

"Homewrecker," she muttered. "I can't believe you'd break up—"

"Okay." I stood. "I think it's time for you to go, and for the record, my wife was cheating on me, and the lady you just insulted was the one who, though in a backward way, discovered it for me—"

"But—"

"Leave." I gritted my teeth. "Before I call the police."

"Asshole," she said under her breath before stomping off.

Yeah, I'd made a scene.

I was still shaking.

"Jessie." Isla reached for me.

I sighed and stared at her outstretched hand, then took it. I wasn't that guy, the one who yelled at fans. The one who lost his fucking mind in public.

That wasn't me.

I'd been trained by Vanessa to keep calm in front of others, always smiling, always fake.

"Thank you," Isla whispered. She stood and pulled me into her arms and then braced my face with both of her hands. "You know, you're pretty protective of the woman who ruined your life."

I kissed the inside of her right wrist and whispered back, "You didn't ruin it—you saved it."

# Chapter Forty-Eight

ISLA

"This is . . ." I put my hands on my hips while Jessie looked ready to strangle Goo-Poh where she stood.

I didn't want to offend her.

But the last thing I wanted was to get married in the old church with its red carpet, red pews, red walls, and weird-looking wooden cross hanging down the middle.

It reminded me of a vampire book.

And not a good one.

"This is where your parents were married, where I was married, this was where—" Goo-Poh stopped midsentence when the ancient minister walked into the sanctuary. He looked like he'd been around since the beginning of time, had a long white beard, and was missing every hair on his head. He had more wrinkles than a bulldog, and something about his inability to walk more than two steps without taking a break didn't give me confidence that he would make it through a ceremony. "No," Jessie breathed out next to me. "Hell no."

"Careful, you're in a church."

"Am I? Because I think I saw a dungeon on the way in, and the pastor looks pale enough to feed off the souls of anyone who walks past the door."

I snorted out a laugh, the minister was just . . . very . . . old. Ancient.

"His heart may legitimately stop during the ceremony," Jessie whispered. "How's that for memories?"

I smacked him in the stomach. Goo-Poh made her way back over to us, her face a mask of worry as she pressed a hand to her mouth like she was holding back tears. I'd only ever seen her cry twice, both times my fault. "It is not available until two weeks from now, but we've already chosen the dates and the bridal bed has been delivered. I've ordered food."

Yeah, that was news to me.

What food exactly did she order?

Did I even want to know?

"Goo-Poh." Jessie stepped forward and wrapped a massive arm around her small frame. "I have an idea, feel free to shoot it down—"

"I probably will."

"I know." Patient, patient man. "But you only get married once . . ."

He cringed.

I inwardly groaned.

"Start over," Goo-Poh ordered. "I don't like how the conversation is going, choose your words carefully. Now, begin."

My skin started to itch as Jessie cleared his throat and then locked eyes with me while speaking. "Isla deserves something elaborate, something as classy as her—why don't we let her pick, and I'll foot the entire bill."

Goo-Poh never talked about money.

It was frowned upon.

Especially in a church.

So I expected her to either go on a hunt for holy water or spit on the ground, instead she looked up at him and slapped his cheek lightly. "You're a good man."

My mouth hung open, and I almost swallowed my tongue when she followed that with a little cheek pinch. "Thank you."

"Well." Goo-Poh pulled away from Jessie and crossed her arms to face me. "You need to pick a location in the next six hours to stay on schedule. Can you and your man do that, or do you need my help?"

Jessie must have seen the panic in my eyes. He quickly pulled me to his side and said, "We've got it. I know you still have a lot on your plate, so let me know if there's anything else I can do."

"Find the location and I'll stop off at the florist." She pulled out an ancient-looking notebook, flipped through the highlighted pages, stopped, pulled out a green marker, and made a little check mark, then checked her wristwatch and wrote the time down. "Call me when you know."

And then she was shuffling off like she was getting chased by the cops.

I sighed and looked up at Jessie.

He choked out a laugh, coughed, and tried to hide his smile.

"Not a word," I said with clenched teeth.

He nodded. "I don't think that's possible . . ."

"Jessie, I'm warning you!"

He placed his hand on my lower back and ushered me out of the giant sanctuary. "So, you learned all your highlighting from Goo-Poh?"

I groaned. "You're dead to me."

"Hey, what are you like at scrapbooking stores, does your brain actually explode or do you just orgasm right next to the washable markers?"

I gave him a shove. "You can't say *orgasm* in church!"

"Orgasm." He grinned cheekily. "See? Totally fine, not getting struck down, not—"

A boom of thunder sounded.

We both jumped a foot.

"Shit." He jerked me to his side. "It was supposed to rain today, this means nothing, but just in case I'm wrong and you're right, let's get out of here."

We ran hand in hand onto the street just as the first raindrops fell. More followed, and by the time we reached his car we were both soaked through.

It was a warm rain.

I lifted my arms and did a little twirl while he walked around to open my door.

"Sorry." I grinned.

"Do it again," he breathed.

I tilted my head. "Do what again?"

"Twirl in the rain."

"I wasn't twirling," I lied.

"It was adorable." He pulled me into his arms and then very slowly twirled me. "And you looked so damn free and happy in that moment that I wish I could have captured it."

"This guy," I said out loud, pressing a hand to his chest. "What am I going to do with you?"

He leaned down and brushed a warm kiss across my cheek. "Whatever the hell you want." He kissed my chin, then my neck. "But if you're in the market for suggestions, I have a few." His hands wrapped around my waist and inched higher to my breasts, right there in the middle of the street.

I didn't care.

"Oh? What kind of suggestions?" Goose bumps broke out across my skin as his teeth tugged my ear.

"I'm finding I have this fantasy of you in red—all the time. It gets me so hard I can't even think straight . . . but there's a lot of lace, and I use my teeth to pull down your lingerie, and the sight of your ass facing me, well, let's just say it's enough to drive me insane . . ." He tugged my ear again. "But first—"

"First?" My body was ready for him, hell, I would have said yes if he asked for a quickie in the back seat.

"First"—he pulled away and sighed—"we have to find a place to get married."

"Oh, that."

"Yeah, that."

"Goo-Poh gave us six hours, what are we going to do?"

"You're going to tell me your dream wedding . . . and I'm going to make it happen."

My heart thudded against my chest so hard I could swear he heard it. "But, Jessie—"

"Let me give this to you."

He looked so earnest, so sincere, his eyes never left mine as I nodded and then whispered, "Okay."

# Chapter Forty-Nine

*JESSIE*

We were closing in on the eleventh hour, and we'd yet to find an available space. Numerous texts from Goo-Poh kept coming in, reminding us that we needed to get married on that date for the blessing to take place. It sounded ridiculous, but the more anxious Isla became, the more I knew it was important. Besides, the public was going wild with the fact that I was getting married again, this time to a woman who made it her job to help celebrities break up their own marriages.

We had one more stop. I could tell Isla was doubtful, but the place was new, and after texting Colin in a panic, he'd suggested it since he knew the owners.

It helped that I was willing to pay anything.

Hell, I'd give them my spleen if it meant Isla had a smile on her face.

It made no sense.

My reaction toward her.

My feelings.

The way my gut churned in protest whenever I thought of not having her in my life, the panic that ensued when I imagined walking into my kitchen and finding it clean.

I shoved the thoughts away and pulled up to the building. On the outside it looked like a plain warehouse.

"Are we meeting the mafia?" Isla joked while I wondered if I had the address wrong. I double-checked the text as Isla balanced on her heels, walked up to the one and only door in the front of the building, and rang the bell.

The door opened, revealing an elderly woman who looked like she could be Goo-Poh's sister, only older. She had gray hair at her temples and small, black spectacles that matched her black pantsuit.

"I've been expecting you." She held out her hands to Isla and tugged her inside, then eyed me up and down as if to say silently, *Eh, you'll do.*

I followed them into a large lobby with huge chandeliers, which opened up into a banquet hall that could hold at least five hundred people. White curtains covered the walls, lights of every blinding color filled the room.

Three weeks ago this would have been my own personal hell.

Lights everywhere.

Color.

Chaos.

Instead, it made me smile.

The universe had a weird way of doing things. My first wedding had been huge, everything was white—Vanessa had wanted it to be black and white and even instructed guests on what to wear.

And yet here I was, staring at what looked like a leopard-print orange light on a white backdrop.

Of course.

Isla was off chatting with the woman in hushed tones, and then Isla hugged her and practically bounced over to me.

"So?" Her excitement was contagious.

She did a little jig. "She said they can fit us in on our date and at a discounted rate."

"Discount?" My eyebrows shot up. "How the hell did you manage that?"

"She thinks her daughter-in-law is cheating, we made a sort of trade." She put her hands on her hips. "So instead of paying ten grand for the day"—I shrugged at the amount—"you're paying three!"

"You didn't have to do that." I tugged her into my arms.

"Just like you didn't have to offer to pay, or propose, or—"

I silenced her with a kiss, I didn't want her remembering those things, the things I was forced to do, when if I could do them all over again I would have savored them more, I would have made them better.

My phone buzzed in my pocket.

I pulled away with irritation and reached for it.

Why the hell was Blaire calling me?

"Who is it?" Isla must have noticed my confused expression.

"Your best friend." I sent the call to voice mail. "I'll call her back."

Isla's phone started ringing.

She pulled it out of her purse and sighed. "Blaire again, hopefully everything's okay, I'll just answer really quick." She tapped the screen. "What's up?"

Her eyes narrowed at me. "Yeah, he's right here, yeah, we were actually heading back to the house and—" She made a face. "Yeah, just meet us there."

She hung up and stared at her phone while crushing anxiety washed over my body, paralyzing me to my spot on the floor. "Everything okay?"

"Yeah, she just sounded . . . pissed."

Fuck.

"Did she say what about?"

"Nah, probably a client or something. You ready?"

"Yeah." I stopped walking and pulled her against my chest. "Tell me again that you're going to marry me."

Isla felt my forehead. "Kind of don't have a choice there . . ."

"Promise me." I refused to let her go. "Promise."

Isla frowned. "I promise."

I kissed her hard on the mouth and prayed that it wasn't the worst, prayed that it wasn't Danica.

And that I wasn't going to lose the only woman I'd ever really been myself with.

The only woman I had ever truly loved.

# Chapter Fifty

ISLA

Twelve.

The number of times Jessie grabbed my hand and kissed my fingertips while we drove home.

He took the long way.

He stopped at yellow lights.

And every few seconds his eyes would dart to mine like he was waiting for a bomb to drop on our car.

Maybe he was nervous about getting married?

He'd made me promise, so maybe he thought I was backing out?

I was doing it again.

Analyzing.

Maybe he liked holding my hand.

Maybe he liked kissing it.

Maybe I needed to stop analyzing every moment and get my head on straight.

Blaire's car was already at the house. Jessie pulled into the garage and killed the engine, then stared straight ahead.

"You coming?" I reached for my door.

"Yeah," he croaked. "Coming."

I found Blaire pacing in the living room. "Everything okay?"

Her blonde head whipped around so fast I'm surprised she didn't pull a muscle. "Yeah, totally fine, actually. I know we're on a tight timeline, so I was thinking we should go wedding-dress shopping tomorrow?"

I tried to tamp down the giddiness in my stomach but it was near impossible. Jessie came around the corner and kissed me on the cheek. "Just make sure she gets whatever she wants." He pulled out a credit card that looked dangerously like the kind that has no limits and pressed it into my palm. "I'm going to go take a shower."

"Wait." Blaire had a panicked look about her—then again, it was Blaire, she was high-strung, it was her nature. "Can I talk to you about wedding surprise stuff really quick?"

Jessie paled. "Yeah, um, we can go into my office."

He kissed me one last time. "It's been a long day. Why don't you go take a bath?"

"Don't order me around," I pouted, even though that was already my plan.

He slapped me on the ass. "Go."

He gave me one last look—it felt like goodbye, it felt like my heart was getting ripped from my chest, and I had no idea why. Why he was giving me that look, why I felt like he was trying to say something.

Hours later I'd realize what it was.

Guilt.

Sadness.

Betrayal.

It was the end.

# Chapter Fifty-One

No sooner had I clicked the door shut behind me than tiny fists were beating into my back over and over again. I leaned my arm against the door and grumbled, "Are you done yet?"

"No!" Blaire punched me in the kidney. It hurt like a bitch. I winced and turned around to face her, to face what I'd done, what she knew. "I was rooting for you! Both of us were! You've changed, I know you have, so why the hell am I finding out that you've paid someone to spy on us and try to take us down!"

"It's not like that." It was exactly like that. Shit.

"Don't lie to me, Jessie, I'm already pissed enough to pull out my Taser. You can thank your best friend for searching my purse before I got in the car."

Thank God.

"Look, Danica isn't exactly reliable," I said. "She hasn't returned any texts or calls, I'm threatening to sue, so pull whatever crawled up your ass out of the scary, dark place and stop hitting me!"

Blaire smacked me in the chest again, then shoved me. "No! You don't go behind Isla's back, you're not that guy. Did you think she wouldn't find out?"

I sighed and hung my head. "I was desperate."

"No. Shit." Blaire said through clenched teeth. "Danica has everything, Jessie. And when I say *everything* I mean her little hacker abilities are even better than Abby's." She paced in front of me. "She has our confidential files, our records, she has social security numbers, bank account numbers, she has our entire corporation on a flash drive. She showed it to me!"

"Fuck." It was time to panic. "She signed an NDA, so she can't go public with any of the information."

Blaire actually laughed. "You think she *just* wants to go public? Are you insane? She doesn't want to go public, she wants to sell all our clients' dirty little secrets to the highest-paying reporters in the country. She's already gotten an offer for fifty grand from *US Weekly*."

Realization dawned. "How much did she ask for?"

"You really don't want to know." Blaire sighed. "I didn't tell Colin that part, because that would be like Colin to bail your ass out. This is on you, all of this. You set out to destroy Dirty Exes, well, congratulations, as of tomorrow at noon you just did. We may as well pack our boxes now, because our company is about to get sued by every high-profile client we've ever dealt with, including your ex-wife."

I hung my head.

"You know why she started it, right?" Blaire whispered. "The company?"

"Her ex," I answered.

Blaire shrugged. "After they broke up, he blacklisted her . . . she wasn't invited to any more Hollywood parties, he stripped their joint bank accounts of anything and everything, locked her out of their house so she had to get a police escort to get her clothes packed, and even stopped making lease payments without telling her, so it would ruin her credit. He destroyed her, and she made something of herself. I never expected the same from you . . . it seems all men do in her life is make sure that she has nothing—while they have it all."

Blaire shoved past me and slammed the door after her.

With shaking hands I grabbed my cell and dialed Danica's number.

"Please answer, please answer, please answer," I mumbled.

It went to voice mail.

When it beeped, I made sure to speak slowly when I said, "Name. Your. Price."

# Chapter Fifty-Two

ISLA

I got worried when Jessie didn't come to bed. Even after such a short time, I was so used to him being next to me that when he wasn't filling that spot, I automatically knew something was wrong.

When I walked into the living room he was sitting there with an open bottle of wine, holding his phone in his hands like he'd just received devastating news. "You're still up?" I made my way to the couch and sat.

He didn't look away from his phone. "Yeah, just . . . thinking."

"About the wedding?"

His lips twitched. "Question . . ."

"Oooh, are the two hours starting again?"

"Smart-ass."

I stole his wine and took a sip. "What's your question?"

He shifted uncomfortably in his seat then tossed his phone on the table and looked across at me. "When we were in Cambodia, did you think about it?"

Not what I expected.

I'd actually felt something for him a year ago. He'd opened up just enough for me to see the man that everyone else saw. There was a frisson of awareness between us I ignored, and we were friends, up until he started blaming my company for everything. For weeks we'd all hung out together, and then the explosion that was Vanessa occurred—she fell out of the limelight then stepped right back into it by blaming Jessie.

I glanced away then back at him as he took the glass from my hand and put it on the table next to his phone. "There were a few times I felt something between us. I ignored it, but it was there, and one night, after drinking way too much"—he smirked—"I thought about it. I thought about touching you, kissing you, and then I felt so damn guilty because there I was, still married, still trying to use Blaire as a way out, as my fallback, and there you were . . . you."

My throat went dry. "I thought about it."

His eyes flashed. "And?"

"And the real thing is way better than the fantasy of these hands on my body." I gripped his hands and then put them on my breasts and closed my eyes. "This feels like everything."

He squeezed and then pulled me onto his lap. "Go on a date with me?"

I laughed.

He slapped my ass. "I'm serious. I want to take you on a date, a real date . . ."

"Okay." I grinned. "Tomorrow night I'm—"

"Nope, right now. And you just said okay, so no backing out."

I burst out laughing. "This seems very . . . spontaneous for someone who freaked over a blue wall."

"At least you didn't paint it pink," he grumbled. "And it's growing on me . . . you're growing on me."

"Aw, nicest thing a man's ever said to me."

"Hey, weeds are hard to pull, I'm being sentimental!"

"Maybe on this date you just kiss me and stop talking." I gripped him by the shirt and slammed my mouth against his.

He pulled away. "Sorry, but I'm not that sort of guy. It is, after all, a first date." He stood and grabbed his phone, music suddenly filled the air, and then I was in his arms, dancing.

He twirled me around a few times before dipping me. His expression was so serious. And the last few pieces of my heart that I'd kept for myself.

For the just-in-case.

Fell into his hands.

I felt the exchange in my soul as tears filled my eyes.

Jessie Beckett was mine.

And I was his.

"Tell me," he whispered in my ear.

"Tell you what?"

"Everything." He twirled me again. "Favorite childhood memory, most hated color, embarrassing stories, I want it all . . . I want you."

We stopped dancing.

My chest was heaving.

This, this was what I'd always wanted but been too afraid to hope for. "Do you mean it?"

"Yes." His eyes flickered to my mouth. "I'm kind of regretting that whole not-kissing-on-the-first-date rule."

"Bet you are . . ." I teased, gripping him by the shirt and pulling him in close, our mouths a half an inch apart, sharing the same air, existing in the same universe. "I hate the color gray, one time I sent a love letter to Jonathan Taylor Thomas's fan group and sprayed it with perfume, and my favorite childhood memory is baking with Goo-Poh during the Chinese New Year. Your turn."

We stopped moving.

His mouth was still so close to mine I could almost taste it.

"I used to hate the color red . . . now it's my favorite, especially on you. Most embarrassing moment is the day Colin accidentally kicked a ball into my junk and I puked in front of all of my friends. They called me Retchy Jessie for a whole year." My lips quirked. "And favorite child-hood memory I'm going to exchange for favorite current memory."

I sucked in a breath.

"Proposing to you. Dancing with you. Loving you. In a few days, marrying you. Seeing you covered in flour from head to toe. Red. Red. Red. Every favorite is attached to you."

I kissed him.

He didn't stop me, just pulled me into his arms and kissed me back so hard that I felt his heart beating against my chest, felt his erratic pulse as his lips moved possessively over mine. His kiss sent a flurry of sensations through my body as he swirled his tongue and released another spurt of lust between us. A scorching heat took over as he removed my flimsy pajama top and shoved my shorts down. Without warning I was pressed against the wall and then Jessie was filling me, my legs trembled as my knees clamped against his naked hips. Over and over again he rocked in a rhythm I almost couldn't keep up with, his lips still fused to mine. My body closed tightly around his as he flexed his legs and braced an arm above my head.

His husky voice whispered my name, and then he was groaning out a curse. "Isla, you have no idea what you do to me."

"I can feel it."

"It's more than this." His lips grazed the side of my neck as he pushed forward, sending me into a fit of ecstasy. "It's so much more."

His hard thighs pressed against my hips one last time before he clenched his teeth, his greedy mouth took possession of mine, and I was lost as wave after wave crashed over me.

"Isla . . ." His eyes were crazed. "I have to tell you—"

"I love you," I interrupted, my eyes filling with moisture.

He surrendered his mouth to mine again, and hours later, when I woke up in his arms, it never once occurred to me that he didn't say it back.

# Chapter Fifty-Three

Two million dollars.

That was the price for silence.

Money wasn't the issue.

It was the fact that I was paying someone off, someone I'd already given a large sum of money to, to do exactly what I was currently ready to pay her not to do.

Fuck.

She'd texted me an account number with a smiley face and "Thanks for doing business with me."

Me: Proof, deposit all evidence you have at my house. If you ever go public, you'll owe me triple what I gave you, and you'll be imprisoned. My lawyer and accountant will handle things from here on out. Oh and I've also slapped you with a restraining order. Go. To. Hell.

It was taken care of.

The money was in the process of being transferred.

I had nothing to worry about. So why was this soul-crushing anxiety attacking every inch of my body and making me want to ram my fist through the wall?

I shook it off and fired a text to Blaire.

Me: It's done.

Blaire: ????

Me: The Danica business: dealt with. Done, including a fancy restraining order.

Blaire: When you say done . . .

Me: Two million dollars done.

Blaire: YOU DIDN'T!

Me: I had no choice.

Blaire: So instead of coming clean . . . you're just sweeping it under a two million dollar rug?

Me: I have to go . . .

I didn't have an answer for her. Besides, it wasn't her business, it was mine. I needed to tell Isla, I just didn't know how to start that conversation. Oh hey, remember when I was out to destroy your career? Almost did, but don't worry, I paid off the same hacker I paid in the beginning, so all is well. Should we pick out a wedding cake?

Damn it!

My mind wouldn't stop coming up with all the ways she could find out without me telling, so much that I finally just grabbed my keys and headed to the dress shop on Rodeo.

I needed to confess.

Now.

# Chapter Fifty-Four

ISLA

A month ago I ate an entire tub of ice cream while watching the fifth season of *Orange Is the New Black* and convinced myself I was never going to get married.

With Wayne, I'd been looking at dresses, but since we hadn't set a date it didn't make sense to buy something.

With Jessie, the date was set, and now I was struggling to find a stupid dress.

Goo-Poh was supposed to come too, but apparently there was a meeting she couldn't miss, meaning if she did miss it Stanley would gain control of the retirement home. As Goo-Poh often said, "Over my dead, wrinkled body."

Only she said it in Chinese.

And very loudly.

And aggressively.

Tears filled my eyes as I did a slow circle in front of the large mirror. I'd chosen a cap-sleeve embellished lace mermaid gown—it had a plunging neckline and hugged every curve. It wasn't something I would normally choose, but the minute I put it on, the dress felt like it was made for me.

Blaire wiped her cheeks and poured herself more champagne, then stared at her phone for a good five minutes before turning around and giving me a huge smile. "You look beautiful!"

"You think he'll like it?"

Her smile fell a bit.

"Oh God, he's going to hate it, isn't he? It's too risqué with the plunging neckline, and the lace makes it look like I'm going to prom—"

"Isla." Blaire put her hand on my arm. "It's absolutely perfect."

"It's over eight thousand dollars." I winced.

"Great, let's get five!" she hissed under her breath.

"Blaire?"

"You look amazing and he's going to lose his mind." She grinned. "And they lived happily ever after."

"You're not . . . upset that I'm marrying Jessie, are you?"

Her jaw dropped. "Isla, no! I love his best friend, the Jessie train has plowed—" She stopped herself. "Bad choice of words. The Jessie train has moved on to greener pastures and I couldn't be happier for you. Promise."

"Okay, if you're sure?"

"Positive. Now go change so we can swipe his card."

I laughed and very slowly made my way back to the changing room and put on my jeans, tank top, and black blazer. When I was finished, I pulled my hair into a low ponytail, grabbed the heavy dress, and returned to Blaire.

Her purse and phone were lying there, but she was gone.

Her phone lit up.

I glanced down, if Colin was sending her dick pics I was going to poke out my eyes.

She had several missed texts from him, and then Mayday mayday, what's for dinner?

I laughed, typed in her code, and wrote back, Make your own dinner, by the way, this is Isla.

I clicked out of the message and saw Jessie's name.

It was an invasion of privacy, plus they were talking about a surprise the other day, but then I saw "two million" and panicked.

Time stood still.

For five seconds while I read, time stood still.

I didn't realize I was shaking until Blaire pried the phone out of my hand and helped me sit.

The bell to the store rang as Jessie barged in.

He locked eyes with me.

And the dreaded words fell from his lips: "It's not what you think . . . I can explain."

Tears blurred my vision as he approached me.

"Get away," I hissed.

"Isla." Jessie crouched in front of me and tried to pull me into his arms. I jerked away.

"We're in public on Rodeo Drive, lots of cameras," Blaire said under her breath. "Jessie, I'll bring Isla home so you can talk."

"Promise?" He didn't look like he was going to leave.

"I swear."

"Okay . . ." Jessie stood and then kissed the top of my head. "I love you, Isla."

Too. Late.

# Chapter Fifty-Five

## JESSIE

I was losing my fucking mind.

I gave the girls an hour to get back to the house.

It had been five.

Five. Hours.

I called Isla's cell every few minutes and left an apologetic message with instructions for her to call.

Hell, at this point I'd even take a messenger pigeon with a note saying she was alive.

Nothing.

I tapped my phone against my thigh, willing it to ring.

Then texted her again.

I'm sorry.

I'm so sorry.

We need to talk.

It's not what you think.

Isla?

I love you.

Isla: YOU DONT DROP AN I LOVE YOU VIA TEXT YOU COMPLETE
JACKASS!!!!!

What came after that contained enough curse words and memes to
make my mind explode.
But at least she was talking to me.

Me: Isla?

Isla: I'm turning my phone off now.

Me: Where are you? Are you safe?

Isla: Maybe you should ask your little hacker, she seems to know
everything anyway.

Damn it! How much did Blaire tell her?
They didn't even have the full story!
Would it matter if they did?
I wiped my face with my hand and called Colin, he answered on
the first ring.
"No."
"You don't even know what I'm going to say!"
"Uh, yeah, I do, you're going to ask where Isla is, and you're going
to call in some sort of dickish bro code, and I'm going to punch you in
the balls." He said it so loud I held the phone away from my ear.

"The hell are you talking about?" I gripped the phone between my fingers so hard they went numb. "I just want to explain to her. I was trying to do the right thing!"

"You mean after doing the wrong thing?"

"Exactly."

"You're actually making our gender look dumber than it already is, you get that, right?"

"Damn it, Colin! I need to see her, I LOVE HER!"

He sighed into the phone. "I can't, man, just know she's safe."

"It doesn't matter." My control fucking snapped as the panic and anxiety that had been attacking me finally hit full force. I fell to my knees and stared at my very clean kitchen.

And my very white and powder-blue walls.

All the things I hated about myself, all my insecurities, all my failures stared right back, and I had no one to blame but myself.

My house was the mirror of my soul.

Completely, utterly empty.

I hung up the phone and threw it against the wall, not caring that it sounded like it shattered into a million pieces.

A few hours later, my doorbell buzzed.

I was going to kill whoever was on the other side of that door.

I ran to it and tore it open just in time for Goo-Poh to slap me across the cheek.

Apparently I was getting killed first.

# Chapter Fifty-Six

ISLA

Colin gave me a wide berth.

I blamed all men.

And he was a man.

I wanted to hate him too since he was guilty by being the best friend, but he kept my wineglass full, and the sharp pain in my chest was at least lessening enough that it didn't hurt to breathe anymore.

I forced Blaire to tell me everything.

And I was livid.

Livid.

He said he was going to destroy me.

And he did.

Just not in the way he set out to. No, it would have been easier had he kept it all business and ruined my contacts, my reputation. But men like Jessie Beckett, they went straight for the heart.

And I knew mine would never be the same.

Because I gave him all the carefully protected pieces without knowing that he couldn't be trusted with their care.

I wasn't getting them back.

They were too damaged.

And so was I.

Colin's phone started ringing.

Texts from Jessie kept coming on my phone.

And then Colin left the room.

Yeah, I bet Jessie was trying to get information out of him, too bad Colin loved Blaire too much to cave. I heard her threaten him twice already.

I tilted my glass back, not even tasting the red blend, and wiped my mouth with the back of my hand.

"Okay." Blaire pulled the bottle from my other hand. "Not to be the devil's advocate, but you read the texts as he arrived, what if he was coming to tell you?"

"Does it really matter?" I spat. "He still went behind my back! He slept with me while knowingly working with that woman!"

"Right." Blaire nodded. "But if he loves you, which I think he does, why would he still do that? Something isn't adding up. I'm not saying forgive him, I'm saying at least listen to him. I'd like to think he's not that much of an idiot."

"He is." I grabbed the bottle. "Believe me."

My phone went off again. I grabbed it and yelled into the phone, "Call me one more time and you're going to be missing a testicle! It's over, Jessie, GO TO HELL!"

"Isla?" Goo-Poh whispered. "What's over? What's wrong?"

My voice cracked.

And I blurted my sadness all over the phone.

# Chapter Fifty-Seven

I'd never seen a small woman move so fast, she was like a ninja. One minute I was opening the door, the next I was fighting off slaps on the shoulder, the face, the stomach.

"Stop. Hitting. Me." I backed away and threw one of the couch cushions, but Goo-Poh had studied the art of evasion. She jumped out of the way faster than a woman her age should be able to move and kept charging toward me. I almost ran. It wasn't a proud moment.

"You hurt her!" Goo-Poh calmed herself and stopped charging, then said in a low voice, "So I kill you."

I believed her.

She wasn't smiling.

And her eyes were lethal.

She could probably take me out with some sort of secret round-house kick to the neck, tearing my artery in half and making me bleed out in less than three seconds, all over my white house.

Sounds like justice would be adequately served.

Let her take the hit.

I was dead anyway.

My soul was crushed.

My heart didn't even feel like it was beating without Isla by my side. Empty. I was so fucking empty.

"I love her," I confessed as I hung my head. "I love her so damn much, I thought I was protecting her, and when I finally got my head out of my ass I realized it was better to come clean even if it meant she walked away from me forever, but she found out first."

Goo-Poh's face didn't flinch. Either she just had a stroke standing up, or she was actually listening to me.

"I want to marry her. I want to have babies with her." My words tumbled out faster the more I spoke. "I want to build her a fucking house that has color. I want to take care of her, I want to come home to a mess, not this." I motioned around the room. "I want her brand of chaos. Fuck perfection. I just need her. In my life. By my side. Forever."

Goo-Poh twitched, I wouldn't call it a smile, but at least she was alive and showing me some sort of movement, meaning I didn't need to call 911. "Then you need to fight for her. Be the warrior she deserves."

"She won't answer my phone calls, she's sending me middle-finger text messages, and I don't even know where she is." I sighed and collapsed onto the couch, my head in my hands.

"You don't . . ." Goo-Poh sat down next to me. "But I do."

"Really—"

She slapped my cheek again. "Yes, now pay attention."

I swallowed my pride.

Rubbed my cheek.

And listened.

# Chapter Fifty-Eight

ISLA

I flipped through the channels like a woman possessed. What the hell was it? Couples week? Even the Syfy channel had a movie on about two aliens falling for each other.

Lovely.

Even aliens got a happily ever after.

I scowled and turned off the TV, then grabbed my phone.

I hadn't moved from my spot on Colin's couch.

My ass was making an imprint in the soft leather, the longer I sat, the more I wanted to just close my eyes and sleep.

Tears spilled onto my cheeks again.

I was not that woman.

The kind to let herself get defeated.

I was the kind of woman who got pushed down and jumped back up, guns firing. So why was this affecting me so much? Why was his betrayal so painful? Especially considering everything was set up on a lie in the first place?

I wiped my cheeks as the doorbell rang.

"Colin!" I yelled.

He jogged down the hall and sent me an irritated glance. "Didn't know that a broken heart also meant broken legs."

"It's not my house," I snapped right back.

"And yet your ass seems to be melting into my couch." He sighed and unlocked the door, calling over his shoulder, "You're not that girl, the one who gets sad."

Hadn't I just said that to myself?

"Isla!" Goo-Poh's voice was like a gong going off in the living room as she dropped a dress bag onto Colin's hands. "You go get the bags." She left him like that, gaping after her.

He listened.

Men always did when it came to Goo-Poh.

Goo-Poh made her way over to me, and then sighed like she was disappointed. "You look pale."

She gripped my chin between her fingers and narrowed her eyes. I tried to pull away. Resistance was futile. Luckily I kept my tears in as her eyes roamed my face at least a dozen times. She released my chin and turned to Colin, who was just laying down the dress bag. "Why have you not fed her?"

I love that her assumption was that since I looked pale, my blood sugar was low. Sigh. "Goo-Poh, it's not his job to feed—"

She held up a hand.

Colin's eyebrows shot up. "Blaire!" he called out of the corner of his mouth. "Get your ass out here."

Blaire rounded the corner and grinned. "Hi, Goo-Poh."

"Your man hasn't fed Isla."

Blaire gasped in outrage. "How dare you lie to me, Colin!"

I covered my face with my hands, and Colin made a choking noise. "You said you fed her!"

"I didn't—"

I peeked through my fingers while Colin made a face at Blaire that pretty much guaranteed he was going to torture her later. He turned back to Goo-Poh. "Uh, what would you like me to make?"

Goo-Poh straightened. "What are you capable of making that has nourishment for a broken heart and pale skin? We can't do anything about the loose-fitting clothing, but I do pray one day she'll reconsider her fashion choices."

I looked down at my skinny jeans and top. They were Citizen! The woman was crazy!

Goo-Poh cleared her throat. "She must look healthy for the wedding."

Say what?

My jaw dropped.

Colin looked unsure. "I, um . . . pancakes?"

"Pancakes!" I yelled. "That's your solution? Pancakes!"

"Lovely." Goo-Poh pinched his cheek, then slapped it. "You're a smart man."

He exhaled like he'd just been taken off death row.

"Goo-Poh," I said gently, maybe age was finally catching up with her? "I don't think you understand . . . I'm not marrying Jessie."

"Yes"—she nodded—"you are. I already picked up your dress."

I was going to be sick.

Really. Sick.

"Goo-Poh." Tears filled my eyes. "I'm not marrying a man who betrayed me in that way, I can't trust him, I'm not walking down that aisle."

"Yes," she turned around and said, "you are. Now, Colin, let's get started on those pancakes."

She abandoned me for the kitchen.

My jaw was still unhinged.

Blaire looked just as surprised. "What did I miss?"

"She's convinced I'm getting married still . . . you think it's because she thinks I'm pregnant?"

Blaire shrugged. "With all the sex you're having you could be pregnant, you know."

I glared at her.

"What? Just saying." She pulled me in for a hug. "What are you going to do?"

"Eat pancakes." My voice muffled against her shirt. "Murder Jessie."

"You know we'd get away with it easily, we know people," she said encouragingly.

My chest pricked with more pain as I tried to suck in a breath.

The thought of him gone only made me more sad.

I was still angry.

So angry.

But a world without him was like a rainbow without color.

I hung my head to the sound of Goo-Poh yelling at Colin in Chinese. A pan dropped, more yelling.

Blaire wrapped an arm around me. "So, what are we going to do?"

"Let Jessie live . . . save Colin from certain death."

"And the wedding?"

My throat felt like it was closing up. "I wish I knew."

# Chapter Fifty-Nine

I'd sent flowers to her office.

I wrote her a poem.

It sucked, but it was still a handwritten poem, on paper. Red paper.

Luckily, Colin finally agreed to hang out with me as long as I promised not to talk about Isla or ask where she was. Not that it mattered, Goo-Poh already told me.

She was mine.

And I would break through every single wall Colin put up in order to hunt her down and tell her just how much I cared about her.

How much I wished I could reverse my bad choices, and at least confess to her and let her help me solve it.

I told her I wanted to be a team.

And the minute I had a chance to act like it.

I handled things on my own.

The Jessie Beckett way.

The way I was always used to handling things, with my killer smile, money, influence, power.

I handled it like the old Jessie.

When I should have handled it with her.

I was just scared shitless she wouldn't give me a chance to explain, and now I was even more screwed.

Colin's knock was the only warning I got before he jerked open the door to my house. "Hey, so—holy shit!"

I looked up from the couch. "What?"

"What. The. Hell." He did a slow circle and then faced me. I knew what he saw, an explosion of red, a mixture of other colors, life. "Are you okay? Do I need to call someone? Are you . . . have you snapped?"

He whispered the last part like I was a small child.

The walls were painted a muted blue to match the kitchen, and I'd added deep-brown leather couches to the living room, a few spots of color on the throw pillows, and traded in a few of the white kitchen appliances for red ones.

Because. Red.

"Yeah, can't you see the drool, I'm heavily medicated, high as a fucking kite, but I feel great. Did you know that even when the TV's off people are still talking?" I forced a laugh at his horrified expression. "They talk to me. They tell me things."

"Uh, cool, man." He took a tentative step toward me. "What, um, what do they say?"

"Things." Oh hell, this was the most fun I'd had since . . . her. I swallowed past the lump and shrugged. "They say they're trapped."

"Trapped?"

I nodded and whispered, "In the TV!"

"Are they now?"

"Yup, but don't worry. I'm working on a plan to set them free."

"Jessie, maybe we should talk to someone—"

"I'm shitting you, you dumbass." I rolled my eyes. "I'm not having a breakdown, though good to know you'd stick by my side if I was."

"Yeah, I was about ten seconds away from running out the door and calling in reinforcements, so . . . maybe don't put too much faith in our friendship."

"That's why I called you a dumbass," I added.

"Oh, good." He nodded. "So . . . care to explain?"

"Explain what?" I got up and walked into my kitchen to grab a beer from my fridge.

My red fridge.

Hey, I think it matched the rest of the decor nicely, so what if it was a little . . . loud. At least I could sleep now.

The white was driving me crazy.

"You have wall art," Colin said slowly. "Your kitchen looks like a red bomb was dropped in the middle of it, damn, is that a mixer? Do you really have a KitchenAid in here?"

"I've been trying to bake." I shrugged. "What's the big deal?"

"This, this isn't normal." He took one look at the beer in my hand, walked over to my minibar, poured two shots of whiskey, and downed them, then winced. "Normal behavior is getting drunk at a bar, having a one-night stand, going on vacation, or in your case buying a new car in white . . ."

"Hilarious."

"You said color gives you hives."

"Well, it doesn't anymore." I closed my eyes as fresh pain washed over me, and then took another sip of beer.

"Holy shit, are those red barstools?" He pointed.

I gave him a shove. God forbid he'd go into my bedroom and see the purple.

I'd done it on a whim.

I needed color so bad that I literally was ready to take a marker to my walls like a toddler, and then I went to Target.

I just wanted to think.

And I ended up leaving with three carts full of shit that I found great joy in putting in my house. Actual joy.

The only downside was that I wanted her to be with me.

I wanted her to experience it with me.

I saved two rooms for her.

Just like I saved hope in my heart that she'd come back and fill them up, fill the house up with her laughter, her baking.

Just her.

"Lost you there for a minute." Colin waved in front of my face. "You seem like you're doing better than you were."

I lifted the beer to my lips and shrugged, then said, "Still won't tell me where she is?"

Colin looked ready to blurt something when the front door opened. Goo-Poh entered with a few plastic containers of food. She was humming to herself, then stopped in front of me. I kissed both of her thin cheeks before she continued humming and put some of the food in the fridge and some on the counter.

"What. The. Hell?" Colin looked between the two of us. "Did she just? Is that food? What's that smell?"

Goo-Poh went into the pantry and let out a happy sigh, her eyes taking in all the ingredients.

I grinned at Colin. "She likes me for my pantry."

He eyed me up and down. "Yeah. Sure. That's the only reason."

Goo-Poh looked over her shoulder at us, eyed my ass, and then looked back at the pantry.

"There may be a few others," I admitted. "Plus she's helping me get Isla back."

Colin's eyes narrowed. "Would any of this have to do with the fact that she's forcing Isla to get married still?"

"Maybe."

"Jessie . . ."

"No, I don't want to hear it. I have a plan."

"Yeah, last time you had a plan you ended up without the woman of your dreams and going on a shopping spree, and this is just as bad. You can't just force someone to marry you and then try to make it work. That's screwed up, even for you."

"That"—I tipped my beer toward him—"is not the plan. Plus, she went all PI on my ass, why not do it to her?"

Colin's answer was to groan. "Leave me out of this, I'm actually still getting laid, alright?"

"Oh, don't worry"—I looked over my shoulder and winked at Goo-Poh—"I already have a partner."

Colin shuddered.

"What did she ever do to you?"

"Well, she ruined pancakes, so there's that. I still hear the screaming when I close my eyes at night, but other than that? Can't think of a thing." He waved at Goo-Poh, who finally acknowledged him with a curse.

Followed by a hiss.

Colin stumbled back a step and shook his head. "I was missing one ingredient."

"She takes her ingredients very seriously."

Goo-Poh finally made her way back to us only to walk right by and sit on the sofa. She grabbed the remote, wrapped it in plastic, and then smiled to herself.

"What the fu—"

"Shhh." I hit Colin on the chest. "It's a thing. I've learned not to ask questions."

"You do realize your new partner in crime is basically setting up camp in your home, right? She brought you food, man!"

I shrugged. "I'd build a house for Goo-Poh and let her fucking watch me sleep at night if that meant I got Isla back."

"You're either crazy or really in love." Colin slapped me on the back in commiseration, like he got it.

"Both." I sighed as Goo-Poh switched channels. "I think I'm both." She started yelling at the TV.

Colin and I both jolted.

"Maybe give her a wide berth when she's here, though," Colin whispered.

"Yup."

# Chapter Sixty

ISLA

The countdown was on.

I measured everything by time.

It had been seven days since his last text.

A day since another dozen roses had been delivered by Blaire, a clever way around the whole not-knowing-where-I-was part.

He stopped at the office and gave them to Blaire at the door, while I peered around my desk for just a glimpse of his lying ass.

Her heels clicked against the floor and she dropped yet another dozen roses onto Abby's desk. I refused to touch them.

I figured if I did, they'd just prick me like the prick who broke me and make me cry.

I looked back at my screen.

It was a waiting game.

Waiting for the ball to drop.

Waiting for something to get leaked to the press.

But everything was exactly the same.

And to make matters worse, the media was obsessed with the fact that Jessie brought me flowers every day.

We once again had people camped outside our offices.

Which meant if I saw him I'd have to play nice.

I glanced at my planner through tear-filled eyes. The wedding was highlighted in red, several times. I'd drawn balloons.

I was an idiot.

A stupid idiot.

"He's still here." Blaire handed me the same binoculars that I'd been using a few weeks ago to spy back.

I stared at them.

She wouldn't relent. It was like she switched sides when Colin came home a few days ago spouting nonsense about plastic-covered remote controls and hissing.

"I bet he is." I found my voice. "Nothing he says is going to change the fact that he betrayed me, that he was still betraying me while sleeping with me."

Blaire made a face. "Look, I know it looks bad, but what sort of guy just waits for you like that? Clearly he feels something."

"He feels for his dick, and his reputation. And if he thinks I'm still going to marry him in order to save his sorry ass—"

"You will," Abby piped up.

"Excuse me?" I was ready for a fight, angry, so angry that I still felt for him, still wanted him every night when I cried myself to sleep.

She looked away from her computer and grinned. "You're miserable because you love him. Marriage takes work, Isla. Relationships take work."

"Okay, thanks, Miss Perfect Marriage," I grumbled under my breath.

"He cheated," she confessed, head held high. "And if you think for one second that didn't kill a part of me, you're wrong. I noticed the signs, I ignored them because I thought I was the reason, I was to blame . . . and then I just . . . disconnected from him, resented his refusal to communicate, every time he left my house he broke my heart.

I wondered, Is he going out on me? Is he meeting her? Will he smell like her perfume?"

"Wait." Blaire held up her hand. "Is that why you wanted to work for us?"

"It's like my own brand of therapy." Abby grinned. "Want to know the worst part?"

I nodded and leaned forward.

"One time." She made a face. "He cheated once. Granted, that's enough to break someone . . . but because of my own assumptions and fears, because of my resentment, I didn't know. I assumed for a whole year it was still going on. I berated him, I was passive-aggressive, angry, I was a horrible wife. Yes, he made a mistake, but my inability to communicate nearly became an even bigger mistake. We have children . . . they should never be part of that sort of emotional environment." She hung her head. "I finally snapped and found out that he'd been seeing a counselor. I also found out that he not only went to HR and owned up to his mistake, he was willing to lose his job because the woman he'd cheated with was his subordinate."

I covered my mouth with my hands.

"We all make mistakes . . . but when you own up to them like an adult, that's the difference maker. Our marriage is so much better now, probably because we both realize what we could have lost." She eyed the window. "Seems to me he's trying. While you sit there and toss more and more blame on him until he's buried. But let me ask you this—is it making you feel better at all? Or worse?"

"Worse." It burned to get the word out. "So much worse."

"The thing about forgiveness, Isla, that nobody remembers in the midst of pain and betrayal, is that we do it for ourselves—not them. You're only punishing yourself. He knows you're angry, believe me, but right now it's hurting you more than it's hurting him."

I leaned back in my chair.

Blaire's mouth dropped open. "And to think I thought you were just a receptionist. She Dr. Philled your ass."

"Receptionist, bartender, hairstylist—all therapists."

"True that." Blaire gripped my hand. "Thanks, Abby."

"Anytime." She spun her chair back to her computer and started humming. The phone rang, she did her normal spiel, and I just stared at her.

Could it be that easy?

I grabbed the binoculars with shaky hands and stood, then found myself at the window looking out at Jessie.

While he looked up at me.

He waved.

I flipped him off.

Then smiled.

Smug, annoying bastard.

"Hold these." I shoved the binoculars at Blaire and marched toward the door.

# Chapter Sixty-One

There's something both gorgeous and terrifying about a woman in spike heels with tears in her eyes.

Tears you're well aware you put there.

My hands tightened into fists as I watched her make her way across the street.

The click of her heels matched the slow, even rhythm of my breathing as I waited for her to say something.

Do something.

Even if it meant I was going to get slapped.

Kicked.

Maimed.

I held my breath when she finally stood in front of me. She was glorious. Her dark hair tumbled past one shoulder. She was wearing a slinky pink tank top and a leather skirt. When she crossed her arms, the jangling of the bangles on her wrist was the only noise that filled the air.

"Stalking again?" she said in an annoyed voice.

I leaned back against my car. "You've sort of left me no choice."

Already we were garnering the attention of a few reporters who'd been camped outside the building for the past two hours.

"Ah, so now we're talking about choices." She pasted on a fake smile and said through clenched teeth, "Do you really want to go there?"

"I'll go there all day." I took a step closer. "I have nothing to hide anymore . . . nothing to lose. I've already lost the most important thing of all."

She snorted. "What, your conscience?"

"My heart," I whispered, reaching for her face then pulling my hand back at the last minute. "My soul." Ah, fuck it, I cupped her face with both hands and pressed a kiss to her mouth. "I lost you."

She didn't kiss me back but she didn't slap me either. She jerked away and pressed a hand to her forehead. "Please don't kiss me."

"I'll do anything." I ignored the way her rejection made my body go numb. "Anything, Isla."

"You paid someone off," she said. "The same someone you paid to destroy me, and then you slept with me and kept it from me. What other secrets are you keeping? How can I ever trust you?"

"I let my anger get in the way . . . I let my selfishness take away the most important part of my life—you. Give me a chance to prove myself."

"You had a chance."

The reporters were closing in.

I refused to panic.

Instead I fell to my knees and held both of her hands before she could step away from me. "What the hell are you doing?" she hissed.

"Proposing."

"You already did that! They're going to talk, you'll ruin everything!"

The cameras got closer.

Talking got louder.

"Let them know it was fake." I locked eyes with her. "Let them ruin me more . . . I don't care anymore, Isla, if it means I can have you. I love you."

A tear slid from her cheek onto the concrete.

"I miss us," I confessed. "I miss your messy baking and the weird dragon bed. I almost lost it when I saw a fucking chicken, Isla, real tears. Gut-wrenching sobs . . . it wasn't pretty."

She tried not to smile.

It was like a balm to my soul when she couldn't manage it.

And when she snorted out a laugh.

I knew I had her. "I just want you to do one thing."

"Just one?"

"You don't have to forgive me. But I need you to read this." I placed a note in her palm. "And if the answer is still yes . . . you'll know what to do."

She frowned at our joined hands. I kissed the top of hers and stood just as the first reporter made it to our side.

"What were you just doing, Jessie?" a reporter asked.

"Groveling," I said honestly. "Never had to do it before, never wanted to, kind of humbling." I gave her one last look and got in my car.

And it was the vision of a small smile on her lips that gave me hope that maybe Goo-Poh was right, and it wasn't over.

# Chapter Sixty-Two

ISLA

I wasted no time. I locked myself in the bathroom and with shaking hands opened up the letter.

A Target gift card fell onto my lap. I set it aside and started to read the words Jessie clearly handwrote.

> *Isla,*
> *Since you won't speak to me, I think this is the only way to get the words out. I met Danica through a mutual friend. It's true, I hired her to hack your system before I ever really knew what Dirty Exes was—or what it meant to you personally. You see, I had this image of a man-hating company that set out to ruin lives—not save them.*
> *And then I saw your business plan.*
> *And then I read your files.*
> *And then I read your ten-year plan.*
> *And if that wasn't enough to convince me, I spent more and more time with you. My boring white-and-black life suddenly experienced the equivalent of a rainbow shitting on it.*

*You're the rainbow in this scenario, just in case you were confused.*

*I'm the shit.*

*But back to Danica. I hadn't heard from her in a while and I was so consumed with myself—and then so consumed with you—that when I heard you mention her that first night we slept together, I panicked.*

*We were just getting to know each other.*

*And I selfishly chose us, chose what was happening over a confession that might separate us forever, like a dumbass.*

*She refused to return my phone calls, texts, emails. I assumed that she'd taken the money I'd given her and run.*

*Instead, she threatened Blaire. Her price was two million.*

*Which I gladly paid.*

*Because I love you.*

*Because I'm an idiot and didn't come to you first and ask if that's what you really wanted. I just wanted it to go away, I handled it the way the old Jessie would have handled it.*

*But I was wrong.*

*I chose to take care of it and then tell you later. I figured I'd be your hero after you slapped me a few times. Instead you found out from someone other than me.*

*And here we are.*

*If you take away anything from this note, take away this: I'm sorry. And I love you.*

*I never knew true pain until you walked out of my life. I've never deserved it more, and that's the hardest part. I can't argue a case I can't win. But I can hope that one day you'll forgive me.*

*Isla, I want to be with you.*

*Not just for the news.*

*Not just to get a stupid nonprofit to look at me twice again.*

*I want you because I love you.*

*Because I want to be part of an "us."*

*Because I want that us to turn into an even bigger us.*

*I'm ready for that next step.*

*Two weeks ago I proposed.*

*Two weeks ago I fell even harder for the woman I became attracted to over a year ago.*

*Fall with me?*

*I'll be waiting for you at the end of the aisle if you say yes.*

*Oh, and the Target gift card is for you. Go wild. I may have decorated a few rooms, but I left you the best ones. My only request is this: color.*

*Make the rooms brighten my life.*

*Just like you.*

*I love you,*

*Jessie*

Tears streamed down my cheeks in rapid succession until I couldn't see the letter anymore.

Someone pounded on the door, then I heard Blaire's voice. "Isla?"

"What?" I wiped my nose.

"Um, Goo-Poh's here."

Oh hell.

"Okay."

"She wants to know your answer."

"What?"

"To the letter." She yelled through the door, "Oh, and she brought your dress, something about you still getting married tomorrow. I told her she was senile and I think she cursed my future children. Can you maybe come out?"

I wiped more tears and laughed, a real laugh, one that felt like a fresh start. One that made me think of Jessie and his damn Target gift card.

I fixed my mascara-streaked cheeks and opened the door just in time for Goo-Poh to continue her tirade around my office.

She brought food.

Shock of the century.

And she was currently holding out chopsticks to Abby, who seemed too petrified to say no.

"Goo-Poh." I crossed my arms. "Or should I say traitor?"

"I know nothing." Goo-Poh shrugged. "He is a good strong man, and he's sorry. I told him if you would not listen to his words in person, he should put them on paper . . ." That was smart. "So your children can see how romantic he is. It shows good fortune."

And there it is.

I grinned.

Her lips twitched.

I pulled her into my arms for a hug.

She stiffened at first and then leaned up and kissed my cheek. "You're getting married, then?"

"Did I ever really have another choice?" I rolled my eyes.

"No," she said in a serious tone and lightly tapped my cheek. "You did not."

"Thought so."

"Goo-Poh, since it's the day of confessions—"

"What?" She looked so hopeful.

Yeah, Jessie better knock me up soon.

I should be petrified.

Instead it only made me laugh.

With our luck . . .

"I love you," I said.

She nodded and then shoved more food in front of me. "Eat. You look too thin."

Her way of saying "I love you" back.

Close enough.

# Chapter Sixty-Three

## JESSIE

"What if she doesn't show up?" I checked my watch again. Everything was perfect. Goo-Poh had outdone herself, and the owners of the event center had made everything look gorgeous.

We went with soft purple lighting against white backdrops. All of the tables were topped with a dragon—not my doing—and while it was an intimate wedding with only close friends and family, Goo-Poh had managed to fill the entire place with people from her retirement home, Stanley included, though he didn't look happy about it.

"She will," Colin encouraged again, checking his watch too.

It wasn't even that I would be embarrassed to be stood up.

It was the simple fact that she would be saying goodbye.

I wasn't sure I could take it.

And when Wayne and Vanessa walked in and sat down, I was ready to puke my guts out.

"Were they invited?" I said out of the corner of my mouth.

"Nope." Colin nodded to them. "Weird."

"I may strangle those two. I can't go to prison on my wedding day."

"And I can't commit . . . what's the word for killing one's sister?"

The wedding march started.

I sucked in a breath. "Is she here?"

Guests looked around.

Suddenly the doors burst open and there was Goo-Poh, with Isla on one arm and a knowing smile—the first one I'd ever received from her and probably ever would—firmly planted on her face. Head held high, she even winked at me.

And then my eyes fell to Isla.

Her dress.

That dress.

My mouth went dry as my eyes strained to take her in. It had capped sleeves and lace embellishments, but my favorite part? She'd added pieces of red lace on the bottom.

And short red gloves with a red-and-white bouquet.

I'd never been happier to see that color in my entire life.

Her eyes met mine.

And instinct took over.

I ran toward her.

I was done waiting.

I met her in the middle of the aisle right next to Wayne and Vanessa.

"I love you," I said in a hoarse voice. "I'm so—"

She wrapped her arms around me and kissed me, fused her mouth to mine in a way I'd been dreaming of for a week. I picked her up and twirled her as people cheered.

I got smacked in the back. I put Isla down while Goo-Poh shook her head. "After the ceremony."

"Right." I walked with them to the front and looked around. Who the hell was officiating, and why hadn't I noticed that nobody was standing there?

Goo-Poh cleared her throat.

And Stanley, very slowly, went to the front and held out a Bible. "Who gives this woman?"

"I do!" Goo-Poh said, then added something in Chinese.

Stanley stared at her a few seconds before mumbling, "Then do it, already."

"Pain in my ass," Goo-Poh said under her breath before kissing Isla on both cheeks and placing her hand on mine. "You will have good fortune. Many children. You will be happy."

With a nod she went to her seat next to Blaire and pulled out a tissue.

We faced Stanley, who looked like he'd rather be anywhere, hell included, than in this room.

"If anyone is against this marriage, speak now or forever hold your peace." He looked into the crowd.

People gasped as someone stood.

I froze and turned.

Vanessa had tears in her eyes.

Oh, hell no, she wasn't going to ruin this for me.

Wayne nodded at her and patted her hand.

"It's not what you think," she whispered. "I just wanted to say . . . be . . . I'm . . . ." Wayne eyed her like this was her punishment. "Sorry. And be happy." He nodded again and she sat.

"Well, that wasn't normal." Stanley peered around at Goo-Poh. "Alright, marriage is—"

I tuned him out and focused on Isla. On the feel of her palm pressed against mine.

The way she said her vows.

The clear expression of love she sent me.

And hopefully forgiveness.

"You may kiss your bride," Stanley said.

"Finally." I mauled her with a deep kiss, then lifted her into the air while people cheered. When I set her down, she had tears in her eyes.

Mine mirrored hers.

"This is crazy," she said.

"Yeah," I agreed. "But it's right."

"It is," she whispered before kissing me again in front of everyone.

It wasn't until Goo-Poh started yelling that we broke apart. And even then, all I kept thinking was, I can't wait to show this woman our home.

# Chapter Sixty-Four

ISLA

He wouldn't let go of my hand or stop touching me.

I just wanted to leave.

To talk to him.

Kiss him.

Show him his wedding gift.

Instead we were stuck at a reception with old people.

They even brought the ones with the walkers, who were currently trying to perform "Thriller" out on the dance floor.

A cane went flying at one point, narrowly missing the cake.

Goo-Poh just shook her head.

Stanley brought her wine.

I think it was his way of drugging her, because she sniffed it before forcing one of her minions to take the first sip.

Sigh. Some things never change, do they?

I glanced up at Jessie, and some things . . . have no choice but to change.

I squeezed his hand.

"Isla." Wayne's voice had me ready to run for the hills.

Slowly, I turned. Wayne looked . . . tired.

Vanessa wasn't by his side, then again I wasn't actively searching for her.

"Wayne." I cleared my throat as Jessie wrapped a possessive arm around me.

"I hope that was adequate."

Adequate?

"Pardon?" I was so confused. "What do you mean adequate?"

"For everything that happened." Now he looked confused. "The tapes? The information on Dirty Exes? I thought you knew?"

Jessie was the first to speak. "What the hell are you talking about?"

"You didn't get Danica's name by accident. When I noticed the money leaving the account I shared with Vanessa, I knew something was up." Bad idea there, buddy, sharing an account with that woman, I thought. "I confronted Vanessa and she confessed everything: how she set you up and tricked your friend into giving you Danica's name, how she paid Danica double the amount you did for the information she collected. I'm sorry. Had I known, I would have put a stop to it right away."

Yeah, keep her on a tight leash. I shuddered.

"Well, there goes two million." Jessie laughed.

"Oh, Danica's being prosecuted for extortion." Wayne seemed pleased with himself. "The money will be returned after the case is closed. I hope we're . . . good." He looked between us. "I think it will be good for Vanessa to see closure on this end, maybe then she'll say yes."

I gaped.

Then gaped some more.

No words would come.

"I love her." He said it so sheepishly.

By then she was making her way over to us and actually blushing when he turned and grabbed her hand.

Huh.

"She has trouble letting things go," he continued.

Understatement of the actual century there, buddy.

"Ready?" He kissed her neck, she giggled. She met Jessie's gaze then mine and nodded goodbye.

"What the hell just happened?" Jessie said out loud.

"How are you not getting arrested right now?" Colin came up behind us out of breath. "I saw you guys talking like normal adults, so I panicked and ran over as fast as I could."

"Wow." Jessie whistled. "What was that? Twenty feet in five minutes? Well done, I think Stanley sprints faster."

Colin gave us the finger as Blaire reached his side. "What was that?"

"Alternate reality," Jessie finally said. "Apparently Danica was working for Vanessa too. Vanessa was also trying to get dirt on Dirty Exes and paid more than I did, so basically we both paid her to do the same damn job. I stooped just as low as Vanessa, I'm such a jackass."

I hung my head. "Vanessa is sorry in some strange way, Danica is going to prison for extortion, and somehow Wayne . . . loves her and knows how to deal with her level of crazy."

Blaire tilted her head. "Really, though?"

"My sister?" Colin needed clarification. "Vanessa?"

"Yup." I gave my head a shake just as techno took over the sound system. Stanley jumped up and went to the middle of the dance floor while Goo-Poh sat on her throne surrounded by her women.

"Some things can't be unseen," Colin said under his breath.

"Hey, best man, one last job for the day . . ." Jessie slapped him on the shoulder. "Make sure none of the old people get drunk and take off their clothes. We're headed out."

"What?" Colin and Blaire said in unison.

Rachel Van Dyken

"See ya!" I laughed while Stanley grabbed someone's cane and went
to town spinning it over his head.

We laughed the entire way home.

Home.

Our home.

I let out a happy sigh and hoped he'd like what I did with the place.

300

# Chapter Sixty-Five

## JESSIE

I couldn't wait to get her inside.

The minute I opened the door, I was ready to take her against the wall, whisper promises into her ear, strip that gorgeous dress from her body.

Instead, she dropped my hand.

"Isla?"

She crooked her finger at me. "This way."

Dumbly, I followed her down the hall.

She opened the door to her old guest room.

Black-and-white everything.

And then when I looked closer, I could see red.

Red throw pillows.

Red accents in the pictures.

A red leather chair.

"You said to do whatever I wanted . . . but I didn't want to take over the room . . . the black-and-white is you, the red is me, the perfect match."

I didn't let her finish.

Instead I attacked her in the doorway and gripped her hips. "I missed you."

"I missed you." She laughed against my mouth. "Do you like it?"

"Love it. Love you."

I flipped her around and started undoing the buttons to her dress. There were at least seven hundred.

And I died a little bit with each one I undid.

"It's like they're multiplying!" I cursed under my breath as she leaned against the doorframe and thrust her ass out. "Not helping, and it's too pretty to rip."

She glanced over her shoulder and smirked. "Sorry, that must be sooo hard on you."

I was going to strangle her.

"It's hard when you have a hard day like that, and you drink tea that makes it even harder and—"

I ripped the damn dress.

"Not another word." I pulled it down, apologized to my credit card, and thrust my tongue into her mouth before she could utter the word *hard* again.

She tasted like my forever.

The person made for me.

I pulled back for air, her greedy hands were at my shirt, and then her lips twitched and she ripped it open. "All's fair . . ."

"God, you're hot when you get violent."

I couldn't get the rest of my clothes off fast enough. We fumbled around as she rid me of my pants, still kissing me as I stumbled with her toward the bed, and then it was just us.

Skin on skin.

My mouth on hers.

And every damn dream I'd had came true.

I was inside her in seconds.

Filling her completely.

Coming home.

"Isla." I drove into her and pressed a small kiss near her ear. "You're my forever."

A tear slid down her cheek, one I'd created, a good one. She whispered back, "You're mine too."

It was the perfect moment.

Followed by complete surrender on both our parts.

In a room filled with ghosts of our past, present, and future.

After a few minutes of panting, then silence, we held one another like we couldn't believe it was real, that we were together.

I looked over and fell off the bed.

"Are you okay?" Isla reached for me.

"Isla, I love you, you know that, and I'll put up with a lot of shit, but why the hell is there a chicken in this room, and why did it just watch us have sex without making a noise?"

She looked where I pointed, made a little yelp, then ran for the front door.

I was close behind her.

She slammed it shut and grinned up at me. "That, that was all Goo-Poh, I wouldn't give her a key if I were you."

A knock sounded at the door. I scrambled for a blanket while Isla dove behind the kitchen island. Traitor.

"Hi!" Goo-Poh walked right in. "I knew you'd be hungry after making babies, so I brought leftover food." She waltzed right by me. I closed my eyes and prayed the blanket wasn't see-through.

She put the food in the fridge, shut off the kitchen light, humming the entire way back to the door before calling over her shoulder, "Isla, eat the rice, you look pale."

The door closed.

Isla popped up, her cheeks rosy red from embarrassment.

"Yeah, too late," I confessed.

And barely had time to run away as she chased me with a red pillow. Hey, at least it wasn't white.

# Acknowledgments

I always say the hardest part about writing a book is thanking everyone who made it possible. God gets all the honor and glory—He's the only reason I'm on the path I'm on (even though sometimes I'm stubborn and decide to take a detour and end up a total mess), and I fully know what a blessing I am living. I'm so thankful it's hard to even put it into words. To my amazing Viking/Dutch husband, Nate, thank you for being more than just support and encouragement but a partner, an inspiration, someone who "gets" it, especially when I need help plotting something out, though let's be honest, you do tend to go off on tangents, and no, I'm not going to write that book . . . you know which one ;) To my adorable son, Thor, who makes it hard to even want to be at the computer. Next to your daddy, you, my boy, are the love of my life. I see joy in your eyes and my life is better just being next to you, even if it means you're crying or screaming or looking at me with crazy eyes. You are my soul. Thank you to my amazing agent, Eric, for always supporting me and pushing me to be better. I'm so thankful for you in my life. To Maria and the Skyscape team, I'm so honored to be a part of team APub, and the threat still stands—YOU HAVE TO CONTINUE TO LET ME WRITE FOR YOU. You know I would even beg, straight up drive over to Seattle (this is the part where the author threatens said publisher awkwardly). Okay, so I wouldn't go that far, just know that I am so appreciative of everything you do and so blessed to have you!

Maria, your emails brighten my day! And your friendship is everything. My publicist, Nina, dude, it's been an INSANE year, and I have a feeling it's just going to get better ;) Thank you for letting me own my crazy, and thank you for being that rock I need on a daily basis. Jill and Becca, you have made this such an incredible year as well, thank you for all your hard work and picking up the pieces when I call you sobbing into my coffee because I accidentally deleted a chapter and can't remember a word I wrote. You guys are everything. To my beta readers, Jill, Liza, Kristin, Tracey, Stephanie, Krista, and Jessica, you are crucial in the making of a book—I so appreciate your willingness to be brave and tell me when I suck. I love you guys! To my rockin' reader group, the best group on Facebook *dances*, your love and support truly make us feel like a family, and I'm so thankful we have a safe place we can chat about books and all the reasons reading is the best. You have been there through thick and thin, thank you for being such an amazing team and family!

To the readers—even the ones who are actually reading the acknowledgments with a slow eye twitch because they've been up since two a.m.—YOU GUYS, the ones who purchase the book, the ones who get lost in all the words, thank you for taking a chance on me, thank you for reading, and thank you for your continued support. I could NOT do this without readers, and I wouldn't have a job if you didn't exist, so thank you for being passionate about the words, I'll keep writing them if you keep reading them. Bloggers, PAs, publicists, graphic designers—all of the book world, thank you for constantly pushing books and authors. A lot of you do what you love for free just because you love it—know that it doesn't go unnoticed. Thank you. If you want to follow me on social media, hit up my Facebook group, Rachel's New Rockin' Readers, or follow me on Instagram @RachVD. Until next time!

HUGS,
RVD

# About the Author

Rachel Van Dyken is a *Wall Street Journal, USA Today,* and #1 *New York Times* bestselling author known for Regency romances, contemporary romances, and her love of coffee and Swedish fish. Rachel has also recently inked a deal for her Wingmen Inc. series—*The Matchmaker's Playbook* and *The Matchmaker's Replacement*—to be made into movies.

A fan of *The Bachelor* and the Seattle Seahawks (not necessarily in that order), Rachel lives in Idaho with her husband, a supercute toddler son who keeps her on her toes, and two boxers. Make sure you check out her site, www.RachelVanDykenauthor.com, and follow her on Twitter (@RachVD).